CW01418280

A World Apart

A Novel

By

Jon Crawley

ISBN-13: 978-1467919210
ISBN-10: 1467919217

Part 1

The University

In the five year's since J.T.'s appointment to the faculty of Bransome Southern University he had never felt as spaced out as at this moment. Sitting near to the President of BSU, he was soon to rise to give the valedictory address for one of the President's closest henchmen, Vice-president Oscar Wolf. The Great Hall of the Alumni Building had been cleared of its usual rows of metal seats to make way for tables set for the dining pleasure of the Trustees, top university administrators and senior faculty members, local business people and politicos, and their partners. The hall buzzed with their conversation, bursts of laughter rang out, and raucous remarks were shouted from one table to the next as the liberal supply of alcohol took its toll. Waiters and waitresses bustled between the tables, juggling trays loaded with plates and calling orders for drinks and water to their colleagues.

The meal had been long and the food dismal. Between courses J.T. had surreptitiously consulted and amended his notes, which made him a less-than-sparkling dinner companion. The President's wife, Amanda, on his left, had long given up any expectation of interesting conversation, or of the hoped-for gossip on the matrimonial cavorting of the faculty. The time was fast approaching when J.T. would have to get to his feet, adjust the height of the microphone, and launch into his speech. The audience-to-be, accustomed to such events as this, were resigned to having to sit through a tedious and almost certainly mendacious eulogy of the man known, to most of the faculty at least, as the Godfather. The trouble with this kind of public oratory was that it was possible to be interesting or humorous only if you told the truth, and that was totally out of the question. The diners knew that, and therefore the only way to survive the event was to take in as much alcohol as possible consistent with maintaining that essential degree of control needed in order to refrain from the smart-Alec remark which could cost you next year's raise.

Having come finally to the realization that it was too late to make any further amendments to his text, J.T. was now virtually comatose, viewing the animated scene that surrounded him as if through a one-way mirror, an observer hardly touched by his environment. His mind began lazily to review the sequence of events which had brought him to this place at this time, and which had resulted in his being entrusted by the President with this most delicate of tasks.

* * *

J.T.'s first appointment to BSU was as Assistant Professor of Sanskrit. He was never sure exactly how he had come to take up the study of this ancient and complex language. He had a hazy memory of a commencement party at his undergraduate school, when his advisor had told him that it would be a good idea to study Sanskrit at Harvard. Years later, a friend who had been present at the party claimed that what the advisor, who had been spurned by Harvard in his search for a teaching post, had actually said was that Harvard was a snake pit. Be that as it may, J.T. had spent seven lonely years working on a thesis entitled "The Evidence for a Double Glottal Stop in the Locative Case in Middle Sanskrit". Having finally gained his Ph.D., although in fact it had really amounted to a nil return, he found himself in a quite unique labor market. For some years there was not a single job in sight in his field. He worked as a waiter, and drove a car rental courtesy bus, but when an academic job opportunity finally did appear, he was the only candidate. The Department of Classical Languages at BSU had convinced the Dean of the College of Liberal Arts that the decline in the study of Latin, a language redolent of Western cultural imperialism, presaged a vast resurgence of interest in the ancient cultures of the Orient, an area of study sadly neglected in Western universities, and that Sanskrit was the cutting edge in this revival. J.T. had been appointed, and for several semesters he had offered First Semester Sanskrit, and An Introduction to Indo-European Linguistics, but not a single one of BSU's 11,000 students had opted for his courses. Faced with the certainty that he was about to be vocationally challenged, J.T. had seized the opportunity of an opening for an Assistant Dean, and had begun a new career as a university administrator. It was in this way that he first came into contact with Oscar Wolf.

Wolf had recently been appointed as Vice-President in charge of International Affairs, and had swept into his sphere of influence any aspect of the university's activities that had even the most tenuous international connection. Wolf was the least academic of any university administrator that had been seen on the campus of BSU in living memory. It was rumored that he had a degree in educational administration from a university which granted degrees on the basis of life experience, but if that was the case he never displayed the slightest evidence of what that experience might have consisted of. The day after taking up his appointment, Oscar immediately set about changing everything in BSU that he could legitimately lay his hands on, and a few other things as well. No program was too successful to escape his axe, no judgment too hasty if it appealed to him. Administrators were moved from one post to another, some were fired, never knowing why, and new ones appointed, usually with no conception of what it was they had been hired to do. The only person who dared question him about this orgy of random change was Elvira, his wife, to whom he explained: 'I have to let the bastards know I'm here. Otherwise they'll wonder why the hell I was appointed.'

One of the beneficiaries of the swathe that Oscar cut through the administration was J.T. On hearing of his knowledge of a foreign language, Oscar had immediately decided that J.T. was the ideal man to take over from the former Director of Study Abroad, a woman of considerable standing in the field, whom Oscar had fired by mistake, having confused her name with that of a quite different person who had been caught falsifying expense claims. On being informed of his error, Oscar had said, 'Aw! What the heck!' The miscreant had continued to work for the University, eventually rising to a senior position in the Treasurer's Department, while the puzzled and angry former Director went off to work for a competitor university.

One of the first tasks that Oscar undertook was to conquer the Middle East for BSU. Surveying a map, which showed the University's activities around the world, Oscar spotted a large gap without any flags. He sent for J.T.

'I want you to set up a meeting,' he paused for a moment, and then his forefinger shot out, 'there.'

J.T. leaned forward to see where the Vice-presidential finger had landed.

'The Kingdom of El Baku. Right?'

'Right!'

* * *

The meeting was to be held in the conference suite of the El Baku International Hotel. It was the most expensive hotel in the kingdom. The conference suite, which could have been in Los Angeles or Minneapolis, was violently air-conditioned, so that anyone coming in from the 100 degree exterior caught his breath, and a number of the participants had turned up the collars of their seersucker jackets.

Oscar Wolf entered the conference room, flanked by his aides. He was a short, stocky man in his fifties. He took the chair at the head of the table, his aides shuffling their chairs around in order to be within whispering distance. There were glad cries of welcome from the sycophants who formed a substantial proportion of the twenty-four people in the room. They had all traveled here to El Baku within the past twenty four hours or so, nearly all of them from BSU itself, summoned by Wolf at very short notice, so that many of them had been forced to fly business class, or even first class, with a clear conscience. 'Hi Oscar! Good to see you! How's it going? Great commencement speech last week. Really something! You really heaped shit on that guy from Stanford.'

The chirping died down. Oscar took command. 'Well, we haven't exactly got a fixed agenda here. Just an opportunity to kick about a few ideas about future developments in this part of the world.' Oscar raised both hands in an evangelical gesture.

'Well, what do you think?' Twenty-four pairs of eyes were fixed on him, hypnotized, filled with trepidation. This had to be the shortest opening address to a meeting in the history of human communication. Was it a trick? Had they all been brought here from the other side of the world for a kind of initiative test? Would the first person to speak get a raise? But what if you said something that contradicted the as yet unstated master plan? That might be the end of a promising career for somebody. Viner cleared his throat. Viner was the chief sycophant, skilled in the delivery of meaningless platitudes.

'Well, Oscar, I guess we all know what you want. You want BSU to be really big in this area. We need to bring American educational know-how to bear on the many problems they face here, and by God we're all behind you in this. What is needed is a feasibility study, to clarify our objectives, and to set out the main lines of future development.'

Oscar Wolf nodded. It was impossible to guess from his expression, or lack of it, whether he agreed with Viner's profound analysis or not. He remained silent, looking straight down at the tips of his fingers, spread out on the table before him. Down towards the bottom of the table Ken Charles raised his hand. Charles had been Director of the University's program in Botswana, until that program had recently folded. He now had some hopes of directing the new program in El Baku, as he had worked for Oscar years before.

'Oscar,' he began, 'we must think big here. There's no point in setting up a program unless we have a throughput of at least 450 students a year. That way we can get a sizeable faculty, provide the range of courses that is needed, and begin to develop a graduate program. We need to find a facility that can cope with these numbers, and enough money to finance it for three years before we begin to make money.' He sat back, feeling that he had focused the discussion in exactly the way that was needed. Oscar was great in his way, but he needed help sometimes to get the issues clear. Silence reigned again. Wolf seemed not to have heard. Then suddenly he jerked his head round to his assistant, Lou, seated beside him.

'What about it, Lou?' Lou was a veteran. He knew how to cover his ass.

'I can draft a proposal for the Trustees, Oscar. Then it's your baby.' The Vice-presidential eyes swept around the table. 'O.K. I guess that will do for this morning. After lunch there is a guided tour of the town. This evening there is a reception for the representatives of El Baku University.' He picked up the unused pen that had thoughtfully been provided by the hotel conference staff, along with a notepad. The hotel had also arranged to tape the proceedings, to be transcribed, and presented that evening to all the participants. Oscar rose and headed towards the door.

J.T. was incredulous. He looked at his neighbor, an expert in educational theory.

'Have we decided something?' he gasped. The educational specialist, conscious of the dangers of careless talk, had perfected the art of speaking without moving his lips.

'We won't know until we read about it in the campus newspaper,' he said.

* * *

The reception was splendid. Tables laden with a mixture of Arab and western dishes, gleaming silverware laid out on the most expensive table linen. The guests entered, some in European dress, but mostly richly garbed in traditional Arab fashion. There were academics from El Baku University, representatives of the Government of El Baku, and the Rector of the University, a prince of the royal blood, Prince Ahmed. They mixed with their American hosts, some interpreting conversations for their less skilled companions. Oscar stepped forward and was introduced to His Royal Highness Prince Ahmed.

'Hi!' the Prince greeted him. 'Great to see you here. Harvard, class of 74.' He omitted to mention that he had stayed at Harvard for only one semester before deciding that, in view of the demands the teachers were making of him, affairs of state in EI Baku were too pressing to allow the luxury of further study.

'It is a great pleasure to be here, Your Highness. We want to build a really close relationship between our two universities and our two countries. I know that we have a great deal to give to each other, and to learn from each other.' Exhausted by this unusually lengthy speech, Oscar stepped back while the prince was being introduced to other members of the American party. Oscar turned to Lou. 'Where's the booze? I gotta offer this guy a drink.'

'No booze,' Lou replied. 'Can't be done. It's not allowed.'

'What the hell are you talking about? Not allowed! We had plenty in the suite last night.'

'Special arrangement,' said Lou. 'Not possible in public rooms like this.' Oscar seemed stunned.

'Why not?'

'Religion,' said Lou. 'It's against their religion.'

Oscar was now becoming really agitated. 'Garbage! I've seen these guys drinking in the States. They pour it down as quick as you or me. Get me some booze.' Lou decided that this was not the time for an argument, and withdrew as if to seek out the required alcohol.

The Harvard man had taken the center of the floor. Everyone stopped talking and adopted the respectful poses expected on such occasions.

'I am deeply pleased today' - he gave a magisterial wave of the hand - 'to welcome the representatives of BSU to our country. On behalf of my uncle, His Majesty the King, I welcome you all.' There was a wave of polite clapping and murmurs of approval. He pressed on. 'It is the policy of our Government and our University to develop intimacies with Americans at all times.' Further applause, accompanied by one or two whoops from the more impressionable Americans. Prince Ahmed bowed, and gave a blessing to the audience. 'It is typical of the friendliness, and generosity of our great American allies,' he made a dramatic pause in order to emphasize his point, 'in this regard as in other fields at present being discussed between us, that they are willing to set up a university here in El Baku in order to convey to our people their knowledge of modern technology and business methods.'

J.T. blinked. BSU was not known for its technological prowess. In fact he could not think of one department which would qualify, except perhaps the Hospitality and Food Technology program. They did fine lunches for the faculty, their cheesecake was particularly good, but he could not believe that that was what Prince Ahmed had in mind.

The prince was warming to his theme. 'It is sometimes thought that Arab countries are wealthy. This is far from being the case. Our expenses are very considerable, and we therefore welcome the opportunity for our young people to receive free education in this way.' He bowed again to Oscar Wolf who looked as if he were about to choke. Oscar looked around for Lou, who was presumably still in search of booze. Prince Ahmed was clearly waiting for a response. Oscar took a pace forward. His right hand traced several shapes in the air as he sought for suitable phrases.

'Your Highness, I guess we are all grateful for your kind words here today. I bring greetings from our President, Fred Zuwicki, who is unfortunately unable to be here today due to illness.' This statement caused some consternation among the Arabs, who found this reference to the President of the United States very puzzling. What had happened to President Bush? Had he died and been succeeded by this man of whom they had never heard? And now the new president was ill. The stability of the most powerful country in the world seemed suddenly to be questionable. It took a few moments for the information to be elicited that the reference was to the president of BSU, and for this information to be translated for those who were still in a state of shock, so that Oscar could continue. 'I guess, however, that there must be a certain failure of communication here,' Oscar mopped his brow, in spite of the fact that the temperature in the room now resembled that of Anchorage in February. 'Regarding free education, I mean. We are a private university. We have to pay our way. We charge high fees. Well, not high exactly, but not exactly low either. We have come here to offer you the best of American educational know-how, but at a price.'

Those among the Arab delegation who could understand what Oscar had said were looking concerned; those who could not were still exuding undying friendship. Prince Ahmed looked first bewildered, then irritated, and finally positively angry. His followers quickly adjusted their expressions. The Prince flung his robe over his shoulder in an unmistakable gesture of challenge.

'Your colleague, Mr. Kenneth Charlie, has assured my advisors that there will be scholarships for those who need them, and furthermore that most of the teaching will be conducted in Arabic. Otherwise we would not agree to having you here at all.'

Oscar jumped as if he had been shot. Ken Charles, a few feet away, cried out in anguish. 'Your Highness, I said that we could provide some scholarships. That's what you told me to say, Oscar. I guess we had in mind about...five. I also said that we could provide some language instruction for those whose English was not up to scratch. That's all I said, I swear.'

Wolf was used to being in tough bargaining situations. He saw himself as the epitome of the American executive - in control, powerful, propelling the situation in the right direction. He knew the product that he was selling, and he was not going to be railroaded by anybody, prince of the blood royal or not. He prepared to issue his ultimatum.

'Well, Prince, I guess you have just got to realize...' He had hardly started when Prince Ahmed swept his robe around him, turned on his heel, and went for the door. His retinue, taken by surprise, hurriedly divested themselves of plates, forks, napkins, and rushed out in his wake.

*   *   *

Oscar Wolf was not in the best of moods. He was in the office of the Ambassador of the United States to the Kingdom of El Baku, and the ambassador was a man whose language at the moment was anything but diplomatic.

'Why in hell's name didn't you consult us before you got into this fucking mess?' Oscar was not used to being spoken to in this way - except of course by Fred Zuwicki.

'We don't have to consult the damned government before we do anything. We're one of the top universities. We operate all round the world.'

'Yeah, I've heard about it,' the ambassador sneered. I heard about Botswana. And what about the Japanese fiasco. I read about it in the consular report. One of your faculty members gave the CEO of Nissan a D- in Management Techniques.'

Oscar blew up. 'Oh, sure. If you'd seen what crap that guy wrote about labor relations - create a family atmosphere in the workplace, cradle to grave support, never fire anybody. What the hell kind of garbage is that?'

The ambassador flung up his arms. 'Perhaps you could learn something from the Japanese about how to do business abroad. You certainly have fouled things up in El Baku.

Oscar finally lost his temper. 'Look you sonofabitch! I don't have to take this from you. Get off my back!' They were standing toe to toe, glaring at each other. The ambassador turned away, and went behind his desk. He gestured to Wolf to sit down, and with a visible effort to control himself he began again.

'Look Mr. Wolf, I have spent the last eighteen months working my butt off, putting together a deal with these people that is essential to the foreign policy and security of the United States. Then you fly in and in one day the whole thing is in ruins. Prince Ahmed has reported to the king that your word is not to be trusted, and it has been made clear that we - the U.S.of A. - are in the doghouse. Do you understand what I am saying?'

'O.K! O.K!' Wolf showed no contrition. 'You've got your problems and I've got mine. So what! This guy Ahmed got it into his stupid head that BSU was going to provide free education for hundreds of his peasants, teaching them how to run oil wells and to build trucks, and in Arabic to boot. What kind of a nut is he? I have to cover costs and turn back the overheads to the Treasurer. I tell you I'm out of here tomorrow.'

It was the ambassador's turn to lose his cool. 'I warn you, Wolf,' - the finger that was pointing at Wolf was definitely a smoking gun - 'if you try to leave tomorrow, I will see that you spend 48 hours in the immigration detention block at the airport, so help me God. And they don't have air-conditioning in that little shack, let me tell you.'

'You can't do that. I've got my rights,' Oscar screamed at him.

'In El Baku you don't have any rights. If you get flung in the can, I will of course bring to bear all the diplomatic pressure of the United States available to me on behalf of one of its distinguished citizens, in order to get him out of a hell-hole of a foreign jail. I reckon I can do that in about 48 hours, or at any rate within the week.'

Wolf looked at him in disbelief. 'What in Christ's name do you expect me to do?' The ambassador was now icily cool. He leaned forward, speaking very distinctly.

'You will go to Prince Ahmed. You will tell him that you will build his damned university in El Baku; that tuition will be nominal; and that a large part of the teaching will be in Arabic. You will smile and bow as you do it, and you will express astonishment that anyone could have got the impression that you ever intended anything different. Understood?' The last word was a pistol shot.

Wolf was speechless. He babbled incoherently for some moments, and then he exploded. 'You're crazy, out of your tiny mind. That would cost BSU about 20 million dollars a year. I could never sell that to Zuwicki. He'd fire me. He'd castrate me!'

'Oh he'll do it, I promise you,' the ambassador's face was rock hard. 'Because if he doesn't, his sweet little operation will never get another single dollar of government money for research. We'll cut you off under Title 24, "conduct likely to bring the reputation of the United States into disrepute, or tending to damage its interests abroad". And I've already cleared this with Washington. You'd better believe it.'

* * *

Stavros Williams sat looking out of the window of his office in the high-rise Franklin Delano Smith Administration Building. His own rise through the university hierarchy had been as meteoric as it was inexplicable to his colleagues. His career had been marked by a series of disasters, most of them extremely costly for the University, after each of which he had been promoted. Not of course that Stavros saw his career in that way. For him every stage had been a victory over the unfairnesses of life, against the unbelievable attitudes of those that disagreed with him, or stood in his way.

At present he was contemplating his latest triumph. The Trustees of Bransome Southern University had requested (i.e. demanded) that a study be undertaken of the extent of discrimination against women on the faculty, if such there should be, and Oscar Wolf had passed on this task to Stavros. Why the Vice President for International Affairs had been entrusted with this delicate internal matter was one of the impenetrable mysteries of administrative policy at BSU, and why Oscar Wolf had chosen Stavros Williams, of all people, to conduct the investigation was equally obscure. Stavros decided that the only way to conduct this investigation was to interview every female faculty member, a not inconsiderable number. His interviewing method leaned towards the 'participant observer' model, rather than the 'survey questionnaire'. That's to say that he favored a lunch or dinner with the interviewee as the best method of putting her at her ease. The resulting shock waves that radiated outwards through the university community testified to the fact that Stavros had certainly had a significant impact upon the objects of the investigation. If a survey had been conducted of those female faculty members who had experienced Stavros's research techniques, the results (on a scale of 1 to 5) would have looked rather like this:

1. Very Satisfied 5% (An Assistant Professor of Sociology, recently appointed who was prepared to do anything for tenure).

2. Satisfied 10% (Two Teaching Assistants who were considered by their female colleagues to be nymphomaniacs).

3. Very Unhappy 68.5% (i.e. every sane and balanced woman in the sample).

4. Homicidal 10% (two unreconstructed feminists).

5. Suicidal 5% (one 'mature' faculty person who actually believed what Stavros said).

The clamor that arose as Stavros scythed through the female faculty members soon reached the notice of the Authorities, and to his chagrin, Stavros was ordered to stay his hand. No further interviews were to take place. When ordered to report to President Zuwicki in person, Stavros pointed out that the only explanation of the faculty's reaction to his activities was that he was beginning to uncover facts that were unpalatable to them. These faculty members did not suffer from discrimination against them - in fact they were totally incompetent. They all ought to be fired. Zuwicki looked at Stavros in undisguised admiration. Here was a man who was actually saying the things that he, Zuwicki, had been thinking all these years, but could not possibly say. He had two choices. He could fire Stavros, and gain kudos with the female faculty, or he could promote Stavros, move him to another job, and get a junior staff member to write the kind of report the faculty wanted. Zuwicki knew the value of having people around on whom he could heap the blame for mistakes, and this guy was a real beaut. It was thus that Stavros Williams became Assistant Vice President for International Affairs at Bransome Southern University.

* * *

Janice Hart was thirty-two, blonde, with a trim figure, slim legs and well-formed breasts. She was not strikingly beautiful, but her face had a calm, charming quality that accurately reflected her character. She had worked at the University for four years, and had been drafted into Oscar's office to work as assistant to Oscar's assistant, and like everyone else she had a title - Assistant to the Assistant to the Vice President for International Affairs. The rule seemed to be that the more junior the position the longer the title. Since she had been working for Stavros Williams she had endured a great deal at the hands of Oscar and his assistant. Oscar's particular specialism was the kind of bad language, accompanied by gestures of serious obscenity, that enhanced his ego, but which made others feel dirty and invaded. Stavros aped his boss in this as in other ways. At an office party some months earlier, Stavros had maneuvered Janice into a corner, and had tried to fondle her breasts and her butt. She tried to force her way out, but he had pinioned her with one arm so that she could scarcely breathe. The only course open to her was to scream for help, but he wasn't actually raping her, and to embarrass her boss in that way was not a good career move. Later she regretted that she had not made a scene, and went to personnel to report the incident. They advised her to let the matter drop. 'Would anyone else who had been present at the party give evidence against Stavros?' Well, hardly. They all liked to be able to eat and pay the rent. Stavros continued his assault on Janice. He persistently tried to date her, offering to take her with him on business trips, or to nightclubs, but she had equally persistently refused. Then one lunchtime, when almost out of habit he offered to take her for a drink, he was gratified to hear her say that she would like that very much.

'They always come round in the end,' Stavros thought with satisfaction. 'The longer they resist the harder they fall.' They went to a bar a few minutes from the office, one that was frequented by administrators and faculty members. Stavros placed his hand on Janice's right elbow in a proprietarily way, and guided her to a table in a corner. He was aware that colleagues envious of his prowess, who were mentally checking off another Stavros conquest, were noting this procedure. They all detested him for his self-adulation and the slick judgments he produced on any and every subject, but they flattered him nevertheless, because of his closeness to the centers of power.

He ordered drinks, a club sandwich for himself, a salad for Janice. They discussed university politics, the perennial and inevitable subject among colleagues at BSU. His position on this subject was one that made it impossible for others either to oppose his views or genuinely to agree with him. He would bitterly criticize the upper echelons of the university from the President down for their authoritarian behavior, but he himself practiced exactly the same techniques on his subordinates that he attacked in his superiors. Conversations with him therefore took the shape either of a procession of formal aquiescences on the part of his hearers, or silent disagreement. On this occasion Janice adopted the former approach, nodding agreement as he ranted on about the incompetence of one, or the fascism of another, and making small noises of disbelief that people could behave in the ways described. Tiring of this, Stavros became amorous, taking her hand across the table, asking if they couldn't see a little more of each other.

'I've always felt that we had a lot in common.' He looked deeply into her eyes. 'It seems a pity that we don't make waves together.' Ignoring what to most women might seem to be a hysterically funny line, Janice squeezed his hand.

'Are you very busy this afternoon? Why don't we go for a drive? It's such a beautiful day.'

Stavros could hardly believe his luck. He quickly paid the check.

'Why don't we leave separately,' Janice suggested. 'I'll take my car. It's less well known around here than yours. I'll pick you up at the corner of Summer and Pleasant.' When she drew up he slipped furtively into the passenger seat, and almost immediately his hand slid along her thigh. She smiled at him and removed his hand.

'Later!' She drove steadily through the city traffic.

'Where are you heading?'

'There's an area I know, to the north of here. About twenty minutes.' The city streets gave way to suburbia, the apartment blocks replaced by low frame-houses surrounded by neatly cut lawns. Then these began to thin out to be replaced in their turn by farms, farmed no longer, but still with all the trappings - barns, old carts, wheels, horseshoes casually mounted on doors and beams.

'I don't know this area,' Stavros said. 'Do you come out here often?' His tone of voice, and the thinly disguised leer that accompanied it, indicated that he thought he had at last discovered the resident university nymphomaniac, a quest that he had been pursuing single- mindedly for a long time.

'No, not really. My Aunt Charlotte lives near here. I visit her occasionally.'

'How much further?' He was getting very excited by the nearness of her. She was having to fight harder to keep his hands away.

'Careful. You'll make me wreck the car. Be patient! Only a few minutes now.' She turned off the road on to a dirt track leading through a field of tall grass, and parked in a circular clearing, turning the car to face the direction of the road. Immediately his arm went round her shoulders, his mouth sought hers, and a hand began to move up inside her skirt, swiftly heading for the top of her thighs. 'Not here,' she said, pushing his hand down. 'Not in here. It's too...sordid. Let's get out.' He was surprised.

'We could get in the back.'

'No. It's such a beautiful day. Let's be in the open.' She placed her hand on his left leg, just below his crotch, and gave it a firm squeeze.

'Boy, you really are something.' He could hardly speak for excitement. He scrambled out of the car, moved quickly round to her side as she got out, put his arms around her and kissed her hard, trying to push his tongue into her mouth. She detached herself, and taking his hand she led him into the long grass for fifteen, twenty yards. His arm was round her waist, pulling her to him, thigh to thigh as they walked. He was kissing her hand, making excited yelping noises like a puppy about to be let off the leash.

'This will do. No one will see us here.' She put both hands on the lapels of his jacket, pulling it back till it slid away, dropping to the ground. He was pawing at her, trying to unbutton her blouse, caressing first one breast then the other, running his hands down over her bottom, totally out of control. She did not resist him, but dropped to her knees, and began to unbuckle his belt. He kicked off his shoes and she drew his pants down, until he kicked those off also. He was transported with delicious excitement. He pulled her to her feet.

'It's my turn now. Let me undress you.' Fumbling he undid her blouse and it slid to her feet. He began kissing the swelling flesh that rose from the top of her bra, pulling one side down to expose a nipple.

'Come down on the ground,' she pleaded, and sank back to her knees. He followed her and she pulled off his shirt, buttons ripping at cloth. His hands were unhooking the waistband of her skirt, then his fingers were inside the top of her tights, to pull them down over the softness that he could now feel for the first time, and which was driving him mad with lust.

'Darling, lie down on your front,' she pushed him gently to the ground. 'I want to give you pleasure.'

Dutifully he turned on his stomach, now wearing only underpants and socks, although there was no way he could lie flat out. He bent his left leg up to make it possible to bear the pressure on his organs. He was whimpering. 'Please let me take you. I can't wait.'

'Yes you can. I want it to last as long as possible.' She caressed his back, and then gently she drew off his underpants, with some difficulty unhooking them from him at the front. She continued caressing him lower down his back, and he groaned in ecstasy.

She leaned down over him till her breasts brushed his back. 'I've got to put something in,' she whispered. 'Be patient. It won't take a moment. Don't peek will you. It would embarrass me. Don't lose it. I'll be quick.' He heard her move back towards their clothes, then a scuffling noise as she maneuvered herself in the long grass.

'Hurry!' he called out in a strangled voice, as he lay face down, naked except for his socks. 'I'm desperate. This is driving me mad.' He'd never before been in such a subordinate role with a woman. It made him think of the men who let women whip and abuse them. There was a kind of delicious pain to it. Would she never come? It seemed an eternity, and he was beginning to feel that he might indeed lose it, when there was the sudden sound of a car motor starting up.

'What the hell is that?' Startled he sat up. Was there another car in the vicinity? Had someone been watching them all the time? 'Janice, where are you?' He got up on his knees, looking over the long grass in the direction in which she had moved. 'Janice!' His voice took on a hysterical edge. The sound of the car was retreating now, moving towards the road. Half crouching, his hands over his privates, he ran towards the clearing in the grass where the car had been parked. Nothing, no sign of the car, no sign of Janice. He began to panic. Had the car been stolen? He tried to remember if she had locked it. Almost certainly not. They had been so filled with passion. But where was she? Had she been kidnapped? He must get dressed. Not bothering to crouch any longer, he ran back to where they had stripped off each other's clothes. There was the patch of downtrodden grass. And then the awful truth began to dawn. There were no clothes there. They had all disappeared. Nothing. Not a stitch. There was only one possible explanation. Janice had taken them. She had collected them up as he lay there, taken them to the car, and driven off. It was incredible, but that is what must have happened. Was it some ghastly joke? Would he hear the car returning in a moment, and see her laughing face as she saw his embarrassment? He returned again to the clearing. Anger began to rise in his breast. He screamed.

'Janice, you come back here. You lousy, fucking bitch. I'll kill you.'

He jumped up and down with rage, forgetting for the moment that he was stark naked, reminded only by the acute discomfort that these exertions caused him. He wept with rage.

'Bastard! Whore! Bitch!' He sank to the grass. 'I'll kill you. You won't get away with this.'

* * *

Late that evening, as dusk was falling, a figure slipped into a phone booth. A close observer would have noted that the figure was unclothed, except that a sock had been carefully arranged over its most delicate appendages, and retained there with one hand, as the figure, crouching as it ran, cried out incoherent oaths and blasphemies.

'Operator. I want to make a collect call. Quickly, please.'

'Yes, sir. I will be as quick as I can. Would you let me have the number you wish to call, please.'

'I don't know the number. I haven't got it with me.'

'Then you must call Information, sir.'

'But I haven't got a dime. This is an emergency, operator.'

'I'm sorry, sir. If you haven't got the number there is nothing I can do. If it is an emergency please dial 911.'

'You silly bitch. It's not that kind of emergency.'

'I am reporting you to the police, sir.' With an animal cry, the figure threw down the handset, and ran for the open fields.

* * *

The BSU program in El Baku had been running for nearly a year. Severely scaled down from its original plan, and much to the annoyance of the government of the Kingdom, the University had put most of its effort into setting up a School of Business, and today Ken Charles was to open the teaching program with a seminar entitled "Business Efficiency: The Global Approach". He entered the newly built and expensively furnished seminar room, already occupied by the first intake of students recruited from the industrial and commercial enterprises of El Baku. As he walked to the podium the audience rose respectfully to their feet. Ken waved to them to resume their seats, and arranging his notes on the lectern, he launched into his address.

'It gives me great pleasure today to open the El Baku School of Business of Bransome Southern University. We see it as our mission to bring to you the most up-to-date knowledge of the theory and practice of management, in order that the techniques and experience that have served us so well should also be available to you, and at the end of this course you will be able go out into the world of international business as ambassadors both for El Baku and for BSU.' Charles leaned forward resting his elbows on the lectern. "My message to you today, is that we now live in the Global Village. The world is one market place. We must rise above local customs and cultural differences to create the homogenous executive. The man or woman...' His eyes swept the room searching for a potentially homogenous woman, but the audience was unrelievedly masculine, 'who can slot into a position anywhere in the world, East or West, and perform there as a modern business executive should.'

Charles fixed his audience with a glare. They seemed less excited by the prospect of becoming homogenous than Charles had expected; indeed there was a certain restlessness in the group, suggestive more of distress than appreciation. He put this down to the impact that his words had had upon students who had perhaps never before come into contact with such a powerful intellectual stimulus. He returned to the attack.

'The fundamental principles of management are universal, unaltered by time or place. They are,' he thundered forth, 'Connecticut, Maine and Pennsylvania.' He paused to allow the students to get this down. Only one or two were making half-hearted attempts to take notes.

'CT, ME, PA.' Charles emphasized the importance of this stage of the lesson by pointing in turn to three or four of his audience, and intoning with ecclesiastical fervor, 'CT, ME, PA. Creative Thought, Management Enterprise, and Program Application.' This was it. THE KNOWLEDGE! They should be electrified, gasping for more.

They were moribund. Nevertheless, Charles wound himself up to embark upon the exhaustive exploration which was required fully to grasp these principles, but as he was about to give forth again, one of the students, rather older than the others, rose hesitantly from the back row. He raised his hand high in the air.

'We have not got the English.' Charles looked at him uncomprehendingly.

'Not got the English? What on earth do you mean?'

'We have not got the English.' The student sat down. Charles looked around in amazement.

'Are you telling me you don't understand English?' He pointed at one of the students in the front row. 'Do you understand English?'

The student gave him a friendly smile, but said nothing.

'Do any of you understand what I am saying?' Getting no reaction from the class, he stormed from the room, turning into the office of the Director of Academic Affairs, a mild-looking young man, sitting at his desk reading the latest copy of the *New York Times* flown in from the States.

'What the hell is going on here?' Charles screamed at the top of his voice. The Director of Academic Affairs, having eventually grasped the drift of Charles' complaint, pointed out that the recruitment of students was not his responsibility. That was done through the agency.

'Get them on the phone. Now!' After some minutes of heated conversation with the agency, Charles flung down the phone, sat down heavily, and put his head between his hands. 'I don't believe this. I just don't believe it.'

The Director of Academic Affairs maintained a diplomatic silence. Eventually Charles raised his head. 'They advertised the course, in Arabic. The advertisement did not say that the course would be taught in English. They say that we did not tell them the course would be taught in English. We've got twenty-four students for the next fifteen weeks, none of whom understands a word of English.'

Forty minutes later Charles returned to the baffled group of students, accompanied by Salim, a liaison officer of the El Baku government. Salim explained to the group that for the rest of the semester he would be acting as interpreter for the course teachers. Prompted by Ken Charles, he informed them that for the rest of the morning they would move into the laboratory, for their first lesson on the most vital piece of high technology in the armament of the modern executive, the computer. Showing some enthusiasm for the first time, the students moved down the corridor to a spacious room furnished in steel and glass, and provided with 24 of the most state-of-the-art computers available. The empty boxes in which the computers had been delivered from the United States still stood in the corridor. Charles explained, through Salim, that unfortunately the technician promised by the government of El Baku had failed to turn up. Salim made no attempt to mimic the contemptuous tone with which Ken Charles had conveyed this information. Charles had therefore set up the laboratory himself, but had no chance to test the network yet. There might therefore be some minor teething problems.

After a brief introduction to the computer, which nevertheless took quite a time to deliver because the interpreter had taken a degree in Medieval English Literature and was not well up in the vocabulary of computing, Charles gave the order to the enthusiastic students to "Switch On", and twenty-four arms were simultaneously extended towards the machines. It has to be said that the resulting explosion was not as great as some rather biased reports have suggested. In fact only four of the machines actually exploded in the sense that the screens blew out. Most of the others simply sent out a shower of sparks, and then began ominously to smoke. The fire that engulfed one machine was quickly extinguished. As for the remainder, their screens merely glowed extremely brightly for a few seconds and then went black. The injuries sustained by the students were minor, and except for one young man, who claimed that his London-tailored suit was burnt beyond repair, they took the situation in good part.

*   *   *

It was 10 a.m. Ken Charles was finishing his memo to Oscar Wolf complaining that the company which had supplied the computers had totally failed to take into account the voltage of the local power supply, when the telephone rang. 'BSU in El Baku. Ken Charles speaking. Can I help you?' The voice at the other end of the line was deep, American and authoritative.

'This is Jason Roberts. Counselor at the Embassy. I'm at the airport. We have a problem. Please get down here straight away. I'll be at the immigration desk.' The connection was broken before Charles had any chance to ask for clarification of the nature of the problem. He shrugged, put the phone down and set off for the airport. Twenty minutes later he pushed open the swing doors of the airport lounge, and found the American diplomat clearly trying to soothe a very irate official of the El Baku immigration service. On seeing Charles the big American excused himself, and turned to the BSU administrator.

'Are you expecting a Dr. Llewellyn-Proctor? His demeanor was anything but friendly.

'Sure am. Going to do a week's teaching for us. Good academic record. Should go down very well in El Baku.' Charles was glad to have the opportunity to show off to the Embassy how well the program was going. 'Is there some kind of a problem?'

The Counselor snarled:

'Problem? The problem, or one of the problems, is that your Dr. Llewellyn-Proctor is an Israeli.' Charles recoiled as if he had been struck.

'No. I can't believe it. Dr. Llewellyn-Proctor teaches at the University of Southern Georgia.'

'Right! Lives in America, teaches in America, is married to an American, but is an Israeli citizen.'

'Oh God! Aren't they going to let him in?'

'Him? Ha, ha! Him?' The Counselor seemed not to be wholly in control of himself. 'Do you have any idea what you are saying?'

'Yes.' Charles could not understand what his problem was. 'I'm asking if they are going to let him in. I've got students expecting to be taught.'

Roberts grasped Charles's arm rather roughly, pulled him across to a door at the side of the arrivals lounge before which a heavily-armed guard was posted, and flung the door open.

'Dr. Charles, let me introduce you to Dr. Mike Llewellyn-Proctor.' Before an astonished Ken Charles stood a short, extremely attractive woman in her early thirties. Her hair formed a great cloud of black curls. She wore a low-cut white silk blouse, a black miniskirt that very nearly covered her hips but nothing else, and high stiletto-heeled shoes. It was doubtful if she was wearing more than one further small item of clothing. Charles was dumbfounded.

'But you can't be. I don't understand.' Later when he had a chance to talk to her in a more relaxed setting, he asked her how an Israeli woman ended up being called Mike Llewellyn-Proctor, for God's sake. It sounded, he suggested, more like someone who had just stepped off the Mayflower.

'Well, my husband did, or at least his ancestors. That takes care of the "Proctor" bit. My parents were Jews who escaped from Germany in 1939, and settled in Wales. My Dad decided to change his name from Liebermann to Llewellyn. That helped at that time in Britain. They moved to Israel in '61 and I was born there. They moved on again soon after that and ended up in Atlanta. They did not apply to change my nationality. It didn't seem necessary. I had the best of both worlds.'

'O.K. But what about "Mike"?'

'Oh, my parents gave me the name Michaela, but I prefer Mike.' Charles felt pretty sore. How could she be so insensitive to the situation in El Baku. These people considered themselves at war with Israel.

Jason Roberts had pulled out all the stops to prevent her from having to spend her time in the Arab kingdom in a detention cell.

The authorities would have deported her immediately, but there was no suitable flight out for three days. Finally they had agreed that she could leave the airport if Charles vouched for her, and provided that when she left she was decently covered up. Roberts sent to the Embassy for his raincoat, and for a scarf to cover her hair, and clad in these she went out into the blistering heat of the early afternoon in El Baku. She had objected vociferously to all this, but when it became clear that the only alternative was a cell, she eventually accepted the situation. The final shot came from the immigration officer:

'Remember, she's not to leave the compound.'

As the taxi carried them away from the airport at a hair-raising speed, Mike loosened the scarf from her head, and opened the raincoat, displaying her legs to the full.

'What was that about the compound?' she asked.

'All the Europeans and Americans live in a special section which is fenced off and kept under guard.' Charles explained.

'O.K. But you have to leave the compound to teach, or whatever.'

'Of course.' Charles sought for the right way to make his point. 'But we don't employ female teachers here. It is very difficult for them. Women can only leave the compound if they are dressed in accordance with the local customs.' A glance through the taxi window was all that was needed to identify the nature of the local custom regarding female attire.

'You're joking of course.'

'No, I certainly am not joking. How can an Israeli be so ignorant of Arab custom?'

'I was very young when we left Israel. You don't come up against it much in Atlanta.' He looked sideways at her as she stared out at the narrow streets of the town. He found it difficult to believe that she was as naive as she implied. In other respects she certainly did not appear to be naive!

'You haven't come here to carry out some Israeli military operation, I hope.' He was suddenly seized by the most awful premonition of disaster.

'And where do you think that I concealed my weapon?' She opened the raincoat really wide for his inspection, and he had to admit that it would not have been easy for her to conceal very much in her clothing.

'Anyway, how am I going to teach my classes?' she asked.

'I guess we'll have to transfer them into the compound. It's only a small group. If necessary you can teach them in my living room.'

'And I have to stay in that place until I leave for my return flight, right?'

'Right!'

* * *

It was just after 6 p.m. The central square of the town of El Baku was cooling off from the oppressive heat of the afternoon The shadow cast by the mosque that formed the west side of the square was lengthening, and had already reached the middle of the open space. The call to evening prayer was over. The people of the town were beginning to go about their business, drinking coffee, and haggling over purchases in the sukh. The north side of the square consisted of the El Baku International Hotel and the Embassy of the United States, whilst across from them was the grim-faced barracks that formed the headquarters of the El Baku police.

A group of five women, heavily veiled, entered the square from a side street, and set off towards the opposite corner. The *burkha*, the long black robes that reached from the top of the head to the ankle, were of better quality than those of the townswomen, and the masks that surrounded their eyes were modestly, but richly decorated.

They glided towards the center of the square where, reaching the area of bright sunlight, they formed a circle. As if at a signal, emitting high shrill cries, they bent down, each took the hem of her *burkha* in her hands, and with wild ecstatic gestures they simultaneously threw them over their heads and to the ground. They were revealed as young attractive women, dressed for the most part in western-style clothes that would have been considered to be almost matronly in New York or London, skirts hardly above the knee, but which were outrageous in El Baku, particularly for Arab women. The only one who was dressed in a more provocative way was a short dark-haired woman wearing an extremely brief miniskirt and a white silk blouse. The women shook free their long hair, and then, in the most modest fashion imaginable, each of them pulled out from the top of their dress or blouse, a bra, no doubt specially loosened for the occasion. They twirled these garments around over their heads, and then with a quick application of a cigarette lighter, the five items of feminine attire soon lay smoldering on the ground.

From the moment when the women's cries first rang out across the square, everyone present was transfixed by the demonstration that was being enacted there. Even when they removed the *burkha* there was no movement from the guards on duty outside the police barracks. But with the incineration of the lingerie, the police came to life, one ran inside the barracks to alert his comrades, and three others set off across the square pulling automatic pistols from their holsters as they ran. The women scattered in different directions, three of them running for the narrow streets that led from the square into the maze of alleys that made up the old town. The police caught two of them before they could reach the edge of the square, one made it to the entrance of the sukh and disappeared. Of the other two, one ran into the main entrance of the El Baku International Hotel, and the other, the woman in the miniskirt, ran towards the open gate of the Embassy of the United States. A tall, burly U.S. marine, hands on hips, barred her way.

'Excuse me, ma'am. Please state your business.' Mike, for of course it was she, jumped up, threw her arms round his neck, and hanging there, kissed him passionately on the mouth. Having endured this attack for rather longer than was consistent with correct military discipline, he struggled to disengage her, and as they fell apart, she slipped past him into the Embassy's grounds, found an open door, and disappeared into the building.

* * *

It was a sunny spring day in Bransome. The oppressive heat of summer was still some weeks away, and Oscar Wolf was humming quietly to himself as he entered the impressive portals of the Woodrow Wilson Administration Building. He took the elevator to the top floor, by-passing the fourth floor complex which housed his office, and those of the other Vice-presidents, for he had received an urgent summons to attend personally upon the President, Dr. Fred Zuwicki.

He passed through the outer office furnished with comfortable chairs and low tables bearing neatly arranged copies of the Alumni Bulletin, through the reception area, where he was greeted by two immaculately turned-out ladies, through the office of the Secretary to the Assistant to the President, guarded by a burly campus policeman who saluted stiffly, through the anteroom of the President's Office, bedecked with the University flag, the state flag and the Stars and Stripes, and into the office of the Secretary to the Personal Assistant to the President.

'Good morning, Mr. Wolf. I will tell Miss Adams that you are here.'

Miss Adams, who was reputed to be a direct descendant of the second President of the United States, was a formidable personage, the guardian of the gate to the President, without whose approval there was no hope of access to the inner sanctum. Indeed, so impressive was she, that when the visitor was finally led into the vast office of the President himself, the sight of the insignificant-looking individual seated at the massive desk was a considerable anti-climax.

'Hi, Fred! What's up?' Oscar was never inclined to obsequiousness, or to unnecessary small talk. Zuwicki sat silently as Oscar took a seat on a low couch and arranged himself comfortably.

'Oscar,' Zuwicki began, his voice quivering with suppressed emotion, 'You stupid bastard! What the hell do you think you're up to? What kind of a shitty operation are you running in El Baku?'

Oscar had become accustomed to the somewhat flowery language affected by his boss, but this seemed a little extreme even for him. Zuwicki clearly had not finished.

'I've got the stinking State Department on my neck. Your people out there have created some kind of international crisis that's likely to engulf the whole of the Middle East, maybe the whole damn world. One of your faculty is holed up in the U.S. Embassy claiming political asylum, and the Israeli Government has demanded she be released. The program director is under house arrest, and is about to be deported. The Government of El Baku is demanding that Clinton should apologize for American involvement in an Israeli plot.' Zuwicki's voice took on an hysterical edge. 'You will recall, Oscar, that I was forced into this program very much against my better judgment. What have you got to say?'

Oscar looked at his president in horror and dismay. 'How can this be? I've heard nothing about it.' He grasped at straws. 'You're sure it's our program? El Baku? Maybe it's all a mistake.'

'Mistake? Mistake?' The hysteria in Zuwicki's voice was taking over. 'Sure it's a mistake. And you made it. I've talked with the Ambassador there. Some crazy broad did a public strip tease and then bolted for the Embassy.'

'But where does Israel come into it?'

'She's an Israeli citizen.'

Oscar gave up. It was too difficult to grasp. He began to hum quietly to himself again. Zuwicki rose to his full 5 feet 5 inches.

'Oscar, you'd better sort this out, and quick, or else you'll be an ex-Vice president. And by the way, where were you when this broke yesterday evening? I had ten people scouring this town for you. Not a trace!' Oscar quivered. He had been in a small but very comfortable motel at the time - with a friend.

'I was out of town. At a convention.' Zuwicki suddenly went berserk. 'Get out! Get out of here. And on your way out, go and see Bill Wilkinson. He's after your hide too.'

Oscar hurried from the room, seized by panic. Wilkinson was the VP for Legal Affairs. A request to meet with him usually spelled trouble, as if things weren't bad enough already.

Wilkinson was dictating to a secretary when Oscar put his head around the door. Wilkinson motioned him towards a chair and continued dictating, for what to Oscar seemed an eternity. This was clearly a deliberate insult to Oscar. They were, after all, colleagues, both VP's. They were also potential rivals for Zuwicki's job, if he should depart, and Wilkinson's treatment of Oscar at this moment signaled that the former felt that Oscar's star was falling rapidly. Oscar rose from his chair, a scowl on his face. Wilkinson waved at him.

'Be with you in a moment, Oscar '' and he continued to dictate for another two long minutes. When the secretary had left, Wilkinson brought together the tips of his fingers, elbows resting on the desk, and pursed his lips.

'Oscar, I need to talk to you about your Assistant, Stavros Williams.' Oscar had been expecting another blast about El Baku, and this change of subject emboldened him. The old aggressiveness returned.

'What's my Assistant got to do with you, Bill?'

'Nothing, thank God,' Wilkinson gave a shudder of distaste, 'except that I spent a large part of the night rescuing him from the state mental institution.' Oscar sank back in his chair. What now?

'It seems,' Wilkinson continued, 'that he was picked up by the police yesterday afternoon, at Jonesville, about ten miles out of town. They found him in a field, after a report was phoned in by a local resident. He was stark naked.' Oscar was now sure that he was fast asleep, and that this was a dreadful nightmare. Reality couldn't be this bad. Wilkinson was speaking again.

'They took him to the station and provided him with some clothes. All that they could get out of him was that he worked for you, and they called your office. One of your people volunteered to go and identify him. A person called...' He paused and consulted a notepad, 'Janice Hart. When she got to the station and was shown into the interview room where Stavros was being held, he went absolutely ape, and tried to kill her. It took four cops to hold him down. They put him in a straightjacket and hauled him off to The Pines.'

Wilkinson paused for effect. He was not disappointed. Oscar Wolf looked like a prizefighter about to go down for the count. He seemed incapable of speech, so Wilkinson continued. 'I was informed of the situation, went out there, and I was able to get him released. I had to guarantee that you would be responsible for him. He has to report to you at 8 a.m., noon, and 8 p.m. Neither of you must leave town.' At this Oscar finally found his voice and exploded.

'You sonofabitch. I'm not his nurse. I've got to go to El Baku. Its urgent.'

'Sorry, Oscar. There was no other way to get the poor bastard out of there. Yeah, I heard about the El Baku business. The State Department got on to me first, and I had to pass on the bad news to Fred. That was a short time before I was contacted by the police about Stavros. I guess you've got a lot on your plate.' Wilkinson looked suitably concerned about the difficulties in which his colleague found himself. Oscar raised a clenched fist to heaven, found his feet and lurched from the room.

* * *

J.T. watched the marker lights flash by as his plane touched down on the runway of El Baku International Airport. With Oscar and Stavros confined to Bransome city limits there had been no-one else to send on this most delicate of missions. At least he had been to El Baku before, even if only for forty-eight hours.

Counselor Jason Roberts, was waiting for him at the gate, to lead him to the official limo that was to take him to the Embassy, where he was to stay as a guest of the United States. Roberts had nothing personal against J.T., but the situation in El Baku was so tense that he was of the opinion that a really big gun was needed to sort out this situation, and BSU had sent this young, junior administrator to cope with an international crisis. Although, he reflected, the last time there had been a big gun from BSU in El Baku had been pretty disastrous. At least this one looked presentable and quite intelligent as well. None of the bombast that he had come to associate with university administrators.

'What's the latest on the situation?' J.T. inquired as they settled into their seats.

'Much the same. Ken Charles is restricted to the compound. Mike is in the Embassy, enjoying herself. Israel is threatening to mount a commando rescue operation to get her out. The Government of El Baku is threatening to break off diplomatic relations with the US. The world price of oil is rocketing. A normal quiet day in El Baku.'

'Why did Dr. Llewellyn-Proctor get involved in this incident?' J.T. asked.

'She didn't "get involved". She organized it. It was an official operation of the Movement for the Liberation of Arab Women.'

'But she is an Israeli.' J.T. was dumbfounded. 'How can that be?' Jason did not reply, but his raised shoulders and outstretched arms were eloquent of the fact that there are some things that a mere man can never hope to fathom.

'What do you think is needed to resolve this situation? J.T. asked.

'First, we have to grovel. A lot of groveling. Of course it will be diplomatic groveling, but El Baku will know that is what we are doing. A regretful message from the President - something like that.' In reply to J.T.'s raised eyebrows he added: 'I mean Clinton not Zuwicki. Then we have to get a safe passage out for Mike. The problem is what do we offer them in return.'

'We could offer to close down the BSU program and leave gracefully, J.T. suggested, thinking of the fervent hope that Fred Zuwicki had expressed to him before his departure.

'We thought of that, I can assure you. But I don't think it would be enough. In any case they can kick you out at any time they want. It's got to be more than that. The fact is,' Roberts was uncharacteristically embarrassed at what he had to say, 'we - the Embassy, I mean - well, we'd rather like your outfit to stay in El Baku.'

'Why on earth?'

'Well, it's a bit difficult to explain, but since BSU has been here life has been in some ways easier for the Embassy staff.'

'In what ways?'

Roberts looked sideways at his companion. This man seemed a cut above the other BSU people with whom he had come into contact. He took the plunge.

'Well, you understand, part of our job here is... intelligence. Up until recently the Embassy staff have been virtually the only foreigners, the only Americans at any rate, in El Baku, and its been difficult to keep a low profile, if you see what I mean.'

'Vaguely ', J.T. responded.

'The fact is that your colleague, Ken Charles, is so incompetent, makes so many blunders, and is such a figure of fun here, that he distracts attention from us. He's a godsend really. And he makes people think that all Americans are equally incompetent. Which fortunately is not the case.'

'So BSU is America's secret weapon in this area. It's a new thought. You don't use any of our people for your intelligence activities?'

'God forbid!' The limo was passing through the gates of the Embassy.

'Well, what can we offer them then?' J.T. was lost for inspiration.

'I'll leave that for the Ambassador to discuss with you.' Roberts got out of the car. 'Let's have a drink.'

'What about the ban on alcohol?'

'Don't you realize that you are now standing on American soil? Come on in!'

The next day Ambassador Anstey received J.T.

'Thank you for coming to help us deal with this little local difficulty,' the Ambassador began. 'I hope that we can find a quick solution.' He looked apologetically at J.T. 'Forgive me if I say that in some ways you are not the ideal person for this job, although Jason tells me that he has every confidence in your ability to deal with it. The fact is that the Government of El Baku is not going to be very happy that BSU sent the Director of Study Abroad to negotiate on a matter which they consider to be of global significance, whatever you or I might think about the importance of a few ladies destroying their undergarments.'

J.T. nodded. 'I understand their susceptibilities,' he said. 'But I am the best the University had to offer at short notice.'

'Quite!' Anstey ruminated for a moment. 'What I suggest we do is to give you a different title. If necessary we can clear it with President Zuwicki. I think he will agree.'

'What had you in mind?'

'We thought that something like Chief Special Assistant to the President would do. It sounds like someone from the White House Office, which might help. They might not ask which President it refers to.'

'That's OK by me.'

'The next problem is what we offer them as a sweetener in order to clear this whole matter up.' Anstey rose from his desk and took an armchair close to where J.T. was seated. He adopted a more confidential tone. 'This is a pretty important moment in the history of the US in the Middle East. We need to get it right.' Anstey looked earnestly into J.T.'s eyes, as if he expected some brilliant comment from the young visitor. When none came he shifted back in his chair and began again.

'I think that Jason has already told you that our attitude to BSU has changed somewhat over the past year. We would welcome a big expansion in your operation here.'

'I see a difficulty there,' J.T. interrupted, 'I am afraid that President Zuwicki would not agree to any higher level of expenditure on this program. He would prefer to close it down. The University loses a lot of money here.'

'I know,' Anstey smiled, 'I persuaded him to try it out in the first place. Money will not be a problem. The Federal Government is now firmly committed to the development of international education, and is prepared to meet the full costs of a project here, as a kind of pilot program.'

'You mean the government will pay for everything? Zuwicki would like that.'

'Yes, I'm sure he would.' There was a rueful note in the Ambassador's voice. Then he returned to his optimistic/forceful mode. 'What we would like is a large university operation that focused on vocational courses, rather than upon the more academic disciplines: tourism rather than physics, hotel administration rather than literature, secretarial skills rather than sociology. That way the country will get the kind of help it needs for development, don't you think, and there will be a rapid turnover of teachers and others passing through El Baku. It. will serve to bring the modern world here as quickly as possible.'

J.T. was rather non-plussed. 'Is that the function of a university? That sort of thing could be done by a kind of technical institute.'

'Let's not be elitist and old-fashioned,' the Ambassador chided him. These are subjects just as worthy of study as any others. And,' he paused in order to drive home his point, 'we are talking about getting your university out of a pit that it has dug for itself, for the USA, and for the whole of the Middle East. Effectively we have two hostages here that we have to set free - Mike, and Ken Charles. This isn't just an academic discussion we are having here.'

'Right!' J.T. remembered why he was sitting in the office of the Ambassador of the United States to EI Baku. 'Right!'

'Oh!' the Ambassador pointed his forefinger at J.T. 'I nearly forgot. There is one condition that we want to put on this package. Ken Charles must be in charge of the whole shooting match. You understand?'

'If that is what you want.'

'It is. Good!' The Ambassador indicated that enough time had been spent on the niceties. 'I suggest that you get on the telephone to Zuwicki, and then we will pray for an audience with His Excellency the Minister of Foreign Affairs who happens to be the third son of His Majesty the King of El Baku.'

'Sir, it is 3 a.m. in Bransome. The President of the University will be asleep. I don't feel that I should disturb him.'

The Ambassador picked up the phone and handed it to J.T. 'Son, just do it.'

* * *

As J.T. entered the Administration building he held the door open for Janice Hart who was about to leave for the day. 'Hi! Janice.'

'J.T. Nice to see you! Have you heard about Oscar's great triumph?'

'No. What was that?'

'He has negotiated this great new program in El Baku. They say it will be the biggest American university operation abroad, ever.'

'Really?' J.T. registered amazement. 'When did this happen?'

'I guess it must have been while you were away. Where have you been? Abroad?'

'Nowhere special. How are things with you?'

'Good. I've had one or two triumphs myself. Let's meet up and have coffee sometime. I'll tell you about it.'

'Great!' J.T. let the door swing to behind her and turned towards the elevator. He rode up to the fourth floor, and turned into the anteroom to Oscar's office. Louise, Oscar's Personal Assistant was waiting for him.

'Hi! J.T. Good to see you. Oscar is expecting you. Go straight in.' J.T. entered the sanctum where the great man sat at his desk, ruminatively smoking a cigar. It was a non-smoking building but Oscar felt that rules like that were for others to observe. 'Hello J.T.! Welcome! Things went well in El Baku?'

'Fine, Oscar. How was it received here?'

'Went down well. Zuwicki thinks that International Affairs did a good job. I'll see that it's not forgotten when raises are being considered.' Oscar began to hum; always a bad sign. He swung his chair round so that he was facing the large world map on the wall.

'You did a good job in El Baku. We're having some problems with the program in Japan. I thought perhaps you might go out there and see what you can do.'

J.T. was somewhat taken aback. He had only been back in the country for a little over two hours.

'That sounds interesting. What's the problem?'

'Well!' Oscar seemed uncomfortable, 'I've been getting a lot of flak lately about the Tokyo program. Seems like the people who run it have very high academic standards, and they upset a lot of the Japanese who come on the courses. That's OK for the faculty, those bums, but it sure makes for a lot of problems with the government of the US. Some of these people are involved with trade negotiations with our government, and then BSU fails them on their economics courses! I've been thinking that we certainly need a program in Japan - it's a matter of prestige - but maybe not in Tokyo. What about say,' looking at the map he picked two cities at random, 'Fukuoka, or Sapporo. I think you ought to check it out.'

'OK. When do you want me to leave?'

'Soon as possible. I've got Stavros making the arrangements, as we speak.'

'Stavros?'

'Sure. I want the two of you to go together.'

'Why Stavros?'

'Don't get hoity-toity. It would be good for Stavros to be out of town for a while. The two of you will get along fine.'

* * *

In Tokyo J.T. and Stavros were shepherded about by a bored young diplomat who privately was of the opinion that the visit by the Americans was a complete waste of time. Fortunately the second leg of the visit would be conducted well away from Tokyo; J.T. in Fukuoka and Stavros in Sapporo. In Fukuoka, thankfully, the *gaijin* would be taken care of by Akiko Takahashi, and in Sapporo a commercial agency would look after Williams san. With a sigh of relief the Japanese delivered his charges to Tokyo airport, and took his leave with much bowing. J.T. boarded the plane, which was to whisk him off to Fukuoka, to be met there by Akiko; Stavros took the flight to Sapporo.

She was twenty-five years old, and her head barely came up to his shoulder. She was very slim; her body like that of a precocious child. Her oval face, framed by severely straight black hair, was not beautiful according to western taste, but for J.T. it came to have an endless fascination. He could never be sure what she was thinking. Whether acquiescence denoted agreement or resignation, whether pleasure was feigned or genuine, he could never be sure. When she laughed, as she often did, he could not be certain whether she was laughing with him or at him. He became intent on trying to get a positive reaction from her, making himself ridiculous by his insistence on knowing whether she really wanted to go to a western-style restaurant, or was only being polite; whether she really wanted to take him to see the city after lunch, rather than go to her room.

For three days she guided him from building to building, office to office. She introduced him to officials, bowing ceremoniously, translating in stiff, halting, but very correct English. She treated him with enormous respect, looking after him, he felt, as if he was a royal personage. She would not allow him to do anything for her, brushing aside any attempt he might make to relieve her of the burden of making arrangements, or dealing with hotel staff. He soon realized that the language difficulty was such that everything was best left to her anyway, and he seemed to float in a vacuum, unable to understand what was being said, and so gradually giving up the attempt to influence the course of events.

Akiko was deeply feminine in every aspect of her behavior and demeanor. No hint of coarseness, no suggestion of provocative or over-assertive behavior was allowed to sully the picture of a completely competent, but supremely female role. Her skirts were long and full, her blouses buttoned high and demurely. Once or twice he reached out to take her arm as they crossed the street, or to help her out of a taxi. She drew away from his touch as if he had assaulted her. He began to feel as if he was offensive to her, until he realized that the Japanese do not touch each other in public, and that in trying to be polite to her he was really insulting her in the eyes of others. There began to grow in him the sense that there was an impenetrable barrier between them, and he was saddened that he could not establish with her the kind of camaraderie that he might have enjoyed with a young American or European woman. He had spent much time with these strong-minded young women. They had joked with him, told him about their boy-friends or husbands, by their very openness shutting out any suggestion that their relationship with him had any sexual dimension. With Akiko, however, the very strength of the barrier between them was charged with sexuality. It was a wall to be broken down, and he became increasingly determined to breach it.

On the fourth evening in Fukuoka there was no formal meeting, no dinner arranged with local officials or university administrators. 'Free time', proclaimed the program provided by the Ministry.

'What shall we do this evening?' J.T. asked Akiko as they left another meeting in which nothing positive appeared to have been achieved.

'Whatever you wish. It is for you to say.' Her negative attitude suddenly angered him. He stopped in the busy corridor of the Mitsubishi Building, and seized her elbows, forcing her to face him.

'What would you like to do? For God's sake say something positive for once.' There was a pause before she responded, and he was afraid that she was deeply offended. Then a smile spread across her face. Instead of pushing him away, her hands clasped his forearms, her fingers pressing into him. Oblivious of the throng passing by, she looked up at him with real excitement in her eyes.

'I would very much enjoy going to a disco,' she said. He put his hands under her arms and almost lifted her from the floor.

'And so you shall.' He laughed down at her. He had a strong desire to kiss her, but thought better of it. 'But you will have to tell me where to go. I would not know where to begin.'

'I know a place. You will enjoy it, I am sure.'

'I'm sure I will, too. Let's get back to the hotel and get changed.' Back in his room, J.T. changed hurriedly, and then had to wait impatiently for Akiko. Eventually there was a quiet knock at the door of his room.

Akiko had changed into a dark red velvet dress that provided the perfect foil to her creamy skin and jet-black hair. It was cut low at her breast, with a narrow row of lace outlining the edge. He was stunned by the change in her appearance, and by the joyful expression on her face. They took a taxi, a process that involved extensive and animated discussion between the taxi driver and Akiko as the car made its way through the narrow, crowded streets. On every side there were neon signs announcing cafes, bars, restaurants, night-clubs, often with a helpful English translation - 'Happy Club', 'No Panty Bar'. The car stopped and there was a particularly vicious burst of Japanese from the driver.

'We must get out here,' said Akiko. 'He does not know where the club is.'

'Didn't you give him the address?' J.T. was puzzled. Akiko waved her hand.

'Yes, I did. But we don't have addresses like you do in America. It's much more complicated here.' With that she set off into the maze of alleys, peering into sinister-looking entrances, until with a cry of pleasure she announced that they had arrived. They plunged down steep steps into a basement doorway that looked to J.T. to be particularly unsavory, and then suddenly they were in a dimly lit, luxuriously appointed entrance hall, being welcomed with low bows by a delightful young woman dressed in a stunning kimono. She led them into a large room. Booths lined the walls, each with a table set for dinner. In the center of the room was a dance-floor, and a counter behind which another lovely girl was playing records for the benefit of two rather self-consciously dancing couples.

They were shown to a table, and the hostess - nobody so beautifully dressed could be described as a mere waitress, J.T. thought - waited for them to order drinks.

'What will you have?' he looked across at Akiko. To his surprise she ordered a vodka tonic. Till then he had only seen her drink orange juice or mineral water.

'Shall we order dinner?' he asked.

'There is no need. They will bring us various dishes during the evening. So that we can dance.' She smiled at him mischievously. He took the hint, and they moved on to the dance-floor. The music was a strange combination of western tunes and Japanese rhythms. J.T., no great dancer, adopted a crab-like wiggle that hugely amused Akiko, who had no scruples about laughing openly at his efforts. They danced, returned to their table to eat elegantly prepared dishes, then again on to the dance-floor. Akiko had an endless appetite for dancing. She blossomed, laughing as she turned and twirled, a totally different person from the professional, closed individual of the past few days. J.T. ordered wine, they drank, then danced again. All thoughts of his mission, or of the problems at BSU, had fled from his mind.

J.T.'s dance style had loosened up considerably, and he adopted a new stance, gently holding Akiko at the waist with both hands, his fingers almost encircling her. Then, as she turned his hand slipped up to her breast and stayed there briefly. She smiled at him, put her hand on his arm, and squeezed gently. They moved closer together, her head almost under his chin, and he felt her body move towards his, pressing gently against him. His leg was between her legs, and as they swayed to the music he could feel the silk of her petticoat sliding across her thighs. He gradually moved his hands down her back until his fingertips reached the base of her spine. They danced that way for a long while, hardly moving, holding each other. The hostesses and the other guests averted their eyes, as if they were not there: they were alone. The music stopped. Slowly they returned to their table, and she made no attempt to stop him from encircling her waist with his arm as they walked.

When they were seated at the table, he slipped off his shoes and began to caress her feet with his. He poured some wine into her glass, and bent across the table to take her hand.

'You have beautiful hands,' he said, and put her fingers to his lips. He became bolder with his caresses, moving his foot further up her calves, almost to the knee. She looked at him across the table, her shy smile responding to his conversation, listening to him talking about the first thing that came into his head, the latest novel that he had read. The hostess served another dish. While she was serving, J.T.'s foot retreated down to rest between Akiko's feet, and they sat, making appreciative sounds as the food was put before them. As the girl withdrew, J.T. raised his glass and they toasted each other, their glasses brushing gently together and lingering for a second as their fingers touched. As he attacked the food enthusiastically J.T. began again to raise his foot the length of her calf, stroking it with his toes. He shifted slightly to put his foot on the inside of her leg.

'Tell me about your home. Do you live in Fukuoka?'

'No, I live in the suburbs. It takes me about an hour to get into work. I live near where I was born. My parents still live there.'

'I would like to meet them,' J.T. looked intently at her as his right foot touched her left knee, and then with firm pressure he pushed it between her knees, which parted a fraction, just enough to enable him to stroke the inside of her thigh just above the knee. She smiled across the table at him.

'Perhaps I will take you,' she said. J.T. beckoned the hostess. This time he kept his foot in its warm nest.

'Another bottle of wine,' he requested. The wine was brought, tasted and served. She drank again, and looked around the dimly lit room. J.T. shifted back in his chair. He was getting cramp in his leg, but she kept a protective pressure on his foot with her knees. He took another drink of wine. He sat further back in the chair and began slowly to straighten his leg. Gradually his toes moved upwards along her thighs. With each gentle advance her legs opened just enough to make room for his foot, all the time maintaining the pressure of her thighs. His leg was almost fully extended now. The hostess materialized at the table again. She asked a question in Japanese.

'Do you want tea?' Akiko translated. 'Green tea, of course.'

'Yes, please,' he said. Akiko looked down at her cup as the tea was poured. J.T.'s toe had reached its goal. She moved forward in her chair. Her legs opened wider, and he felt her body jerk twice against his foot.

Akiko ordered a taxi, and they drove back to the hotel. They did not speak during the journey. They sat, arms clasped around each other. In his room she undressed him, her fingers deftly undoing his clothing, until he stood naked before her. Smiling, she slipped off the clothes that he had clumsily attempted to remove, until she too was naked.

* * *

The situation in Japan was, J.T. reflected, standard issue for BSU. The program in Tokyo was in fact an extremely well-run operation, but the student body was less than exciting, as most Japanese preferred to attend a Japanese institution, and the ones that were attracted to the BSU program usually had some rather oblique reason for doing so. This led to all kinds of problems. What to do when a minor member of the royal family, with absolutely no academic ability, applies to take a higher degree, having already graduated from the most costly college with the lowest standards in Japan? What to do when a member of the government requests that a seriously unsuitable relative could perhaps be given a teaching post? What to do when a rich parent promises a large gift, provided that the University overlooks the child's disastrous grades? Up till now the reaction to these problems of the Tokyo Director, James Stuart, had been to take the path of moral rectitude. He had refused to bend either to threats, or to bribes. This had earned him the respect, and the deadly enmity of all concerned, particularly Oscar Wolf.

In this situation Oscar would have preferred to bow to both threats and bribes, but to have replaced Stuart, a member of the faculty, in order to appoint a more amenable Director would have been too blatant even for Oscar. A more devious path had to be found. This was not too difficult. Stuart's morals were expensive. The program lost money. Why not move it to a cheaper location, offer the Director a job elsewhere, and reshape the program in the Wolf image? Hence the mission on which J.T. and Stavros had been dispatched.

In truth, Oscar was not really contemplating setting up a program in Sapporo on Japan's northern island of Hokkaido. The fact was that he had to get Stavros out of his hair for a while, and as far away as possible. Other than contemplating a program in Antarctica he couldn't think of a better place to send him. Almost as soon as J.T. and Stavros had stepped on the plane to Tokyo, Oscar had sent a message instructing Stavros to remain in Sapporo for a month to conduct a really thorough feasibility study for the establishment of a program there.

J.T.'s role was different, and much more serious. His job was to close down the Tokyo program, get rid of Stuart, and establish the new program in Fukuoka. Of course, J.T. could not do all of that in two weeks, but he was to lay the basis for it. He had already told Stuart that the Tokyo program was losing so much money that it would have to be wound up, but had not revealed to Stuart the plan for Fukuoka. That would come later. Already Oscar was discussing with Stuart on the telephone what his next post would be. The double act of Oscar and J.T. was working well.

With Akiko's help, J.T. explored buildings which could be used as classrooms, met officials who could facilitate the development of the program in Fukuoka, and contacted universities to identify one which might be prepared to cooperate in the establishment of the program. It was J.T.'s first visit to Japan, and he was fascinated by the way in which the people he met were very helpful and at the same time impenetrable. He really did not know whether he was achieving results, or just being given a polite brush-off. Without Akiko he would have been totally at a loss. As the week neared its end he was more and more absorbed in her, and he dreaded the thought of leaving her. He tried to analyze his feelings toward her. He did not feel in love with her, but her attraction was so strong that he wanted to do anything to keep her near him.

J.T. faxed his report to Oscar on Thursday. He was due to leave for Tokyo, and then to fly back to Bransome on Saturday. Akiko suggested that on Friday they should visit a Buddhist temple that was set in parkland some way from Fukuoka. They set out early on a commuter train, so crowded that they had to be levered into the coach by skilled packers. It was ironic, J.T. thought, that the Japanese, who hated physical contact with strangers, were jammed together in the trains so closely, their bodies pressed so tightly against each other, that there could be no vestige of modesty left to them. J.T., although not tall by

American standards, towered above most of the passengers. A middle-aged woman had her elbow jammed into his groin. As they swayed together between the stations, each acting as if the other did not exist, J.T. would have given a great deal to know what was in the mind of this female, whom he did not know, and would never meet again, but who had for a short time been on more intimate terms with him than all but a handful of human beings.

A few yards distant from the teeming station, they entered the temple park, and were immediately transported to a different world, a world of calm, contemplation and beauty. They entered the temple, the great black figure of the Buddha towering above them, as the sound of a deep-toned bell punctuated the silence. Akiko joined a row of pilgrims kneeling before the statue. J.T. hung back, not wishing to intrude. After a while, Akiko rose to her feet, took a joss-stick, lit it at the flame burning before the Buddha, and holding it in both hands ceremoniously before her, she proffered it to J.T. As he took it from her, the strong scent rising up between them, she said quietly, 'Remember me when you are back in America.'

They spent the afternoon in the park, watching the animals that grazed there, smiling at the children who came to gaze in awe at the strange foreign devil, and then ran back to parents giggling and pointing, parents who bowed apologetically to J.T., and tried to quiet their offspring. J.T. would dearly have liked to have put his arm round Akiko, or bend his head against hers, but he refrained for fear of embarrassing her. His attempts at light-hearted banter, of the kind that lovers affect, were politely but firmly rejected. They dined quietly, and then returned to the hotel. J.T. was fervently hoping that the events of the previous night would be repeated, but on reaching the hotel lobby, Akiko turned to him and bowed deeply.

'I wish you a safe journey to your home,' she said formally.

'Won't you...stay for a while?'

'No. Thank you very much. I must go.' Without further explanation she bowed again, turned and left the hotel. The next morning J.T. took the plane to Tokyo and began the long journey home.

* * *

As J.T. entered the office Oscar was sitting at his desk, smoking a cigar, and humming quietly to himself. It was as if J.T. had never been away.

'J.T.! Good to see you. I read your report. Great! Let's do it.'

'Exactly what do you have in mind, Oscar?'

'I want you to go back to Fukuoka and set up the program. Take six months.' J.T.'s spirits rose. Back to Fukuoka. Back to Akiko. 'By the way " Oscar continued, 'you'd better keep in touch with Stavros. Keep an eye on him.'

'Do you mean that you're setting up a program in Sapporo as well?'

'Hell, no! Are you crazy? One program in Japan is enough. No, I'm sending Stavros to Sakhalin.'

'Sakhalin? In Eastern Russia. A large island just to the north of Japan?'

'Dead right! A closed territory until the Soviets fell apart. No other American outfit has a program there.' Oscar looked quietly proud of this notion.

'But is it suitable for a program?' Even J.T. could not help but question this latest brainwave of the great man. 'I thought it was a few fishermen's huts, and some decaying nuclear installations.'

'That's what Stavros has to work out. I've told him to take three months to write a report. Anyway,' Oscar continued, 'Stavros needs time away. I worked hard to get him out of the country. I don't want him coming back now.'

'What happened to Stavros? He wasn't his usual self on our trip to Japan.' To himself J.T. thought, 'And a good thing too. The less like himself Stavros is the better.' No reply was forthcoming from Oscar who was studying the map again. The humming increased in volume. Fearful that some new and potentially threatening idea was about to be born, J.T. inquired:

'When do you want me to leave for Fukuoka?' Oscar waved his cigar.

'Tomorrow will do.'

In fact it took J.T. two weeks to arrange his affairs before he found himself back on the flight to Tokyo. On his arrival he sought out the bored young diplomat who had acted as his guide on his earlier visit. They took lunch in a sushi bar. After some desultory conversation J.T. asked the question that had been on his mind for weeks. 'By the way, can you tell me how to get in contact with Akiko?' The Japanese seemed puzzled for a moment.

'Ah! You mean Takahashi Akiko san? Did she not tell you? You were her last assignment for the Department. Her husband's company has transferred him to Europe.'

In Fukuoka J.T. went through the motions of establishing a program, without the slightest enthusiasm for his task. He found suitable premises, applied for the necessary permits, employed secretaries and caretakers. The major problem was to find a Director. He made inquiries amongst the American expatriate community in Tokyo and other cities, but no suitable candidate emerged. He asked Oscar Wolf to search for someone at BSU, but the cost of sending a Faculty member to Japan with the salary, housing allowances, travel costs, and other expenses that were involved, exceeded the bounds even of Oscar's flexible budgetary arrangements. J.T. began to despair of ever finding a satisfactory person, and contemplated taking over the position himself, on a semi-permanent basis. Fukuoka had memories for him that had become painful, but it was in many ways the ideal place to which to withdraw from the world. Situated on Japan's southern island of Kyushu, not far from Nagasaki, it was remote from the more cosmopolitan cities such as Tokyo and Osaka, and indeed the mere sight of a Westerner provoked notice and comment from local people, as J.T.'s experience when walking in the park with Akiko had demonstrated.

After some weeks of frustrating endeavor, J.T. paid a visit to Fukuoka Christian University, an institution originally founded by American Methodist missionaries. The President of the University and his senior colleagues received him with the greatest politeness. After a tour of the campus, the President took J.T. to lunch at a traditional restaurant on the outskirts of the city. It was like no other restaurant that J.T. had ever experienced. The one-story building seemed to be nothing other than a private home. The lady of the house, in traditional dress, bowing low before President Sakuradani and his guests met them at the door. After removing their shoes they were led into a long narrow room furnished only with a long, very low table set on the *tatami,* the rush matting that covered the floor. J.T. sat rather awkwardly on the floor, legs stretched out beneath the table, shifting from one buttock to the other, conscious that the Japanese seated around the table were supremely comfortable, legs crossed, perfectly balanced. Throughout the long meal, which consisted of twelve beautifully presented courses, the food was served by the proprietress who entered the room on her knees and shuffled from guest to guest. The *sake* bowl at the side of J.T.'s plate was always full, after every sip that he took it was replenished.

There were ten people at table. The President sat J.T. at his right hand, and on J.T.'s right was seated the only woman amongst the guests. She introduced herself as Kasuko Henderson. She spoke perfect English, with a slight American accent.

'I am your interpreter. Normally there would not be any female guests at a function like this, but in your honor an exception has been made. I am married to an American businessman and we live here in Fukuoka. I have myself lived in the States, in California, for five years. I am a graduate in Sociology of the University of California at Santa Barbara.' J.T. looked at her as if at a miracle - he knew that he had found his Program Director.

* * *

The string of messages from Sakhalin had become more and more difficult to interpret. Every week for seven weeks, Stavros Williams sent a report to Oscar, with a copy to J.T. in Fukuoka. The reports were long and rambling documents, mostly concerned with the minutiae of life in Sakhalin, and with the problems with which Stavros had to cope, just to stay alive. How to obtain light bulbs, the quality of the toilet-paper, the intricacies of the transport system, and above all, the nature and complexity of the plumbing and sewage facilities. A whole report of 16 pages was devoted to this last subject, written with a sensitivity that would bring tears to the eyes of the more tender reader. The potential for a global ecological disaster was stressed.

Back in Bransome, Oscar did not read these epistles. His overriding interest was that Stavros should remain safely far away. When an internal auditor questioned the large requisitions for Rubles from Oscar's department, he sent a strong memo to the Treasurer pointing out that Stavros's mission was vital to the University, and that its purpose was top-secret; an action which was to win him considerable praise at a later date. J.T. on the other hand read the reports with a kind of hypnotic fascination. Each one started out with a long survey of the shortcomings of an area of life in Sakhalin, the incompetence of the local authorities, and the likely consequences of this both for the local population and the universe at large. But instead of concluding that Stavros should be repatriated to Bransome immediately, each report turned into an affirmation of the belief that the one person, who could turn this situation around, and in doing so secure the future of the human race, was Stavros Williams. Armed with the necessary technical assistance, and with a few trusty aides, Stavros could single-handedly transform the electricity supply, the educational system, the transportation and sewage of Sakhalin. It was clear that Stavros had become unhinged.

It was the report of week 8, however, that changed the future course of history. The document consisted of a proposal that BSU set up a

Technical Education Unit, funded by the Government of the United States, which, under the leadership of Stavros Williams, would lay the foundation for the propulsion of Sakhalin into the 21st.century. The proposal was addressed directly to President Zuwicki of Bransome Southern University, with copies to Oscar Wolf and to J.T. J.T. received an urgent message to contact Vice President Oscar Wolf immediately.

'J.T! Have you read Stavros's latest?'

'Yes, I have. I'm worried about him. I think he's in a bad way, mentally I mean.'

'Never mind that. Zuwicki has been in touch with the State Department. They are so pleased with our program in EI Baku that they are prepared to finance Stavros to the limit. Zuwicki is delirious. The overheads will save our Admin. budget. I want you to get over there straight away. You are the nearest person to him. It's only a few miles away. I'm looking at the map now. Get over there and keep Stavros on the right lines. This is big.'

'But Oscar! Do you think that Stavros is the right person to direct this program? I've felt for a long time that he is on the edge of a breakdown. Did you read his plan to ship raw sewage from Sakhalin to Los Angeles for the tomato industry?' For a moment Oscar was distracted from his main purpose.

'Why raw sewage?'

'It's the only kind they've got.'

'Ah! I see. Look!' Oscar's tone became Vice-presidential. 'State has read all Stavros's reports. They insist that he should direct the program. They think that BSU has a unique resource in its administrative personnel.'

* * *

As J.T. descended from his plane at Kasakov he was met by a very different Stavros from the man he had last seen nearly three months before. Stavros had grown a beard and a long drooping moustache. He was dressed in a smock and loose trousers. He looked like an off-duty Russian Orthodox priest. He bowed gently to J.T. in greeting, then embraced him, kissing him on both cheeks.

'Stavros! Its good to see you.'

'J.T. I've found myself.'

J.T. suppressed the rather obscene riposte that rose to his lips.

'Well, that's great, Stavros.'

Stavros led him to a small battered car. They climbed in and drove to the house where Stavros was rooming with a local family. Once there, over a bowl of steaming hot tea, J.T. explained that the State Department had approved the Technical Education Unit proposal, and that a flood of Rubles was on its way.

'I tried to telephone you but I couldn't get through.'

'I know. That's one of the problems I intend to deal with,' Stavros replied.

'How will you start to tackle all these problems?' J.T. inquired.

'The sewage. It's the key to everything. It's the biggest resource of the island. Get the sewage right and everything else falls into place. That's the lesson of the Industrial Revolution.'

'What will you do with it?'

'Pump it around.'

'Pump it around?'

'Exactly! I see that you understand.'

'Well, not altogether.'

'Heat exchangers. That's the secret.'

'Ah! I'm not well up in that area. Sanskrit is my specialty.'

'Just what we need.'

'Sanskrit?'

'No. Heat exchangers. I found an old Encyclopedia Britannica here. It revolutionized my thinking. You pump the sewage through a heat exchanger. It extracts the heat from the sewage, and you can use the heat to generate electricity. Then we can tackle the transport problem, the telephone system, everything. But we have to start with the sewage. We'll pump it all over the island, with heat exchangers in every town and village.'

'What about LA and the tomatoes?'

'That's what we do with it when it's really cold.' Stavros was concerned that J.T. really understood. 'When there's no heat left in it, you see.'

'Ah! I didn't think that the population of Sakhalin was that big. Do you have that much sewage here?'

'Oh, no! You seem to have missed the whole point. We shall pipe all the sewage from the mainland to Sakhalin. At the present time they pour most of it straight into the sea. Such a waste of heat! There will be millions of tons of it. From all over Russia. That's why it is so important that we can send it to Los Angeles when it is cold. And it will be an expression of the gratitude of the people of Sakhalin for the help that the US is giving.'

J.T. was silent. The whole conception was so grand; it took quite a leap of the imagination to grasp it.

'There's one other thing,' he said. 'The State Department are sending ten observers to monitor the program.' Stavros was delighted.

'Great,' he said, 'I'll get them working on the sewage immediately.' J.T. contemplated the new Stavros, seated before him.

'Stavros, what happened? You sitting here in this kitchen, in a remote part of Russia. Dressed like that. It's light years from the way you were in Bransome.'

'J.T. I went through a kind of religious conversion. I was wasting my life, chasing after women, power breakfasts, that kind of thing, when what I was really interested in all the time was sewage. I believe we are all like that really, deep down inside.' He leaned forward and rested his hand on J.T.'s shoulder. 'Just think. What is the one swear word that we Americans use all the time?'

'You mean...'

'Exactly.'

'You know, Stavros, I don't think that there is a great deal for me to do here in Sakhalin. You've got it all worked out. I'd better get back to Fukuoka.'

* * *

Back in Fukuoka J.T. called Oscar Wolf.

'Oscar, Stavros is insane, stark, raving mad.'

'Was he threatening to kill anyone?'

'No, he was very calm.'

'Did he have any clothes on?'

'Yes, of course. He was dressed like a priest.'

'That's all right then. He's obviously recovered. Don't worry. What could go wrong?'

'He wants to pump sewage from Moscow to Sakhalin, and then ship it to LA'

'Sounds harmless enough. J.T., you seem to be under something of a strain. Take the day off. Better still! Take the week off. I need someone to go to Ploiesti.'

'Ploiesti?'

'Zuwicki was having dinner the other evening with the Secretary of Education, and he told him that we have a program in Ploiesti.'

'But we don't.'

'You know that. I know that. But Zuwicki doesn't know that, or he didn't. He got confused with the program in Plonsk.'

'But we don't have a program in Plonsk either.'

'Ah! Right! I was thinking of Plobsheim. Anyway, that's what he said.'

'So?'

'So the Secretary of Education said, "Great, we need a base there for a big education exchange program we've just negotiated." So now BSU is that base.'

'But, we've nothing there.'

'That's why I said I needed someone to go there.'

Two days later J.T.'s plane was circling Bucharest preparing to land at Otopeni airport. This would be his most difficult assignment so far. His knowledge of Romania was minimal, he had no contacts there, and he had already been warned that he could not ask for help from the US Embassy. As Oscar Wolf had put it: 'If the Department of Education knew that we didn't have a program in Romania they would not be very pleased, and to tell the State Department that we are going to set up a program in Ploiesti which the Department of Education thinks is already in existence, might cause some difficulty. So you're on your own.'

J.T. turned to the passenger in the next seat with whom he had struck up an acquaintance since they had boarded the plane in London.

'I'm staying at the Hilton for a couple of nights before I go on to Ploiesti. Can I give you dinner? I would welcome your advice about what to see in Bucharest, as I've never been before.'

'I'm staying at the International. It's just round the corner from the Hilton. I'd be delighted to have dinner with you. This evening, if you would like.' The speaker was a woman in her late twenties, dark-eyed, a full round face, a generous figure. She had told J.T. that she was returning to Romania for the first time for ten years, having escaped to England after leaving school. She was biting in her assessment of the situation in Romania, telling J.T. that it was very different from the other countries of Eastern Europe. There had been a palace revolution, no more. The Communist old guard was still in control.

Passing through immigration J.T. experienced for the first time a sense of unease at the scrutiny of officials whose attitude was less than welcoming, who conveyed the feeling that foreigners were not wanted in their country. The drive from the airport revealed a city with a faded grandeur, showing the scars of years of Communist rule. To enter the newly established Hilton Hotel was like a re-entry into the West, an island of familiar modernity.

At 8 p.m. J.T. was in the lobby waiting for Galia Ionescu. She arrived twenty minutes late, full of vivacious energy, kissing him on both cheeks as if they had known each other for years. Her English was extremely good, but sprinkled with charming eccentricities. She led him to a small restaurant in the Ulita Blanarilor, and they settled into a booth.

'Shall I order the meal?' she asked, 'or can you speak Romanian?'

'No, I'm afraid I can't. I am an expert on linguistics, so that I can understand something of quite a wide range of languages. But please do order.'

After the waiter had left the table, Galia looked at J.T. with earnestness in her dark eyes.

'I read that many American colleges have very strict codes of sexual behavior. Does your University do that?'

'Yes. Ours is pretty strict.'

'That is very good. I approve of such things. Too many men in Europe think that to pinch a woman's bottom is a sacred male privilege. I read that in America, if a man and a woman go out together for the evening, the man has to state what his sexual intentions are. Is that true?'

'Well some colleges recommend to their female students that they try to clarify such issues beforehand, so that the man should not have any false expectations.'

'And they each have to sign a paper saying exactly what they expect to get from the evening?'

'I have seen that suggested in some cases.'

'Oh, that is so good. I like that. What are your sexual intentions this evening?' J.T. looked at her in astonishment.

'I don't have any. What I mean is that I had not thought about it before you mentioned it.' Galia twisted her face into a pained expression.

'That is not very flattering. You did not give it even a little tiny thought?'

'Well, of course, I did think that you were very attractive,' J.T. did know where to turn, 'but I did not think that on such short acquaintance any question of sex would arise.'

'But surely the code of sexual conduct has to operate right from the first moment. Otherwise we might be misunderstanding ourselves.'

J.T. was becoming exasperated. 'Look, I have no sexual aspirations or expectations this evening. You are quite safe. If you like I'll write that down and sign it.' Galia was indignant.

'Do not worry. I can look after myself.' Her expression softened.

'Anyway, perhaps your intentions might change as the evening goes on.'

'I promise you, you will be the first to know.'

She sat back smiling. 'Good! I like this American way. It is so open. Not like Europe where the men are trying to put the hand up the skirt under the table.'

'You wouldn't like that?'

'I might. But only if you had written it on the paper. What are you going to do in Ploiesti?'

Her manner of switching rapidly from one subject to another unnerved J.T.

'I am going there to set up a new program for my university.'

'What kind of program?'

'A program in Education.'

'It sounds pretty vague.'

'The plan is still in its early stages of development,' J.T. conceded.

'What is your university?'

'Bransome Southern University.'

'Never heard of it. Is it any good?'

'Pretty good. Well, reasonably good. Anyway the students pay a lot of money to attend the University.' Galia was clearly not impressed.

'I am going to Ploiesti,' she announced. 'We will travel together.'

'I didn't know you intended to go to Ploiesti.'

'I didn't. But I do now. You will need someone to direct your new program. Someone who speaks English and Romanian.'

'You mean you? But I couldn't just appoint you. I would have to look around; advertise the position.'

'Ha! You don't know anything about Romania. If you go about it that way you will end up having to appoint some Communist Party hack.'

J.T. felt that he was losing control of the situation. 'But I know nothing about you. What is your educational background?'

'I have two degrees from English universities. In Theoretical Physics and Astronomy.'

'But this a program in Education.'

'I know all about education. I am very educated. I certainly know about Romanian education. I went to school here.' As if the matter were settled she changed the subject again. By the time that the dessert was served, a heavy Romanian pudding, J.T. was exhausted.

'I'm jet-lagged,' he said. 'Why don't we have breakfast tomorrow, and discuss your ideas.'

'What? It's only 9.30. We must go dancing. I know the only place in Bucharest to go dancing.'

'How do you know all these things? You've been away for ten years.'

'Ah!' she said, as if it explained everything, 'I'm Romanian.'

Three hours later, she delivered J.T. to the door of the Hilton. His eyes were glazed, and he could barely walk. Galia was very happy. She kissed his cheek. 'Goodnight. See you at breakfast!'

Two days later they took the train together to make the short journey northwards to Ploiesti. They found a comfortable, if old-fashioned guesthouse near to the Oil Museum, and took two rooms. The next few days were spent trying to penetrate the bureaucratic mess in which J.T.'s mission had soon become entangled. Without any official backing, either from the Government of Romania or the United States Embassy, Galia explained, there was only one way forward - bribery, and on a fairly large scale. With great difficulty J.T. reached Oscar Wolf on the telephone.

'Oscar, I will have to stay here much longer than a week. This is going to be much harder than we thought. It will probably take me a month to get an office set up.' There was a silence at the other end.

'J.T.! Exactly where are you, and what are you talking about? Speak up, I can hardly hear you.'

'I'm in Ploiesti, in Romania, setting up a program for the Department of Education, remember?'

'Ah, yes! I remember. O.K! I wondered where you were. We had a great office party yesterday evening. Not the same without Stavros, of course. He's doing a really good job in Sakhalin. The State Department is full of praise. Seems they are putting in another twenty observers to monitor his program. And a lot of piping.'

'Good! I'm delighted. Oscar, I need twenty-five thousand dollars, in cash, as quickly as possible.'

'What's it for? Renting a building?'

'No, it's for the petty cash, Oscar. It's difficult to be too detailed on the phone.'

'Petty cash? O.K! I'll arrange a bank transfer into Romanian currency, whatever that is.'

'No, no! I need it in dollars; small bills; urgently, by courier.' He gave the address of the guesthouse. 'By the way! I think I've found a Director for the program. She really knows her way about here.'

'O.K.! J.T. I hope that she is not the reason you need to spend a month in Romania.'

'Goodbye, Oscar. The connection is getting very bad.'

'Darling, I've got us an appointment tomorrow with the Director of Public Affairs for Ploiesti.' Galia was excited. J.T. could not be sure whether the form of address, 'Darling', was a Romanian equivalent of the normal theatrical way of rendering "You guys", or if Galia had some more affectionate intention in using this term.

'Good! Do you think we'll need to take any of the slush?' The parcel of dollars had arrived that morning.

'No! Not take it with us. That would be too crude. But we should make some oblique reference to it.'

'Like, we have twenty-five thousand dollars in a brown paper bag. How much would you like?'

'Don't be so cynical. These people have to make a living. Times are very hard here.'

'Galia, what are we trying to achieve here?'

'We are trying to win the approval of the Director, so that we can obtain a license to operate as an educational institute, so that we can get zoning permission to use a building for that purpose, so that we can legally employ people to work for the program, so that we can open a bank account to pay them, so that...'

'OK! I know all that, Galia; I've done that kind of thing all over the world. But why do we have to bribe this Director in order to do all that?'

'Because he is the real power in this city. Without his say-so we will get nothing.'

Two hours later they were in the office of the Director of Public Affairs. His attitude towards them was extremely cool. With hardly a greeting he gestured to them to sit down, and then waited for one of his visitors to speak. Galia started off with a long introduction in Romanian and then switching to English, she said:

'J.T., I have explained that you have come here to establish an education program. Could you tell the Director exactly what the program aims to achieve?' J.T. pulled himself out of the reverie into which he had fallen while she had been talking to the Director. One problem in answering the question was that he did not know what the program was supposed to achieve, because no one had yet told him what the Department of Education needed from BSU in Romania. Every effort he had made to drag that information out of Oscar had failed. The second problem was that increasingly over the past two weeks he had become obsessed with thoughts of Galia, thoughts which always followed the same path, starting with a pleasant dinner, and ending with a particularly detailed account of a love scene, the like of which neither he, nor perhaps anyone else, had ever experienced. Whenever his mind was allowed to wander, the same sequence, each time embellished with a new refinement, began to take over his mind. The burst of Romanian from Galia had left his mind unoccupied, and the love sequence immediately started to run. The difficulty was that once it had begun it was almost impossible to break off. He had tried speeding it up, or jumping forward to the final climactic moments, but neither technique was wholly successful. The Director was waiting.

'I have been sent to Ploiesti by Bransome Southern University and the Government of the United States of America,' J.T. began ponderously, 'to initiate an important educational program in order to establish cross-societal links between our two countries, resulting in a deeper knowledge of the history and cultures of the United States and Romania, and which, by developing an environment of trust and mutual understanding, will make possible future collaborative projects aimed at the improvement of the social, economic and cultural quality of life in this great country.'

Galia's eyes had taken on a glazed expression during this performance. Whether the Director had understood a word was not immediately clear, but he and Galia fell into a rapid discussion in their native language. J.T.'s mind began to run the Galia tape again. He had just reached the point at which, after many long and passionate kisses, Galia had begun to swoon with desire. He picked her up in his arms, her head hanging back to expose the long sweep of her neck down to her bosom, the swelling breasts straining at the thin material of her negligée. He moved towards the bed, lowered her gently onto the satin sheets, and put his head down into that soft, perfumed nest that was yearning for his touch, when suddenly the Director and Galia rose, shook hands and J.T. was being ushered from the room.

He was flustered. 'What happened?' he asked as they made their way out of the building.

'We agreed that the Director should become a consultant for your program. He will assist you in any way he can.'

'That's very good of him. You should have given me the opportunity to thank him.' She looked at him with amusement.

'You were hardly conscious. What's been the matter lately? You seem distracted. Anyway,' she went on without waiting for a reply, 'you have thanked him. To the tune of ten thousand dollars, to be paid immediately.'

'My god! That's a bit steep. What do we get for our money?'

'Everything! At any rate, anything that's available - at a price.' She took his arm, and nestled against him as they walked through the stream of workers intent on finding a place to eat their lunchtime sandwiches. He could feel the pressure of her breast against his arm. 'The first thing is that I now have an apartment. He said I could move in tomorrow. It sounds pretty nice, and the rent is reasonable. It belongs to his sister.' She looked up him, mischief in her eyes. 'I'm bored with the guesthouse. If you are very good, perhaps you can move into my new apartment, for a while.'

The next evening, having spent the day establishing themselves in the apartment, which occupied the whole of the second floor of a mid-nineteenth century house in a quiet section of Ploiesti, they sat down to their first meal in the high-ceilinged dining room. J.T. handed Galia a sheet of paper across the table. It looked rather like a shopping list.

'I thought it was time I began to observe the code of conduct.' he said. 'These are my intentions. I hope you approve.'

She studied the list, checked off items 1 to 5, carefully deleted item 6, shaking her head and reproving him with a raised finger, and then checked items 7 and 8. She signed the paper and returned it to him. She raised her wineglass. 'That sounds very good,' she said. 'I like it.'

* * *

Three days later Oscar called. 'J.T., I want you back here as soon as possible.'

'But Oscar there is so much to do here. I can't leave now.' Wolf could detect the anguish in J.T.'s voice in spite of the five thousand miles that separated them.

'This is important. You can leave that new Director in charge, what's her name, Coucescou?'

'Ionescou.'

'Whatever. I'm putting you in charge of a new outfit - the College of International Affairs.'

Part 2

THE COLLEGE

That summer in Bransome had been particularly hot. The town was somnolent, most of the townspeople having driven to the mountains for their vacation. The faculty had dispersed to all parts of the world, making pilgrimages to any academic shrine that would pay their expenses. The offices of the Administration were also depleted, with administrators and secretaries taking their annual leave. One office, however, was extremely active, with lights burning on into the night. The offices of the College of International Affairs were situated in a new and very elegant building, which had been constructed with great rapidity, and much federal government money. Workmen were still putting the finishing touches to decorations and fittings, putting up signs and completing the paths around the building. The office of the Associate Dean, J.T., was a hive of activity, telephones being installed, filing cabinets being delivered, secretaries testing word processors, and students hired for the summer helping out in every possible way. J.T. himself, slightly bemused by being at the center of all this activity, had withdrawn into his inner office, and was attempting to ignore the chaos in the rest of the building.

The effect upon him of his encounter with Galia had lasted for many months. Forced to leave Ploiesti he had tried to maintain the relationship that had flowered so dramatically in those few days after they had moved into the apartment. He was still in frequent contact with her at a business level, but his attempts to engage her in a more personal correspondence, which would hold out some promise of future involvement, had failed. Depressed, he had thrown himself into his work, but although a long time had now passed since his new appointment, he still had not quite recovered his former ebullience. He had few friends in Bransome, and although the university was large, the town was small, and offered little distraction. His colleagues were either totally absorbed in their work and boring, or totally uninterested in their work and committed to bizarre life-styles that effectively excluded him. He had tried to work up a friendship with an Associate Dean of Students who, bored with the daily round, was into bungee jumping, and spent every available spare moment traveling to any likely site within several hundred miles in order to plunge off cliffs, bridges and tall buildings. The initial excitement of this relationship for J.T. began to pall, however, when it became clear that he was very much an outsider at these events. He would toil to the top of some distant cliff carrying the Associate Dean's equipment, only to witness her rear view as she plummeted below, and would then retrieve her equipment while she exchanged whoops of triumph with her fellow jumpers. He should have foreseen that she would suggest that he should join her on one of these jumps, but when the offer came, one evening in the afterglow of a celebratory dinner, he was not prepared. By failing to make the depths of his terror fully apparent, he found himself being tutored in the necessary techniques, and then on one fateful afternoon, standing helmeted and uniformed at the rail of a bridge over the most beautiful gorge in the Southwest, with a fond decanal arm around his shoulders, surrounded by her jumping partners giving advice and encouragement. When it became apparent that he was not going to jump, had never intended to jump, and never would jump, the relationship cooled, and no further invitations were extended.

Janice Hart, left without a job after Stavros had departed, had become J.T.'s assistant. He came to depend upon her quiet efficiency, listened to her advice, generally acted upon it, and delegated large swathes of his work to her. Each morning she appeared, neatly dressed, her blonde hair always well groomed. At 5 p.m.she left for her apartment on the outskirts of town. He knew little of her private life, and less of her hopes and aspirations. She was always reserved with him, and he felt that she did not want him to intrude. Occasionally they took lunch together, but always discussed work or the latest developments in university politics. Once she was about to tell him of her triumph over Stavros, but at the last moment decided against it.

J.T.'s mission was to develop programs around the world similar to those he had established in El Baku, Nagoya and Ploiesti. Bransome became the center of a network of academic activities of great variety. Each program was tailored to the needs of the particular location - agricultural economics in Sao Paolo, distillation sciences in Dublin, and fashion design in Aberdeen. J.T. no longer traveled to these locations to establish programs. He had trained a small team of specialists who were perpetually on the move, armed with a checklist of the steps necessary to the creation of a successful program. J.T. coordinated and controlled their activities from the gleaming communications center that had been installed at the heart of his new headquarters. When fully operational he would be able to communicate by satellite with 24 centers simultaneously, by day or by night, without having to go through public telephone or radio systems. Vice President Oscar Wolf had given him virtually a free hand to run the College, provided that he delivered programs at the right speed. Even the finances of the College were detached from the normal university controls. 'Don't worry about it,' Oscar told him. 'Think big. This is something entirely new in the world of education.'

With all that was happening at BSU, Oscar had become a celebrity on the conference circuit. His papers on the philosophy and methodology of international education were received with adulation by audiences hoping to steal the formula that would enable them to get a piece of the action. The first time that Oscar had been asked to give such an address, to the

Conference of Senior University Management, the insistent ringing of the bedside phone had rudely awakened J.T.

'Hallo! Who is this? It's 2 a.m. for God's sake.'

'J.T. This is Oscar!'

'Hi, Oscar! Good to hear you. What's the problem?'

'I need your help, J.T. I'm giving a speech in Boulder tomorrow evening - I mean this evening - today. Can you come over and give me a hand?'

'What now, this minute, Oscar?'

'J.T. this is serious. I'm catching a plane at 10 a.m. I need your help.'

By the time that J.T. had reached Oscar's house, a splendid pseudo-mansion, set in a woodland park, had read the three lines of incoherent notes that Oscar had produced so far, and grasped the nature of the problem, it was nearly 3.30. He set to work on the word processor. Oscar sat quietly watching him for a while.

'J.T. Would you mind if I take a nap?'

'O.K. Oscar. I should have something for you by eight. We'll go over it then.'

At nine Oscar, breakfasted and briefed, took off for the airport humming happily to himself. 'Thanks. J.T! See you.'

Invitations for Oscar to speak began to arrive almost week by week. After another hysterical midnight summons to J.T. for help they developed a more rational system. Oscar's secretary automatically channeled all requests for speeches to J.T., who advised Oscar which ones to accept, and sent the draft speech to Oscar a few days ahead of time. They would meet over lunch the day before Oscar flew off to make his presentation, and discuss any difficult points. This became so much of a routine that soon neither of them thought anything to be odd about it, and as Oscar's international reputation grew, and the demands for his thoughts expanded, J.T. depended more and more on Janice to supervise the activities of the office.

Soon after Christmas Oscar Wolf dropped into J.T.'s office.

'How's the speech going for IATABS?' The Convention of the International Association for the Teachers of American Business Studies was to be held in February in New Orleans.

'It's O.K. I should have a draft for you in a couple of days.'

'Fine! By the way, I thought that maybe you ought to come along to this bash. Make a change for you. Bring Janice. We'll be staying with Jim Holcombe.'

'Holcombe? The poet?'

'Right! Never met him myself, but the President of IATABS knows him, and he thought it would be more interesting for us than staying in a hotel.'

The Holcombe's met them at the airport. Jim Holcombe was a bulky, cheerful, relaxed character who immediately put his visitors at their ease. His wife, Julia, was tall and beautiful, with well-groomed reddish hair, about eight or nine years older than J.T.

'O.K. guys.' Holcombe's mode of address was not exactly poetic, J.T. thought. 'We'll take you to our little shack, and then we'll fill you in about this evening.' The little shack turned out to be a mock ante-bellum mansion in the Garden district, with about twenty bedrooms, and as many bathrooms. The BSU party were installed in attractive bedrooms overlooking a semi-tropical garden, and after showering and changing clothes J.T. went down to the grand drawing room. Oscar Wolf was already there, clutching a large gin and tonic.

'Welcome to New Orleans! I hope that you will have a good visit here.' Julia Holcombe led J.T. across to the drinks set out on a table, and served him. 'You've come here just at the right time. We're in the middle of Mardi Gras. We'll watch the parade and then we're meeting some people for dinner at Antoine's.'

The Holcombe's had rented a limousine to take the five of them to the parade, and as the car reached the fringe of the French Quarter it became entangled in the crowds of revelers on their way to watch the carnival procession. They stopped the limo and set off on foot.

'If we get separated we'll meet you at Antoine's at eight.' Holcombe called as they were swept away by the crowd. On all sides laughing people streamed towards the route of the parade. They wore all manner of funny hats, false noses, and fancy dress. J.T. and Janice lost Oscar almost immediately. They pushed their way through narrow streets lined with European-style houses, their wrought iron balconies overlooking the cobbled roads. Young men were shouting up to the girls leaning over the balcony railings. One boy carried a placard with the message "Show us your tits" as he progressed along Royal Street, and from time to time a beautiful woman would undo her blouse or shirt and lean right over the balcony to wave, bare bosomed, to the crowd below. Music blared from almost every cafe, and as they made their way along Bourbon Street hustlers tried to tempt them into strip joints or gay bars. Through the opened doorways they glimpsed scantily clad women dancing on tables, women in cages moving sinuously to strangely oriental music, and transvestites, beautifully made-up, dressed in breathtaking gowns, luring men in to buy expensive drinks.

J.T. maneuvered Janice through the good-natured crowd and found a vantagepoint just before the first float arrived. There was a magical quality to the slanting evening light as the float bearing the carnival queen turned into the street. A classic American blonde, dressed in white, surrounded by her fair-skinned attendants, she waved regally to the crowd as ragged black flambeau carriers whirled and danced around the moving float. Float after float, each an elaborately devised tableau depicting episodes in the history of New Orleans, passed before them, each float manned by white men and women expensively outfitted in period dress. Streamers, fake coins, and beads were being showered over the spectators who competed for them as if they were of great value. At the end of the procession, as if to emphasize the most recent phase in the city's development, came half a dozen floats loaded with men dressed in the most flamboyant costumes imaginable. Brightly colored peacocks, dressed to emphasize their sexuality, some nearly naked, their skins every shade of color from deep black to freckled pink, they proclaimed their way of life in every movement, every gesture. As the last float disappeared, and the street cleaners took over, Janice and J.T. turned away, bemused by the images of a society so full of contradictions. The evidence of the persistence of racial and class divisions, stretching back to colonial times, alongside new and very different norms of social behavior, was disorienting.

The restaurant gleamed with fine silver and glass, the menu was a ravishing combination of French and Creole cuisine, the wine list offered French and Californian vintages priced up to a thousand dollars a bottle. The Holcombe's had invited two other couples, so that the whole party was seated in the center of the restaurant at a great round table. J.T. had been placed next to Julia Holcombe, across the table from Janice, Oscar and their host. As the meal progressed the talk became more lively and uninhibited. A waiter refilled glasses as quickly as they were emptied.

'I have read a great deal of your husband's work,' J.T. leaned towards Julia. 'I admire it greatly. You must be delighted at his winning the Gehlin Prize.'

'Hell, no!' was the unexpected reply. 'I think all of that is a load of shit.' J.T., who was in the act of taking a long draught of the Chateau Neuf du Pape, choked and sprayed some of it over the mahogany. Julia leaned towards him, putting her hand on his thigh. 'I'm so glad that you are visiting with us, J.T.' She looked at him in a way that made it seem that she had been waiting all her life for this moment. 'I have lived with that ridiculous hypocrite for fifteen years. He's never had an original thought in his life.' Her hand moved higher on J.T.'s thigh, and she leaned closer to him. He could not avoid looking down at her bosom, her dress revealing almost the full majesty of the upper half of her body. He hurriedly took a gulp of wine.

'Does he know what you think of him?' he asked.

'Of course not! He thinks I worship the ground he walks on.' By now Julia was almost in J.T.'s lap. He was having increasing difficulty in conducting a conversation while her hand tightened on his leg.

'Everyone will be watching us.' he said into her ear, which was hovering perilously close to his mouth. Janice, however, seemed not to have noticed how closely J.T. and Julia were entangled. She was listening intently to Jim Holcombe who was regaling his audience with some of the bawdier examples of Elizabethan poetry.

Julia smiled sweetly across at her husband.

'The trouble with that sonofabitch,' she cooed, is that he can talk about it, but he can't do it.'

'Can't write poetry? J.T. gasped. 'I'm sure he has written some of the best...'

'You know what I mean.' She was nibbling his ear. 'He's useless in bed. I can tell that you'd be great.' J.T. gave an involuntary shiver. He had witnessed some strange behavior in his time to be sure, but no one had ever spoken to him in this way before. He had met this woman only four hours earlier and here she was talking about bed. They hadn't even got as far as the main course yet, for God's sake.

By the time that dessert was served everybody was very merry indeed. Holcombe was loudly intoning Shakespearean sonnets in an authentic sixteenth-century accent, to a somewhat bemused audience. The woman on J.T.'s right, to whom he had been introduced at the beginning of the meal, but to whom he had said virtually nothing, was singing black spirituals quietly to herself. Holcombe called out:

'Who would like a brandy?' Several hands were raised. 'J.T., brandy?' J.T. felt that he was losing touch with reality - distinctly woozy! He waved indecisively at Holcombe. Suddenly Julia unwound her legs from J.T.'s, and stood up.

'Darling,' she called across at her husband. 'J.T. and I are going to get a breath of fresh air.' Nobody seemed to hear. J.T. hardly had time to replace his glass on the table before Julia grasped his unwilling hand, dragged him from the table, and pulled him out of the restaurant into the cool evening air. He steadied himself on a very willing arm, and as they walked through the crowded street, Julia took his hand and pressed it closely to her side.

'I'm not wearing any panties,' she said in a matter-of-fact tone of voice. The world was veering out of control, but it was very clear to J.T. that he would be failing in his duty to his hostess if he did not take this matter seriously. At least he ought to check it out. They turned into the darkened entrance to a shop. His hands went down her back, and one handful after another of her ankle-length skirt came up, until it became clear to him that Julia was indeed a woman of her word.

The next morning, when J.T. made his way gingerly to the breakfast room, he found Janice already there, talking to Jim Holcombe. She barely acknowledged his greeting, and continued her conversation.

'I went out for a walk earlier on,' she was saying. 'There were these two men sitting in an automobile a few yards along the road. Big, burly fellows, they looked like gangsters. Then when I turned the corner, there was another one lurking in the garden. When he saw me he turned away, and walked round the back. It made me quite frightened.' Holcombe reached out a large hand and patted her arm reassuringly.

'No need. Those are security people. We have to be careful here, you know. Times are difficult.'

'Well that's a relief,' and she turned back to her cereal. J.T., with some difficulty, focussed on her. He sensed a certain coolness.

'That was a really good meal last night.' J.T. addressed his host. 'Thank you very much.'

'Glad you liked it. I think everyone had a good time.'

'Some more than others,' Janice said rather acidly. At that point Oscar Wolf entered, and slapped J.T. on the back. J.T. put his hands to his head and groaned.

'Boy, were you loaded when you got back last night, J.T. Where did you disappear to?'

'I think that I made a tour of the French Quarter.' He looked out of the corner of his eye at Holcombe. 'I started out, I believe, with Mrs. Holcombe, but I think we got separated somewhere.'

'Julia's a great girl for showing off New Orleans to visitors,' Holcombe was quietly proud of his wife's hospitable orientation. 'She said that you had a great time. Where did she take you?' J.T. was saved from having to make an attempt at answering that question by the arrival of their hostess herself.

'Good morning everybody. What a beautiful morning! I think this is the best part of the year in New Orleans. I thought we might drive into the country today. We could visit some of the splendid old houses in Mississippi. Who would like to come?' It turned out that Holcombe had to write some poetry, Oscar was going to go over his speech for that evening, and Janice was rather tired.

'That leaves you and me, J.T. We'll leave in half an hour.' J.T. would have preferred to go back to bed, but soon found himself being driven westwards across a very long, low bridge over the waters of the delta of the Mississippi River. By 10.30 they were in fertile farmland, passing through small semi-abandoned towns, Spanish moss hanging from gnarled old trees, glimpses of stately houses through the foliage.

* * *

Oscar Wolf, accompanied by J.T. and Janice, was seated in the back of a long, black official limousine as it swept towards the New Orleans Royal Hotel where the IATABS convention was being held. In the front, beside the driver, was seated one of the security guards that Janice had spotted at the

Holcombe's house that morning. It was 5.0 p.m., and Oscar was scheduled to give the key-note address, following a reception, at 6.0. The streets were full of workers returning home, the traffic was heavy. The tall downtown buildings were dwarfed by the massive new conference center and hotel, which could accommodate, it was said, 3000 participants. As the car turned into the entrance, J.T. was surprised to see that police barricades had been set up, cops were everywhere, including a small detachment of officers mounted on horses. Behind the barricades, heavily outnumbered by the police, demonstrators had gathered, and as they spied the limousine they began to shout and to wave placards. J.T. strained to read them. "Save Islam from Western Influences", "Hands off Japan", he read, and strangest of all, "Stop the Sewage Swindle". The car drew up at the front of the hotel. The security man sprang out, police gathered round Oscar and his companions as they moved towards the doors, amidst a great deal of shouting and the blaring of bull-horns, as the police kept the demonstrators in check. Inside the lobby J.T. turned to the security man.

'What on earth was that all about?'

'Just some weirdo's. Think nothing of it. Things like this happen all the time in this town. You get used to it.'

The corridors were thronged with the convention participants, all wearing their identification tabs. The mandarins of the business schools, their graying hair brushed back in elegant waves, mingled with the upwardly mobile aspirants, male and female, who fawned on them, and then moved away to mock their manners and pretensions. From time to time a way would be cleared for the passage of a foreign ambassadorial delegation or the entourage of the president of a great multinational corporation. Several rooms had been prepared for the pre-convention reception. A vast featureless room big enough to house three 747's was available for the hoi-polloi, with trestle tables set with sandwiches and cheap wine; a room decorated in the fashion of the French Second Empire for the red badge-holders, denoting their status as minor officials of the Association or academics reading papers to the convention, and the VIP suite, lavishly provided with canapés and champagne for the bigwig officers of the Association and their honored guests. Oscar of course had a blue badge, providing the entree to the holy of holys. J.T., as the hanger-on of a VIP, had a red badge, and Janice had the white label of a mere foot soldier. Oscar was swept away by the First Assistant to the President of the International Association for the Teachers of American Business Studies, and J.T., spurning the Second Empire, accompanied Janice into the aircraft hangar where eighteen hundred conferees were intent on getting through the maximum amount of free wine that could be drunk in forty-five minutes - quite a lot as it turned out. Janice and J.T. knew no one, so they stood together, sipping the wine, not because they were enjoying it, but because they had nothing else to do. All around them, the conversations turned on the demonstration outside the hotel, speculating on its origins and meaning. J.T. looked earnestly at Janice.

'Did you notice that one of the placards mentioned sewage?' he asked. 'I thought that rather odd.' She looked at him coldly.

'No doubt they have public health problems of every kind in this city.'

With supplies of wine running out, and conversation flagging, they moved towards the auditorium, where the seats were already filling up. J.T. looked around and was surprised to see the number of security personnel that were posted at strategic points. The platform party entered. The President of the Association moved to the podium.

'It is an honor to introduce to you this evening our key-note speaker, Oscar Wolf, Vice President for International Affairs at Bransome Southern University. Oscar is without doubt the most distinguished figure in international education in this country, and indeed, perhaps in the world. His knowledge of the field, his original and brilliant ideas, and his very real achievements, are an inspiration to us all. Oscar, we are proud to have you with us this evening, and we know that you will set this convention on the right track, as you have done for so many other ventures in the past.'

Oscar took his position before the microphone.

'Mr. President, Your Excellencies, Ladies and Gentlemen. I can think of few tasks I would undertake so willingly as to open the 12th. Annual Convention of the International Association of Teachers of American Business Studies, here in this great city of New Orleans, and in the presence of the most distinguished men and women of the State of Louisiana.' Oscar launched into his speech. J.T. was surprised to see how well Oscar read it. Almost as if he understood what he was saying. True he occasionally left out a vital word or phrase, but nobody seemed to notice, and the faces of the audience, fixed raptly upon him, were evidence of the awe in which he was held.

Soon, however, J.T. became bored by hearing his own words read out, and his mind began to wander. He still played the Galia tape from time to time, but it had become rather stale, and since he no longer had any real expectation of experiencing the reality again, rather frustrating as well. He was, however, surprised and intrigued, when a new tape began to run in his head, which featured Julia Holcombe in the leading role. He was lying in bed, in the Holcombe's mansion, when the door opened quietly, and Julia slipped inside, closing the door after her. She was wearing a lace negligée, rather similar in fact, J.T. noted, to the one Galia used to wear, and moving swiftly towards him she knelt by his bed. He sat up, turned to her, and took her in his arms. She smiled, and her head went back, her lips slightly parted so that he could see the even white teeth, and between them, her tongue pinkly flickering. With his left hand he caressed her long, softly descending hair, and at the same time his right hand moved down her back until he could feel, at the base of her spine, the beginning of a sweet furrow. Julia took his hand in hers, and placed it over her breast. He felt her nipple rise under his palm. He bent his head towards her, and she closed her eyes in anticipation of his kiss. At that moment the tomato hit Oscar Wolf. It was one of those large Italian tomatoes that you use to make a *trecolore* salad, and it was very ripe. It burst squarely in the center of Oscar's forehead, ran down his nose and chin, and dripped onto his shirt and tie. The silence in the auditorium was total. Oscar, equal to the occasion, took a tissue from his jacket pocket, wiped his face, and barely lifting his eyes from his script, said, 'The value of such an international education in meeting the varied and complex challenges of life today cannot be exaggerated.' The applause was deafening. The audience stood and cheered. Three security guards darted forward and captured a small male figure trying to break for the exit. After everyone had calmed down, Oscar resumed his speech, and having completed it, left the platform to a tumultuous ovation.

That evening there was a gala dinner in the aircraft hangar. Oscar was the guest of honor, feted on all sides. The President of the Association made a speech praising Oscar's bravery, in phrases which would have been more appropriate had he single-handedly won the Second World War, colleagues grasped his hand in theirs, welcoming him back from the battle-front, grateful that he was unmarked, and two attractive young Assistant Professors, Oscar's arms round their waists, posed for the photographers of the national press. On all sides there was speculation about the reasons for the attack. Saddam Hussein and Colonel Gaddaffi were the favorite culprits, though no one was able to offer a convincing explanation of the *modus operandi* adopted for this particular outrage. Oscar did not reappear at the Holcombe's that night, but everyone had had so much to drink that they were hardly capable of noting his absence. At the convention the next day there was something of a panic when Oscar failed to appear for the meeting of the Executive Council. The police were alerted, and a search of the hotel was begun, only to be abandoned when Oscar was found fast asleep in bed with one of the Assistant Professors. A communal sigh of relief was accompanied by a grudging admiration that one man could live such a full and fulfilling life.

J.T. spent days of boredom in the convention, wandering from one excruciating session to another, alleviated only by evenings spent in the magnificent restaurants of the French Quarter, followed by sessions in the jazz cafes until the early hours of the morning. On the last night, before the return flight to Bransome, he was lying in bed, in the Holcombe's mansion, when the door opened quietly, and Julia slipped inside, closing the door after her. She was wearing a lace negligée, rather similar in fact, J.T. noted, to the one Galia used to wear, and moving swiftly towards him she knelt by his bed. He sat up, turned to her, and took her in his arms. She smiled, and her head went back, her lips slightly parted so that he could see the even white teeth, and between them, her tongue pinkly flickering. With his left hand he caressed her long, softly descending hair, and at the same time his right hand moved down her back until he could feel, at the base of her spine, the beginning of that sweet furrow. Julia took his hand in hers, and placed it over her breast. He felt her nipple rise under his palm. He bent his head towards her, and she closed her eyes in anticipation of his kiss...

* * *

As the flight to Bransome roared westward, J.T. turned to his companion in the next seat:

'What was that all about, Oscar?'

'What was what all about?'

'The police barricades, the security men, the tomato?' Oscar looked out of the aircraft window.

'Beat's me!'

'You must have some idea. Why would anyone do that to you? Who was that guy that they arrested?'

'Some kind of a nut. The police said that he had escaped from a mental institution. Nothing to worry about.'

'I must say that you are taking it all very calmly.'

'No good doing anything else, is there?' Oscar pointedly opened a magazine, and no more was said before the plane landed at Bransome.

* * *

The pace began to heat up at the College of International Affairs. Oscar Wolf began to demand more and more programs in ever more obscure locations. He made more and more appearances at conventions, seminars, and briefing sessions, all over the world. J.T. found himself working longer and longer hours, writing speeches and directing the work of the College. He hardly had time for any social life, dragging himself off to the apartment at nine or ten, slumping in front of the TV, with a sandwich and a gin and tonic. The efficiency of the office began to suffer. Documents were sent to wrong destinations; a visiting Congressman was refused entry to the building because the guard had not been alerted to his arrival. 'Sorry, sir,' the guard apologized later, 'but this guy looked like some kind of mobster.' Not surprising really, because that was what he was. President Zuwicki received a letter from a student in an African center complaining that BSU staff there were unsympathetic to local customs, displaying a typically Western arrogance towards the Third World. On investigation it transpired that the program director had made disparaging remarks, in public, about the standards of plumbing in Solario, after the toilet in his apartment had suddenly begun to spew sewage vertically into the air instead of ingesting it as one might reasonably expect. As Zuwicki pointed out, the correct response would have been to compliment the Republic on its advanced technical development, make a gentle inquiry about the differential effects of gravity in the southern hemisphere, and invite the Minister of Public Works to a lavish dinner with a great deal of drink, necessitating the subsequent use of the facilities.

After a while even Oscar became aware that something was amiss. He called J .T .to his office.

'J .T .We are being subjected to an efficiency audit.' He gestured towards a remarkably nubile young woman sitting by the side of his desk. 'Meet Rebecca Vogelsang. She is a partner in the management consultants, Hickspeed, Lohnro, Finklestein and Vogelsang. She is going to make a complete study of your operation and report on it to me. I expect to get some very positive recommendations about how to tighten up our procedures.'

The next three weeks were extremely invigorating. The minions of Hickspeed, Lohnro, Finklestein and Vogelsang invaded the building demanding detailed information concerning every aspect of the operations of the College of International Affairs. The accounts were minutely perused, each member of the staff was closely questioned about their work, the office files were opened to inspection, and J.T. received daily visits from Rebecca Vogelsang requesting clarification of the information culled by her subordinates. For J.T. this was the most confusing period of his life, presenting him with dilemmas that had never before had to face. Rebecca Vogelsang was characterized by an incredible degree of self-confidence in approaching subjects about which she knew absolutely nothing. No rebuff dented this self-confidence, however extreme.

'J.T. I see from the files that the program director in Solario has the use of a Jeep provided by the University, as well as an official car. Surely that is excessive for a relatively small program in Illinois?'

'Solario is in Africa. The director, or a member of his staff, has to travel hundreds of miles through the bush every week.'

'I thought Solario was in Illinois. I used to go there as a child. My aunt Mathilda had a very nice house there. Unfortunately after she died the house deteriorated and the family had to sell it for a song.'

'There is a Solario in Illinois, but our program is in Africa.'

'O.K! I understand what you are saying, but even so the expenses he has been claiming seem excessive. I see that in December last year he put in for

$531.09 for salt tablets, anti-malaria shots, and mosquito netting. When I saw that I thought, "Oh boy! Illinois wasn't like that in winter when I was a kid." I mean that's summer stuff. The rule is that he should claim for expenses within a month of making the purchases. He seems pretty lax in his accounting procedures.'

'Solario is in the Southern Hemisphere, not far from the equator.'

'O.K. I'll mention that in my report, but it seems that there is quite a lot of scope for tightening up here.' When the report eventually came out there was, inevitably, a reference to slack accounting procedures in Solario.

The main problem for J.T., however, was that Rebecca was unbelievably attractive. She was honey blonde, with faultlessly regular features, long slim legs, and above all an ample and firm bosom. Her smart office suits, low cut blouses and pencil-thin skirts showed off her figure to perfection. Seated across from J.T., her legs crossed, her upper body leaning forward earnestly in the quest for truth, she could have portrayed the College of International Affairs as a den of thieves and opium addicts and J.T. would have forgiven her.

* * *

Although he had been overworked before, the added burdens and delights of the arrival of the management consultant nearly tipped him over the edge. Each day he yearned to see her coming into his office to ask him ridiculous questions, her long hair floating, her blouse open down to button number three.

'Hi, J.T! I just noticed that you are a Sanskrit buff. That sounds really fascinating. You'll have to show me how you play it some time.' All J.T. could think about was button number four. After a week he was close to desperation.

'Rebecca! Would you have dinner with me?'

'Sure J.T. It goes with the job. How about tonight? I'm staying at the Apollo. Meet me in the lobby at 7.30.'

In the restaurant the same bizarre game was played. Rebecca would ask dumb questions which J.T. would try to answer as honestly as possible, whilst in reality he was lusting after her to the point where he would have said anything to achieve his goal. Meanwhile she was terribly earnest about her assignment, determined to get to the root of the problem.

'J.T., what is the objective that you are aiming to achieve?'

J.T. looked at her in consternation. Did she realize that for days his sole preoccupation had been how to get her into bed? No, she must be talking about the College. He'd never even thought of an 'objective' in relation to his work. To satisfy Oscar, and keep his job? That wasn't the kind of answer she was expecting. It had to be something more high-minded.

'Well, of course I feel that our mission is to spread American ideals of higher education throughout the world.'

'How admirable!' She stretched her arm across the table and took his hand in hers. Her eyes were shining. 'Tell me what those ideals are. I so want to hear about this.' J.T. gulped inwardly.

'Well, excellence, of course, and the opportunity to develop to the fullest the potential of the individual.'

'That is wonderful. I have never before had the opportunity to discuss educational philosophy with someone like you J.T. Most of my assignments are much more down-to-earth. Like what advice to give to people making parts for automobiles, or the best way of organizing dog shows.'

'How are you able to do these things, Rebecca? Forgive me, you seem so young. Have you ever worked in the automobile industry? Or run a dog show?'

'No, I haven't actually done those things, but I took an MBA at Sampson, and I saw an advertisement for a partner in this management consultancy, I applied and got it.'

'A partnership! That was a pretty high level to begin at.'

'Well of course they were looking for somebody with capital to put into the business, and Daddy has always been very generous. But that is enough about me. Let's talk some more about your educational philosophy. Why don't we go up and continue our discussion in my suite.'

The suite consisted of four rooms, plus a bathroom with a Jacuzzi, and a sunken tub large enough to hold a football team. Rebecca poured two large brandies, handed one to J.T., and pointing to one of the bedrooms, she said:

'You'll find a bathrobe in there. There's no reason why we shouldn't relax as we continue our discussion.'

J .T .was far from relaxed, but he stripped off, donned the bathrobe and returned to the lounge. Indeed he was so far from being relaxed, that he decided to retain his shorts as the only way to prevent his enthusiasm for further discourse from becoming too prominent.

When he entered the lounge he heard water being run into the tub. Gripping the brandy glass he made his way to the bathroom door. Rebecca, her robe loosely tied, was bending over to test the temperature of the water. One breast hung deliciously from the toweling, and her right leg was bare to the top of her thigh. She turned as he entered, and called, 'Come on in. It's just right, I think.' She opened the robe and let it fall to the floor. J.T. had never seen anything remotely as beautiful as Rebecca's body. Her breasts were full, but taught, the nipples turning up slightly; her stomach was superbly flat, and as he looked further down, he saw that the Mount of Venus rose steeply up from her abdomen so that the soft froth of blonde hair was prominently displayed, and then subsided invitingly into the gap between her legs.

Rebecca stepped down into the bath. As she turned he saw the long slim hips, the tight, rounded buttocks, and caught a glimpse of blondeness from the rear. Every movement was a thing of beauty. She sat at one end, the water reaching only a little above her waist, took her glass in her hand, and gestured to J.T. to join her. Self-consciously he dropped his robe and for a second considered getting into the bath still wearing his underpants. Concluding that that would make him look even more ridiculous, he quickly dropped them and jumped in. Rebecca observed him as he entered the water and sat down at the other end of the bath.

'Education is such a fascinating topic. There is so much about which I would like to have your views. Do you think that the work you do really helps to empower your students, to give them real control over their own future?' J.T. took a deep swig at the brandy.

'Well, that depends.' He hardly knew what he was saying. 'We run such a variety of different programs. Some do, some don't.'

'That's what is so refreshing about you J.T. You are so honest. You make no attempt to bullshit me. So many of the men that I meet have only one thing in mind, whereas with you I can have an intelligent conversation on a man-to-man basis.'

'I'm glad you feel that way, Rebecca.' His heart sank.

'I do, I really do.' She set down her glass, and moved along the bath to kneel in front of him. She squeezed some soft soap from its plastic container, and began to lather his shoulders and his chest. 'It seems to me that someone in your position must be constantly evaluating progress, planning the next move, assessing the virtue of what you are doing.' She rinsed off the lather. 'Stand up!' He obeyed blindly. She took more soap, and with her long slim fingers thoroughly massaged every part of his lower body, sliding her hand between his legs to ensure that he was clean between the cheeks of his bottom, working on the skin between his legs, and drawing her soapy fingers again and again caressingly along his penis. ' After all, knowledge is of no use unless you share it with others.' J.T. was unable to speak. He slumped back into the bath and began minutely to soap her, she arching her body to lift her lap clear of the water so that he should not miss any part of her.

'I think my skin is beginning to get wrinkly,' she said. 'Let's go into the other room.' She took a towel and led him into the master bedroom, dominated by a massive bed. He toweled her gently, taking particular care to get her pubic hair really dry so that it was gorgeously frizzy. She took his hand and led him to the bed, lay down on her back and stroked his head as he leaned over her.

'Let's talk about your future plans for the College. You must have lots of exciting ideas about what to do next.' J.T. had now had an erection for almost forty-five minutes. He was in agony.

'Rebecca, the only thing I want to do is to make love to you. Please!'

'J.T., I thought you'd never mention it. Fuck me! Quickly!'

* * *

He was in love, hopelessly, forlornly in love. He spent all day discussing the minutiae of the programs with her. Each day they went to lunch together. He would rush back to his apartment to pick up clean underwear in the early evening, and then they would go to dinner, go dancing, visit the one night-club that Bransome boasted; and then each night they made love in the big bed at the Apollo Hotel. He was making love every night to the loveliest, without doubt the most beautiful woman in the universe. True, she seemed determined to treat the whole affair as if it were part of her mission to explore the world of overseas study, keeping up a continuous barrage of questions, even in the most intimate of circumstances. It was as if she had to justify sexual intercourse on her expense account, crying out at climactic moments for him to make her understand it all, or pleading that he bring her to see the truth. His normal work was left completely untouched. The office staff was reduced to impotence, being unable to catch his attention for a moment.

As the days passed he became more and more depressed.

'When will I see you again? You'll be back in New York soon and working on another assignment.'

'I'll come back to Bransome to present the report. I always do that in person. Maybe you can visit me in New York before then.'

He was seized by bouts of extreme jealousy. 'Do you go on like this on every assignment? I can't bear to think of you with someone else.'

'J.T. How could you? Let's make the most of the time we have left.'

'I love you, Rebecca. Don't you feel anything for me?'

'Of course I do, J.T., but we lead very different lives.'

He knew that he had no hope. She was a goddess, a being from another planet. She had come into his life for a short while, and soon she would leave again. There was nothing he could do about it, and if he had tried he would just have looked ridiculous. He returned to the apartment, to the sandwich and the gin and tonic, except that now it was two, or three, or more.

* * *

Two weeks later Oscar received the report. Rebecca sent a note to J.T. apologizing that she could not deliver the report in person, as she would normally do, because of extreme pressure of work. 'I hope you will not be upset at anything in the report,' she wrote, 'but I am sure that you will understand that our private relationship could not have any influence on my professional judgment. Were it otherwise, it would have been quite unethical for us to become such close friends as we did.'

Oscar was not in a very good mood when J.T. entered his boss's office to confer about the report, a copy of which J.T. had not yet seen.

'Sit down J.T. We paid thousands of dollars for this report. I expected to get some kind of constructive suggestions about the running of your programs. This damn thing is not worth the paper it's written on.'

'What's the problem, Oscar?'

'Well in the first place this woman Vogelsang cannot spell my name. She puts an 'e' on the end every damn time.'

'At least she's consistent.'

'This is not a laughing matter, J.T. There are some pretty damaging revelations in this report. For example, I did not have any idea that we were involved in prostitution in Japan! How is that going to look when Zuwicki reads this?' J.T. looked at Oscar in utter amazement.

'She says that we are involved in prostitution in Japan?'

'That's what it says here. She says that the College recently rented premises in Tokyo for the purpose of supplying *geishas* for Japanese government officials.'

'But that's ridiculous. I told Rebecca, I mean Ms. Vogelsang, that we had rented a place in the Ginza district to improve liaison with the Japanese government offices there. She must have got it wrong in her notes.' As he said this J.T. remembered the exact circumstances in which he had passed this information to Rebecca in response to one of her urgent inquiries at a moment of some intensity. The position in which she had been at that time, however, was such that it would have been quite impossible for her to take notes.

Oscar shook his head doubtfully. 'Well, it looks bad. She adds a comment about the necessity for universities to maintain the highest moral standards in their overseas programs. And what about this on page 36? I quote: "Bransome Southern University is taking considerable risks in allowing its administrative personnel to invest university funds in gambling activities such as those conducted at Happy Valley racetrack in Hong Kong, particularly as there appears to be no record of the bets placed, and no betting tickets were submitted to the University Finance Office for accounting purposes." What have you got to say to that?' Oscar looked accusingly at J.T., who cradled his head in his hands. What in God's name was the woman doing?

Was she relaying every unguarded remark he had made in their most intimate moments together? What if she had reported what he had said at that time when he had been about to reach the heights of passion and she had asked him...No, surely she would not do that.

'Oscar, I seem to remember saying that Jimmie Lee, you know the guy that handles our recruiting in the Far East? Well I told her that he had said that the University could make a killing at the track, and that I thought we ought to do it, if we hadn't already. It was a joke for God's sake!'

'You had no business making jokes to a management consultant. Those people have no sense of humor. You should know that.' J.T. was learning quickly. Oscar was still in full flow. 'The report is full of this kind of stuff. The worst bits are the one's that deal with you personally. She says that you appear to be almost totally free from day-to-day responsibilities, and that you spend excessive amounts of your time in restaurants and other places of entertainment. And then she says that far too many of your staff, especially the overseas Directors, are *women.* She seems to think that you are running some kind of international harem! And listen to the final conclusion. Again I quote: "Surely it should not be the purpose of an organization of this kind to serve the particular needs of its senior administrators, rather it should be to deliver excellence, and develop to the fullest the potential of the individual."' Oscar sank back into his chair, bringing his hands together in a prayer-like formation, waiting for a response.

J.T.'s morale was as low as it was possible to get. To lose his goddess, and then to be betrayed by her in this awful way. He had no desire even to defend himself. He was silent and defeated. Oscar waited. The silence became oppressive. Still J.T. remained wordless. Oscar began to hum quietly. The humming increased in volume, until Oscar could contain himself no longer.

'O.K. Let's lay it on the line. J.T., I don't take too much notice of this kind of crap. This Rebecca woman uses all this stuff to hide the fact that she doesn't really know what goes on here.' For the first time since he had met Oscar J.T. was impressed by his boss's perspicacity. 'Fortunately, Zuwicki does not know that I asked for this report to be done. I thought I'd keep it to myself. In fact, in a way, it has served its purpose.' With this Delphic utterance Oscar indicated that the interview was at an end.

As J.T. was walking miserably from the room, Oscar called to him. 'Ask Janice to come in. I want her to get started on organizing a convention - a kind of anniversary get-together.' J.T. hardly registered the import of Oscar's words, but dutifully sent Janice off, and then retired to his office, firmly closed the door, and sat glumly in his chair, staring unseeingly into space.

The ensuing weeks and months were painful for J.T. The feeling of having lost face, of having failed in the eyes of Oscar, and of having been used and discarded by Rebecca, were made intolerable by the loneliness of his life. There was no one to talk to, no one to reassure him, no one to comfort him. He became almost a recluse, doing his work and then retreating to his apartment, without any social life or recreation. Several people attempted to draw him out of his depression, but he resisted all such overtures, refusing invitations, avoiding College social functions, eating sandwiches in his office at lunchtime. Janice made two attempts to entice him out to a meal, but on the second occasion she was met by such a coldly-worded refusal that she made no further efforts, and their daily working relationship became more formal even than before. J.T. continued to service Oscar Wolf's speech-making, thinking that perhaps it was this more than anything else which had protected his job after the Vogelsang disaster. And so life continued at Bransome, J.T. virtually alone and isolated at the center of an organization engaged in activities which spanned the whole globe, and which involved many more people than actually appeared on the payroll.

* * *

Part 3

THE CONNECTIONS

Shit!' Ken Charles banged his fist against his forehead. The sound of the air-conditioner running down indicated that the power had failed again. The El Baku electricity supply was simply not up to coping with the demands that the program's new equipment made upon it. The satellite transmitter was powered by a small independent generator situated next to the center, so that contact was maintained with Bransome even when the El Baku supply failed, but it could not provide the power necessary for the overall needs of the center. A powerful new generator was soon to be installed in the compound, but until then this kind of breakdown would recur. The magnificent new communications center was a matter of great pride to Charles, but it was difficult to keep it going. It needed to be kept at a constant temperature, between 60 and 80 degrees Fahrenheit, and as the ambient external temperature at midday was generally well above 100 degrees, if the air-conditioning failed there was a danger that the whole installation would melt down. So every time this occurred Charles had to activate the center's maintenance staff to rush the large stock of ice that was kept on hand into the communications room, and pray that the electricity would be restored before all the ice melted.

Ken Charles lunged for the door, issued his orders, and anxiously monitored the temperature of the room whilst his staff staggered in under the weight of large tubs full of ice. He had already telephoned the engineers to replace the mains fuses in the transformer that supplied the compound, and hopefully it would be at most thirty minutes before full power was restored and the air-conditioning with it. Proud as he was of the high-tech equipment of which he was in charge, he did have moments of doubt about the need for equipment that clearly had cost hundreds of thousands of dollars, and whose principal function seemed to be to insure that his monthly report to Oscar Wolf arrived with all speed. He had standing instructions to give the highest priority to keeping the communications equipment operational, and he put his whole being into discharging that responsibility.

'How much ice is left in the cold room?' he inquired of one of the sweating janitors.

'Only about 250 pounds. We didn't have time to restock properly after the last breakdown.'

'It's melting quickly. Where are those damned engineers?'

The tall figure of Jason Roberts, Counselor at the US Embassy, appeared in the doorway.

'Hi, Ken! I heard that you were in trouble. I brought our electrician over from the Embassy. He should get you back on stream in no time. Can I have a few words in private, please?'

The Counselor had been a frequent visitor to the compound during the past year, giving a great deal of help in establishing the communications center. He seemed to have a benevolent, even fatherly attitude towards Ken Charles, humoring the latter's foibles, such as the frequent polishing of the brass fitments on the generator, or the daily flag-raising ceremony in the foyer of the center.

'The Ambassador has asked me to pass on some information that is highly classified. I know that you will respect his confidence.'

'Of course!' Charles was flattered.

'We are faced with a rather serious situation here in El Baku. It began with the demonstration that was led by your colleague Mike Llewellyn-Proctor. No, don't worry Ken, we are not blaming you.' Roberts was quick to respond to the obvious distress that the memory of that event aroused in his companion. 'It's just that what seemed a harmless prank at that time in reality had a much deeper significance. It was a symbolic event, a sign to a lot of people in El Baku who had been keeping their heads down that the time had come for action.'

'What kind of people?'

'Well, we were not aware at that time - a failure of our intelligence system, I'm afraid - that there was a very strong underground feminist movement in El Baku. A group that is determined to bring about fundamental change in the nature of society here. Of course, a lot of other people, lefties and other subversive elements, are ready to jump on the bandwagon if there is any indication that it is really going to roll.'

'That's quite amazing. This is such a conservative society. Surely they have no hope of success.' Ken Charles could hardly credit what he was being told.

'I'm not so sure. For years we have been expecting a crack to appear in the fabric of the traditional regimes in this area, but we did not think it would happen in this way.'

'So what's going to happen?'

'Well, the policy of the Government of the United States is to give every assistance to this new dissident feminist group in achieving their aims.' He smiled at the blank astonishment on Charles's face. 'I thought that would get to you. You'd expect us to be doing everything in our power to prop up the monarchy and to maintain the *status quo*. That's what we've always done in the past, but things have changed.'

'It's not because of Hillary...?'

'No, no!' Roberts swept the thought aside with a gesture of his hand. 'It goes very much deeper than that. There has been a big policy review, and now our intention is to support democratic movements whenever they attack autocratic regimes anywhere in the world. We are returning to our Jeffersonian roots.'

'Wow!' Charles was stunned. 'What do you think of that?'

'My personal opinion is that it's a load of garbage. It's those fancy young Harvard men at State that have come up with this. They know nothing about the real world. They've never been to places like El Baku. They occasionally take dinner in Oxford colleges, or browse through the bookstalls on the Left Bank of the Seine, but that's about the only experience they have of anything beyond the East Coast of the US. Still, no one cares what I think.'

Ken Charles made great efforts to absorb this extremely disorienting information. 'How does all this affect me?' he asked in a somewhat timid voice.

'This compound, *and its facilities,* may become very important in the coming weeks. The Embassy cannot become directly involved, but we must give all the support that we can to the dissidents, and in particular provide them with communications so that they can get news to the outside world of what is going on. We are looking to you to provide that support. Your new generator will be rushed into position in the next few days. I will post an engineer here permanently to keep you operational, and one of my staff will be here to advise you, day and night.'

'But what if there is any violence?' Charles was rapidly losing enthusiasm for this operation.

'Then may the best man - sorry, woman - win!' And with that heartless remark Jason Roberts departed, leaving Ken Charles in a pensive mood.

The next two weeks were taken up with urgent activities, installing the new generator, stocking up with oil and food. Outside the compound life seemed normal. Women went about their daily tasks, shrouded from head to foot in the *burkha,* masks covering their eyes. Then after dusk one evening, a car drove into the compound with just such a shrouded figure in the back. The car drove up to Ken Charles's bungalow, the woman emerged, and rang the bell. Charles opened the door, and without a word the woman slipped past him into the hall.

'Excuse me ma'am. I'm not sure...'

'Jason sent me.' She ripped off her mask.

'Mike! It's you!' Within seconds the *burkha* was off, revealing the jeans and sweatshirt underneath, but revealing also the AK 47 slung from her shoulders. Ken Charles squeaked in fear. 'Mike! For God's sake what are you doing here with that gun?'

'I've got to get a message to Bransome straight away. Tomorrow is F Day.'

'F Day! What in hell is that?'

'Feminism Day. We are starting our takeover.'

'If they catch you, an Israeli with a gun, they'll execute you. Me as well, likely as not.' Mike laughed, and stretched up to kiss him on the cheek.

'Cheer up, Ken. We are well organized, and we are going to win. But I need to reach our coordinator.'

'Your coordinator! Who's that?'

'Never you mind. Just get me to the transmitter, and leave me alone there for a while.'

Over the next five weeks Mike came and went many times. Always at night, always modestly covered, and always with her AK 47. Meanwhile the Kingdom of El Baku was thrown into chaos. Groups of shrouded women entered public buildings. They retained their traditional dress, removing only their facemasks, withdrew automatic weapons from under their black habits, and set armed guards at doors and windows, politely requesting everyone to leave, including any police that might be there.

His Majesty the King of El Baku ordered the Royal Armed Forces to eject the women from the Main Post Office and from the Railroad Station. As a line of troops advanced towards the Post Office a warning burst was fired over their heads. The soldiers halted, and then conferred amongst themselves. A spokesman, a large, heavily mustached corporal, was appointed, who then turned and approached the captain leading the platoon. The corporal saluted and standing stiffly to attention, he said:

'Sir! It is against our honor to kill women. We would prefer to be executed for disobeying orders than to fire on these women.' The captain drew his pistol.

'I order you to advance on the Post Office. If you refuse you will be shot.' The man stood silent, and unmoving. The officer raised the pistol to the corporal's forehead.

'For the last time I order you to advance on the Post Office.' There was a brief silence, the sound of a shot, and the man crumpled to the ground. The captain ran forward to the group of soldiers. 'In the name of the King,' he shouted, 'I order you to advance on the Post Office, or you will share his fate.' No-one moved. Inflamed with rage, the officer turned, raised his pistol, and ran towards the occupied building. He had covered half the distance when a single rifle shot rang out, and the captain fell forward on his face, blood spurting from a large hole in his back. The soldiers turned away, climbed into the truck that had transported them there, and left the battlefield to the victorious women. In the following days no officer dared to order his men to attack the groups of women who infiltrated into all the major public buildings, and then quietly took them over.

Stalemate! A week passed, in which no move was made by either side. Then the government decided that a gesture was needed. A princess of the royal house was dispatched to the Radio Station where the dissidents had set up their headquarters.

'What is it that you want, my sisters?'

* * *

Ken Charles was worried. Indeed, he was very worried. Mike had not visited the center for five days. She had come every day, without fail, for four and a half weeks. He had lost his initial fear of her visits, and had come to welcome them. She was invariably cheerful, optimistic, full of life. Once or twice she had stayed for a meal instead of rushing off to whatever political or military tasks she normally performed. Ken, a man condemned to the single state by the circumstance that he bored any woman to tears after a few hours of his company, was pitifully grateful for any indication that a woman actually chose to spend time with him. He had become infatuated with her, and began to fantasize about Mike's attachment to him. He had not dared to make any advances to her, simply sitting staring adoringly at her as she ate. For her part she talked incessantly, telling him about her husband, her life in Atlanta, her academic interests, anything except the events in which she was involved.

When she had finished the meal, she resumed her habit, kissing him on the cheek before replacing her mask, and then entered her car to be driven back he knew not where. And now she was not there.

Eventually he could stand it no longer. He called Jason Roberts at the Embassy.

'Jason, I'm worried. The visitor that I've had regularly lately, you know? Well, that person has not been to see me for five days. Do you know what has happened?'

'Not exactly. It's difficult to discuss this on the phone, Ken. I'll come to see you as soon as I can.'

The next day the big diplomat's shadow fell across Ken Charles's desk.

'Hi! I'm sorry I didn't call you earlier. The fact is we don't know where Mike is or what has happened to her. She was last heard of six day's ago, a few hours after she left here, and since then, nothing. We have been looking for her as hard as we can, but so far no luck.'

'What do you think has happened to her?' Ken Charles's voice betrayed his true feelings.

'We think that some kind of deal has been made.' Jason Roberts wanted to be as gentle as possible with this man whom he considered to be a genial imbecile. 'We hope that it will not be too bad for her, but we don't know.'

Ken Charles thanked him, and Jason left. There were other ways of getting information than the American Embassy, better ways. Ken took up the phone.

'Salim. I need your help.'

* * *

J.T., worried about the situation in El Baku, decided to call his boss. 'Oscar, I've been trying for days to contact Ken Charles. I get no reply on the phone and no response from the communications center there. I can't understand it. What do you think we should do?'

Oscar was silent for a moment. 'O.K., J.T. Leave it to me. I'll see what I can find out.' He hung up, and then placed another call. Two hours later he called J.T. over to his office. 'J.T. I want you to go to El Baku again. It's a similar mission to your last one, but it's a hell of a lot more difficult this time. You know that they've been having this so-called feminist uprising there. Well it seems that Mike Llewellyn-Proctor was one of the ringleaders, if not *the* ringleader. She disappeared over a week ago, and it looks as if Ken Charles set out on some damn-fool mission to find her, and now he has disappeared from view as well.' Oscar was annoyed. 'Why don't people do as they're told, instead of frigging off on their own without telling anybody?'

'This is terrible. What can I do about it?' J.T. was somewhat apprehensive about landing up in a Middle-Eastern trouble spot in the middle of an uprising, although he remembered reading that only one person, a soldier, had been killed so far. 'Would it not be better to leave it to the Embassy there?'

'It's the Ambassador who has asked for you. He was impressed by your behavior last time, and he thinks you can help now.' J.T. sighed resignedly.

'OK. If you think it will do any good. But I'm not keen to go.'

'It may be good for you. You don't seem to have any life in you these days.'

'I do my job.' J.T. was on the defensive.

'Sure! Sure! I'm not complaining about that, but you sure ain't a ball of fun to have around.' Oscar Wolf waved a hand dismissively, and J.T. miserably left the office. 'The Ambassador said to make it as quick as possible,' Oscar shouted at the retreating form.

It was like a video replay of his earlier visit. The touchdown at El Baku International Airport, Jason Roberts there to meet him at the gate, being whisked through immigration without any formalities, the limo to the Embassy. 'What the hell is going on?' J.T. was unusually irritable. Jason wasn't his usual suave self either.

'You'll hear soon enough from the Ambassador.' The rest of the drive passed in silence. This time, however, there was no waiting before Ambassador Anstey received J.T. Jason swept him into the ambassadorial office without giving him time to wash his hands.

'Thank you for coming so promptly.' Anstey was very business-like. 'We have a difficult problem here, and we welcome your help. Please sit down.' J.T. and Jason Roberts sat. Another man, who was not introduced, sat behind the Ambassador's chair. 'Let me put you in the picture. Mike Llewellyn-Proctor planned and led a move by a feminist group to take over a number of public buildings in El Baku. It is not clear what their aims were, because they were never made public. One officer was killed by his own men, and the Government very quickly became alarmed that they might spark off a mutiny in the army if they tried to use heavy-handed tactics to deal with the situation. The King sent a female member of the Royal Family of El Baku to meet the leaders of the movement, and some kind of deal was struck. We don't know exactly what it was, but we think that some concessions were made to the feminist leaders, and in return they agreed to surrender Mike to the King, on the understanding that she would not be harmed. Having an Israeli woman stirring up trouble in the Kingdom was more than the Government could bear. As far as we know she was taken to a fortress in the desert, and is perfectly safe. We have made representations to the Government of El Baku, and so have the Israelis indirectly, but the Government says that she was engaged in illegal activities, and that her case will be dealt with as soon as possible.' Anstey paused to see if J.T. wanted to ask any questions, but as none were forthcoming he went on. 'We were talking hard to the Government here, and I think we were making some progress, when Ken Charles took it into his head to go charging off into the desert with some mad-cap scheme of breaking her out of prison. He got nowhere of course, except to get himself arrested, and now El Baku thinks that the U.S. Government was behind the whole thing, and they have stopped talking to us.' He turned to the man behind him. 'Have I covered everything?' The man nodded.

'So where do I come in?' J.T. spoke for the first time.

'We want you to meet with the El Baku Foreign Office people. As a representative of Bransome Southern, Mike and Ken are, after all, your employees. You have to try to convince the Government that they were not working for the U.S. We think that El Baku would like an excuse to get them out of the country, but this time they are going to want assurances that this is not going to happen again.'

'Won't they realize that I have been in the Embassy discussing this with you? Should I have gone straight to the Foreign Office? I could have been briefed back in the States.'

'Yes of course they know that you are here. But diplomacy doesn't work like that. If you had tried to approach them directly they might never have let you in. As it is you may have to wait in the Embassy for three or four days before we get permission for you even to sit in the waiting-room at the Foreign Ministry.'

As it turned out that was not to be the case. The next day Jason Roberts sought out J.T. in the Library of the Embassy.

'OK, J.T., you're on.' They were driven to the Government quarter, a collection of magnificently tall buildings rising out of the desert, some miles out of the City of El Baku. Security was extremely heavy, and by the time they actually entered the Foreign Ministry the guards had a pretty comprehensive and detailed knowledge of their anatomy. They were shown to the anteroom of the Under Secretary, and after only one and a half hours there were admitted to his presence.

'Your Excellency,' Jason Roberts began, 'allow me to introduce the Associate Dean of International Affairs at Bransome Southern University. It is he who has requested this audience in his capacity as the officer responsible for the two persons at present detained by the Government of His Majesty the King of El Baku. In the circumstances I suggest that it would be preferable if I were to withdraw, to allow Your Excellency and the Dean to discuss this matter privately.'

'As always Counselor Roberts you are the soul of discretion. You have our permission to withdraw. Dean, please sit down. We have much to discuss.' Before they began the discussion, however, coffee was served and the Under Secretary, Prince Ibrahim el Said inquired exhaustively after the health of J.T.'s relatives, the state of mind of President Zuwicki, that great friend and supporter of El Baku, and the situation in Bransome, the city and university of which he had heard so much, all of it so very complimentary. J.T. began to think that they would never get down to business when suddenly the mood changed.

'Dean, I have to tell you that the Government of El Baku takes a most serious view of what has happened here. The two people concerned have been involved in subversive acts, one of them in acts of a most serious nature, acts which could involve the death penalty.'

For the first time, J.T. became fully aware of what was really at stake. Perhaps before he had not taken El Baku very seriously. He had been reluctant to undertake the journey to this distant Mid-Eastern desert kingdom, because it interfered with his private grief, his sense of having been abandoned by the rest of humanity. He wanted nothing else but to wallow in self-pity, and not to be distracted by the problems of others. After all these people had brought their problems on themselves. But the mention of death, death for Ken Charles and for Mike Llewellyn-Proctor, put a rather different face on the matter. He resolved to do all he could to save them, but he would make damn sure that they never got him into a mess like this again. The Under Secretary was speaking:

'His Majesty's Government is of course aware that the execution of two foreign nationals, one of whom is an American citizen, is certain to give rise to a potentially delicate diplomatic situation, but the seriousness of the charges - inciting an armed rebellion and an attempted jail-break - leaves us no choice. I am sure that you understand that.' His manner suggested that the matter was now satisfactorily settled, and that his visitor could return home to report that the government of El Baku was dealing with the problem in a reasonable and sensible manner.

'What about the trial? Is it not possible that they might be acquitted, or found guilty of a lesser charge?' Prince Ibrahim's eyebrows rose in a regal fashion.'

'There will of course be a criminal process. But the facts of the case are so clear that it will not be necessary to engage in complex discussion of the matter. It should not take more than ten minutes, fifteen at the outside.'

'What?' J.T. spluttered, 'What if they plead innocent? We'll need to get lawyers over from the States...' Prince Ibrahim's face took on a beatific smile.

'Ah, of course. The Anglo-Saxon adversarial system. Very interesting. Derived I think from trial by combat. I studied it when I was at Cambridge. Of course we don't have anything like that here. It's much too cruel. No, we establish the facts and then we deal with the matter decisively and expeditiously. That way nobody builds up false hopes of getting let off.'

'Expeditiously? What does that mean exactly?' Ibrahim opened the diary that was lying on his desk.

'I think it has been set for Wednesday. The execution, I mean. That's another advantage of our system; it's quick and it's public. I always feel that the long drawn-out procedures that you have in America for carrying out the death penalty tend to lose the interest of the people, and so do not have the deterrent effect that you would wish.' J.T. could not believe his ears.

'Wednesday! Wednesday! That's only five days from today. That's inhuman. I protest!' The Prince looked hurt.

'We are not in the least inhuman. These people are criminals, and must be treated as such. However, this is a civilized society. You may visit the prisoners, if you wish, and you will see that they are being well treated.' Ibrahim seemed to say this in almost a pleading way, as if this announcement was more important than what had gone before. J.T. modified his tone.

'Thank you Your Excellency. I would like to see them as soon as it can be arranged.'

'There is transport waiting for you now. I suggest that you leave at once. It is a three-hour drive across the desert.'

There was a good road for about three miles after they left the government center, after that it deteriorated into a desert track.

Sitting in the front of the Land Rover beside Mahmoud, the Royal EI Baku Marine driver, J.T. was impressed by the weaponry on the two escorting armored cars. 'Do we have to worry about being attacked?' he asked.

'We have to be ready for anything.'

'For example?'

'Bandits. The CIA. Feminists. They are all the same!'

'Do you mean that they are the same people, or that they are all a threat?' The soldier shrugged. J.T. persisted.

'Why do you speak of the CIA as enemies? El Baku and the United States are allies, we are friends.' The soldier averted his eyes from the track ahead long enough to turn his head and laugh loudly at J.T., a laugh imbued with Arab cynicism. At the same time, to emphasize his point, he waved his hands wildly above his head, causing the Land Rover to swerve dangerously. After that J.T. did not attempt any further conversation, but devoted himself to observing the starkly beautiful scenery.

After nearly three hours of a very bumpy ride in a hot dusty vehicle J.T. was pleased when the driver broke his long silence.

'El Khalid,' he said as he pointed through the windshield to a giant rock-face looming out of the desert plain. The medieval fortress which sat at the top of a massive escarpment, seemed wholly inaccessible until a road came into view, winding up the side of the mountain in a series of terrifying hairpin bends. A guard raised the barrier across the road after a close scrutiny of the occupants of the three vehicles and their identity passes, and they began the long, slow ascent. Two further checkpoints had to be negotiated before they reached the plateau at the summit. There nothing was to be seen from the road, other than a wall so high that it completely obscured any buildings that might lie beyond it. They drove round the wall for some minutes before coming to a massive pair of wooden gates studded with iron. Incongruously, video cameras peered down from the walls, and the small cortege waited while they were scrutinized. Then, silently, the great doors swung inward, and the Land Rover and its escort entered. Yet another check was made, and finally J.T. was set down at the entrance to an imposing structure that looked as if it dated from the twelfth century. It did. When J.T. was led into the presence of the Governor of El Khalid, it was to a scene that mixed elements of the Arabian Nights and Alcatraz. The Governor was a large man, with heavy black moustaches, dressed in fine Arab raiment. The two guards behind him wore battle fatigues and carried automatic pistols. A heavily-veiled woman placed an ornate tray on a low table in front of the Governor, bowed and withdrew, walking backwards for the first few yards. The Governor gestured to J.T.

'Welcome to El Khalid. Would you care for some coffee?' He began to pour a thick black liquid into two very small cups, and proffered a plate of sweetmeats towards J.T. 'We rarely get visitors here, and there is little passing trade.'

'Thank you very much.' J.T. reached out his hand towards the plate, but as he did so a guard stepped quickly forward, taking J.T.'s wrist, twisting his arm behind him and pinning him to the floor. The Governor spoke a few words in Arabic and the man released J.T.

'I'm sorry about that.' The Governor was clearly distressed. 'We have a very strict code of etiquette here. You could not be expected to know, of course. How could you, being an ignorant foreigner, as you are? You should bow low before addressing me, and *never* reach out your hand towards me. The servants will bring anything that I offer to you. Also you should address me as "Your Serene Highness". Here in El Khalid you see, I have absolute power of life and death over everybody in the fortress.'

J.T. bowed from the waist. 'I apologize, Your Serene Highness. I had no intention of offending your customs.'

'My dear fellow, you make it sound as if we were savages. That is far from the truth. I myself studied social anthropology at Oxford, and most of my staff are graduates of American or British universities. It is just that certain standards of behavior are expected here, and we all have to observe them. He selected one of the sweetmeats from the dish, and then extended it again to J.T., who bowed deeply, and a servant darted forward to take the plate and offer it to him.

'Your Serene Highness, I am fascinated by this place. How old is it?'

'Here we are not very far from the cradle of civilization, Ur of the Chaldees. Without excavating this site it would be impossible to put a date on it, and we are not about to open it up to the public. This building has its roots in the twelfth century, but I am sure that there was an earlier settlement here. You Westerners often forget that civilization began here, not in Chicago.'

'Your Serene Highness is right to characterize many Westerners in that way; however, I think I can claim to be rather more aware than most Westerners of the achievements of the ancient civilizations. My academic expertise is in the study of Sanskrit.'

'Really?' The Governor was impressed. 'Then we shall be able to have much interesting conversation while you are here. Are you staying for the executions?' J.T. was unable to formulate any coherent response to this question.

'Your Serene Highness...' he waved his hand vaguely, and then recoiled as one of the guards seemed ready to launch himself in his direction again. 'May I discuss this matter - the fate of my friends, that is - with you in a frank way?'

'Possibly, my young friend, but not now. You should know that it is not our way to be precipitate in such matters. First you must bathe and rest after your journey, and I would be pleased if you would join me for a meal this evening.' J.T. thanked the Governor and withdrew from the room with care, anxiously watching to make sure that he did not alarm the guards by any sudden movements.

At six p.m., after he had bathed and rested, there was a knock at the door. At his instruction to enter, a robed figure appeared, and gestured to him to follow. He was led through long corridors until a steel grille, which was opened by a guard, halted them, and they were allowed through. They passed through three more such barriers before they arrived at a solid steel door, guarded by two men carrying machine pistols. The guide indicated to the guards to unlock the door and they were admitted to a small vestibule beyond which there was yet another steel door. There guards thoroughly searched both J.T. and the guide himself, before the inner door was opened and they passed through. The room that they entered was not the prison cell that J.T. had expected. It was large and luxurious. Two women, veiled but richly dressed, were sitting on low ottomans, eating fruit from a large bowl, and sipping sherbet. At the sight of J.T. one of the women rose quickly and ran to put her arms around him.

'Hi! Thank you so much for coming. It's good to see you.' It was Mike Llewellyn-Proctor.

'Mike! Are you OK? I thought you would be chained to the wall.'

'No, nothing like that. They are very kind to me here. Come and meet Leila. She is my friend. We have a really good time together.'

On this occasion J.T. could not stay very long, and there was no time to discuss the situation in the terms which it demanded. So the conversation remained at a trivial level, the quality of the food, the opportunities for exercise, the problem of the heat at midday, and so forth. After half an hour J.T. took his leave, promising to return the next day, and was led back through the long corridors to his room. He asked his guide if he could visit Ken Charles, but if the question was understood it was ignored. The situation was surreal. He was staying in this 'luxury hotel', his every need taken care of, looking forward to what would probably be a splendid dinner, and yet in the same building were his two colleagues who were to be executed on Wednesday. It was difficult to formulate a sensible course of action; it was difficult to concentrate the mind.

The dinner was indeed splendid. The Arabian Nights triumphed totally over Alcatraz. There were no gun-toting guards, there were no barred windows, and there was no suggestion of imminent death. The walls were hung with damask, the low tables set before the Governor were loaded with exotic food, and there was a continuous stream of servants offering dishes, and musicians were playing. J.T. was the honored guest, seated at the right hand of His Serene Highness. The Governor was the model of the concerned host, assuring himself that J.T. was receiving all that he needed, inquiring after his welfare, engaging him in conversation about the state of the world, the American political situation, artistic and cultural affairs. The only subject that he did not broach was the one subject that really concerned J.T., and which was never far from his mind. After some two hours of eating and conversation the Governor gave one loud clap of his hands and immediately dancers appeared, weaving sinuously and sensuously, offering their bodies in principle, if not in practice. In spite of his preoccupation with the fate of his friends, J.T. was distracted by the way that the dancers moved ever closer, kneeling before him in poses so suggestive that he was convinced that they genuinely were attracted to him and to him alone. The group of three girls then withdrew, and there was a general expectant hush.

From between the curtains at the back of the room there emerged the most beautiful woman, her long black hair framing oval olive features, her figure perfect in its proportions.

Slowly she began to dance, her arms twining above her head, her body beginning to sway to the music. She moved towards the Governor's table, every step imbued with sexual innuendo, her magnificent legs thrusting forward, free of the hanging strips of silk which passed as a skirt, naked to the edge of the brief costume which covered her abdomen and which clearly outlined her voluptuous sexuality. She wove towards the Governor, and abased herself in front of him, her head lowered to the floor, her arms stretched out to him. Then she danced away, circling, twisting, whirling. She turned and advanced boldly towards J.T., and only a few inches from him, in time to the music, her body began to tremble, beginning with her head and moving down past her shoulders and arms, her breasts, her stomach and then her hips. She dropped to her knees before him, her legs spread wide, her head thrown back, her bosom thrust out towards him. She began to move her belly, rippling movements that shook her whole body, moving down to a climactic eruption between her legs. J.T.'s mouth was dry. He was completely shattered. As she drew herself erect, to the wild applause of the whole company, the Governor turned to J.T. 'Did you enjoy the dancing of Aleisha?'

'She is the most wonderful, the most beautiful woman that I have ever seen.' The Governor smiled wryly.

'Then my friend, she is yours.'

Soon after J.T. had returned to his room, drained by the experiences of the day, there was a soft knock on the door. When he opened it, there stood a woman, wearing a white robe trimmed with gold, immediately recognizable as the lovely Aleisha, and behind her stood an older woman, dressed in black, carrying two very large bundles. Aleisha spoke a few words in Arabic. When J.T. just looked at her uncomprehendingly, she gestured to be allowed into the apartment, and when he stood aside the two women moved inside, the older one immediately went into the bedroom and began to unpack the bundles, revealing that they contained all the paraphernalia of the female wardrobe.

'What is happening? Why are you here?' J.T.'s voice was slightly hysterical. Aleisha turned to him, and speaking very carefully she said:

'I belong you.' That appeared to exhaust her English vocabulary. Nothing J.T. could do produced any further enlightenment. She had been taught to say, 'I belong you,' and every time he addressed her she repeated this phrase.

To J.T.'s increasing bewilderment Aleisha and her maid withdrew into the bedroom and began what looked remarkably like the beginning of Aleisha's bedtime routine. J.T. retreated into the living room feeling that the situation was now totally out of control. After a while the maid reappeared, made an obeisance, and left the apartment. J.T. went to follow her, only to find that she had lain down in the corridor across the threshold of the door, and was already composing herself for sleep.

Entering the bedroom he found Aleisha, a vision of loveliness, sitting up in bed, wearing the most diaphanous of nightdresses which served to reveal rather than conceal the beauty of her bosom. She looked at him expectantly. There seemed no other course open to him but to retire to the bathroom and change into his pajamas. Hesitantly he climbed into bed beside Aleisha. She looked at him with happiness shining from her eyes.

'I belong you,' she said.

* * *

At 10 a.m. the next day there was a knock at the door, and the guide stood there again. He gestured for J.T. to follow him. J.T. kissed Aleisha on the cheek. 'Don't go away '' he mouthed the words carefully, and indicated that she should stay where she was. She nodded vigorously. They were already becoming very expert at using their hands to communicate with each other. J.T. followed the guide through the same set of barriers and checks as before, but this time they ended up at what was clearly a prison cell. Through the bars could be seen the dejected figure of Ken Charles sitting on the edge of a narrow bunk, his head sunk down, his shoulders drooping. Even the sight of J.T. did not rouse him from his lethargy. J.T.was allowed into the cell, but Charles did not even rise to greet him.

'Ken! How are you?'

'About as well as can be expected of someone who has four days to live.'

'Come on! I can't believe they will do this.'

'Why not?'

'Well, you are an American citizen.' Charles laughed theatrically.

'That's great! Really great! Don't you realize that this whole thing is being orchestrated from Washington? I'm the human sacrifice here.'

'Why do you say that?'

'What are they doing to get me out?'

'I'm sure that there are diplomatic pressures being applied behind the scenes. These things take time.'

'Well time is something I don't have a lot of.'

'Ken, how did you get into this situation? I was told that you tried to break Mike out of here. This place is impregnable. You couldn't get to this cell from the outside unless you had about twenty thousand troops.'

'Right! But I didn't know that. I was set up.'

'By whom?'

'I spoke to a fellow named Salim. He works for the Government here. He said he would help me. He got back to me and said that he had found out that Mike was only lightly guarded, and that a little bribery would do the trick. He supplied me with transport and a guide, who was heavily armed. By the way, all of this will appear in my posthumous expense account for this month at BSU. If I were you I would charge it to "Entertainment". Anyway, we bribed our way through the check points and the main gate easily enough, but when we were inside and making our way through the corridors we were jumped by about fifty men armed to the teeth, and I was flung in here. Then there was some kind of charade where a judge came in, someone read out a lot of Arabic, I was sentenced to death, and that's that.'

'The Embassy arranged for me to come here. They must have some kind of plan.' Ken Charles did not reply. He sank his head in his hands, and after a while J.T. took his leave, perceiving that his presence was doing no good.

Over the next two days he was allowed to see Mike and Ken two or three times a day. At night he enjoyed the delights which are promised only to a select few in the paradise to come. But he was not summoned to the presence of His Serene Highness, and any attempt he made to request an audience was met with blank incomprehension. Finally, on Tuesday, the day before the scheduled executions, he was collected by his guide and taken to the room where he had first met the Governor.

'Doe's the jewel of El Khalid please you?' was his opening gambit.

'Your Serene Highness is referring to Aleisha? She is the most perfect companion a man could hope for, although our conversation is limited.'

'Cynics might say that that is a most admirable arrangement between a man and a woman. I sincerely hope that your future together will be bright indeed.'

'Your Serene Highness was most kind to send her to me, but I must soon leave her.'

'Not at all! She is yours. She was my gift to you. The nature of your praise of her left me no other choice. She is yours forever.'

'Your Serene Highness, surely she is not a slave simply to be given or taken.'

'Certainly not! We do not have slavery here. But she has been attached to my household since she was a child. It was always understood that at some point she would wish to transfer her loyalty to someone else - with my approval of course. Now she has chosen to attach herself to you. You are fortunate indeed.' J.T. decided to abandon this line of conversation. It was not what he was here to discuss.

'Your Serene Highness! Today is Tuesday. You told me that my two colleagues, my two friends, were to be executed tomorrow. I came here to plead for their lives. Neither of them deserves this fate. They are not evil people. They acted out of the best of motives, but they were misled by their emotions, the one for the welfare of her sisters, the other for the safety of a woman that he admires and of whom he is fond.'

'She is married, I believe,' the Governor interrupted. In this country we view adultery as seriously as treason, and the penalty is the same.'

'There is no suggestion of impropriety between these two people, Your Serene Highness. Ken Charles felt responsible for Mrs. Llewellyn-Proctor as a friend and colleague.'

'Then he is responsible for her armed insurrection against the realm of El Baku.'

'I am sure that neither of them saw their actions in that light. I ask you to show mercy to these people. You are powerful, and they are weak.'

'You argue well. Not in the way of a Western lawyer, but in the manner of a person of culture. However, these matters are decided not by people like you and I, but by the will of God. I am to tell you that you are to speak to your Ambassador. Go into the next room and they will connect you to the Embassy.

'Jason! What's going on?'

'Hi! J.T. The Ambassador wants you out of there.'

'But why? I've got to try to save Mike and Ken. So far I've achieved nothing.'

'You've done a good job. Believe me! Don't worry about Mike. It's all arranged. She will be moved out of El Khalid today, and she'll be back in the States tomorrow.'

'What about Ken?'

'He will stay there for a while. The execution has been, quote, postponed, unquote. But the Ambassador wants you out of there. We are sending a chopper. Be ready at noon. One other thing J.T. - bring your women with you.'

'You mean...?'

'Yes, I mean...'

* * *

Forty-eight hours later J.T. was back in Bransome. But he was not alone. After arriving at the Embassy in EI Baku he had had a serious talk with Jason Roberts.

'Jason, We cannot uproot Aleisha and her maid. They have never been out of El Baku. They speak no English. It will be very difficult for them.'

'Look, J.T. There is no alternative. The Governor has made a gift to you, a very significant gift. If you refuse it will be the biggest insult you can imagine. It will be war between El Baku and the US.'

'But what about immigration? What possible reason can Aleisha have for entering the US, let alone the maid?'

'J.T., give us credit for something. The Embassy may not be able to achieve much, but at least we can fix a visa. It's about all we can do nowadays, but we are very good at it. Aleisha will enter the United States on a diplomatic passport, as an Administrative Officer of the Embassy of El Baku, seconded to Bransome Southern University, in order to assist the University with its overseas programs. Her maid will act as her secretary and interpreter.' The sheer audacity of this plan stunned J.T.

'But the maid cannot speak a word of English. How can you pass her off as an interpreter?'

'I didn't say she would interpret into *English.* In any case with a diplomatic passport no one will challenge her. They will be through immigration while you are still waiting for your baggage to come up.'

And so it was.

The impact of J.T.'s arrival in Bransome can hardly be exaggerated. The initial delight at his safe return turned into amused disbelief when it was learned that he had brought two Arab women with him to share his small two bedroom apartment. The natural reaction was for all the staff to issue invitations to him and his female guests to lunch, dinner, cocktails, etc. J.T. avoided all such proposals with excuses about how busy the ladies were with their official duties, but he was outflanked by Julie, one of his assistants, who turned up at his apartment one afternoon when he was at the office, and knocked at the door. The maid opened the door, and when faced with the first visitor since arriving in America she bowed low and wordlessly waved Julie inside. Afterwards Julie described the sight that met her at least forty-five times to her friends. Both the women were dressed in their traditional costume, Aleisha in costly silks, and the maid in funereal black. As nearly as possible they had turned the small rooms into the sumptuous apartments that they had occupied in El Khalid. The walls were covered with the beautiful silks and damasks they had brought with them. In J.T.'s bedroom, clearly no longer a bachelor's domain, the bed was covered with cushions, and the air was filled with delicate scents.

Julie attempted to engage the two women in conversation, but after ten minutes of non-communication she gave up, and trying to convey her friendliness through exaggerated smiles and gestures, she left the apartment. Her re-enactment of this scene when she returned to the office drew considerable acclaim, except that Janice Hart slammed down a file she was carrying and abruptly left the room.

Oscar Wolf asked to hear every detail of J.T.'s experiences in El Baku, and J.T. did his best to describe the atmosphere of El Khalid and what had gone on there, but he hardly mentioned Aleisha. When he had finished Oscar sat quietly staring into space, humming gently to himself, until J.T. could bear it no longer.

'What do you think will happen to Ken?'

'A couple of years in an El Baku jail, I suspect.'

'But that's terrible! Can't we do something about it?'

'I'm sure the State Department is already working on it. But he only has himself to blame. Charging off like that to storm El Khalid on his own. The man's a fool.'

'OK! I know he's not too bright. Indeed, Jason Roberts once said that that was Ken's main qualification for the job in El Baku. But that's no reason to leave him to rot in jail.' Oscar seemed to lose interest in Ken Charles.

'You'd better think about a replacement for him,' Oscar said.

'Are we going to continue with the El Baku program after all that has happened?' Oscar looked surprised.

'Sure. Why not?'

* * *

Summer was fading fast in Sakhalin; the nights were drawing in, and the sparse vegetation was preparing to hibernate. The nighttime temperatures began to plunge, and Stavros Williams began to worry about the effects of frost on piping. A break in the pipe from the mainland would have disastrous effects, not only on his program, but on the whole area including the Sea of Okhotsk and the Sea of Japan. Sakhalin had flourished since the sewage had started to flow, new enterprises had been set up, housing projects had been started, and there had been immigration from the mainland. All this would be threatened by any disruption of the flow of sewage. The main pipeline had now been extended as far as Irkutsk, and plans were in hand to begin work on the section to Krasnoyarsk. Stavros had dreams of a flow of sewage in the spring from as far away as Novosibirsk, Sverdlovsk, and even one day from Gorky and Moscow itself. Stavros himself had achieved the status of a demi-god in the eyes of the inhabitants of Sakhalin. The prosperity which he had brought, the creature comforts which had followed, the promise of future growth and development, and all at no cost to themselves - it was indeed a miracle. They had built a beautiful house for Stavros, almost a mansion. Irina, the daughter of a local notable, had moved in as his "housekeeper", and his table was supplied daily with every delicacy that the island had to offer. Still exuding the odor of priestly sanctity, Stavros presided benignly over all this munificence.

Nevertheless, in the midst of this success, Stavros was worried. He had received anonymous threats, by mail and by telephone, threats to disrupt the whole operation. The exact motive behind these threats was obscure. There were references to 'theft of sewage' and 'imperialist exploitation of our birthright', but the origins of these comments were never made clear. So Stavros continued with the development of his grand design, receiving more and more support from the US State Department, sending more and more technical advisors to the Russian mainland to supervise the laying of the pipeline.

Life with Irina was delicious. Tall and blonde, sensitive and intelligent, she was conscious of the honor of being associated with the most famous man on Sakhalin, but at the same time she was in no way subservient or obsequious. Stavros and she were equals, each with their role to play, each respecting the qualities of the other. True she sometimes found the American's obsession with sewage difficult to understand, but the results spoke for themselves. The two of them shared every aspect of their lives, she speaking her school-book English and he struggling with the local version of the Russian language that he had been studying since his arrival in Sakhalin. Every evening they would sit down to a formal dinner, served by the cook who had been provided by a grateful community, and they would discuss the events of the day. After dinner they would savor a glass or two of vodka, before retiring to bed to hold each other as closely as possible till they fell asleep.

One night, however, this idyll was rudely shattered by the jangle of the bedside telephone. The crackling on the line, which made it almost impossible to make out what was being said, identified this as a call from the mainland. Since Stavros had taken over, the island's telephone system now measured up to the best the world had to offer.

'Speak up! I can hardly hear you. Who is this?'

'It's Krislow.' All the State Department technicians seemed to have Russian names. 'I'm in Novgorminsk. There's a serious situation here. There's been an explosion. We think it was a bomb.'

'A what?' Stavros sat bolt upright in the bed. Irina turned on her side and pulled the bedclothes over her head.

'A bomb. We're not sure yet, of course, but it has all the signs. It was planted directly under the pipeline.'

'My God! Was anybody hurt?'

'No, not hurt. But a lot of people got covered in deep shit. Not only people, but all the buildings around here have a covering of about six inches. So far that is.'

'So far? What do you mean?'

'Well it's still pouring out. About two thousand gallons an hour I would say. Of course that is only a provisional estimate. I will be able to give you a more precise measurement in the morning. The stuff is so thick in the air that we can't get any lights on to the broken section. As soon as we rig up a lamp it gets covered with a thick layer. The worst thing is that there is a strong wind here, and it keeps changing direction. Nobody is safe in Novgorminsk tonight.'

'For God's sake! Can't you turn it off?'

'Fraid not. The nearest valve is at Preskoi, and we can't raise them on the phone. Can you contact Irkutsk and ask them to stop pumping?' An agitated Stavros promised to do what he could, but he knew that the ordinary telephone system would not be able to reach the people he needed.

'Irina, my darling!' He began hurriedly to dress. 'I must get to the communications center.' She nodded her head, and he left, driving dangerously fast along the narrow road to the center. The communications set-up was identical to the one in El Baku, and indeed in every other program site of Bransome Southern University. Stavros knew that he would get assistance from headquarters at any time, day or night. He quickly contacted the duty officer in Bransome, who accepted with equanimity the information that he transmitted, as if this kind of thing was a daily occurrence. After an assurance that all would be done that could be done, Stavros returned to his home and to his bed. But sleep did not easily return, and after several fitful hours, as the sun began to lighten the sky, he went into the living room and turned to the radio, and to a familiar source of information, the BBC World Service. The calm voice of the presenter was working through the regular news items - peace talks in the Middle East, the Balkan question, changes in the Constitution of South Africa, and so on. Stavros, sitting in his comfortable chair, almost began to doze off as the unemotional voice of the British broadcaster droned on. There was a pause, and the next words that came from the radio, still in the most even tones, electrified Stavros:

> Reports are coming in of an environmental disaster centered on the small town of Novgorminsk in eastern Russia. A high-pressure sewage pipe has fractured and effluent is being discharged over the whole area. Sabotage is suspected. The main source of the effluent is Irkutsk, some distance to the west, but apparently the authorities in Irkutsk will not be able to cease pumping operations for approximately forty-eight hours. When the new system of pumping the effluent to Sakhalin for treatment was developed, the former treatment plant was partially dismantled, and it will take time to reinstate it. The scale of the problem is being compared to the Exon Valdez disaster in Alaska, although no-one quite knows what methods will be needed to clean up this particular kind of pollution. Perhaps the most moving aspect of this situation is the fact that the effluent has blocked the drains in Novgorminsk, and as a result, the people who are trapped in their homes cannot flush their toilets.

Stavros sat with his head sunk between his knees. Rarely can a public benefactor have been faced with such a disastrous outcome to his activities. The radio presenter was dealing with other world issues, and then, once again, Stavros's attention was gripped by the broadcast:

> I have just been handed a further report on the environmental disaster in Russia. American technical advisors in the town of Novgorminsk have evolved a plan to bring the situation under control. Wearing special protective clothing and breathing apparatus, they will lower a new section of pipe into the gap created by the

explosion, and in this way control the flow of effluent until the authorities in Irkutsk can divert the sewage elsewhere and permanent repairs can be made to the pipeline.

With a sigh of relief Stavros returned to bed and to the comforting arms of Irina. But the aftermath of that night was, if anything, worse than the immediate disaster had been. The town of Novgorminsk had to be completely evacuated, and the authorities claimed that it would be at least six months before it would be habitable again. There was a threat to public health throughout the whole region, and the cost of cleaning up the town was expected to run into many millions of dollars. The mental anguish suffered by the inhabitants of Novgorminsk was considerable. They had been trapped in their homes for more than thirty-six hours as a thick layer of excrement covered the windows. Few of the doors or windows fitted very well, and the thick brown sludge began to seep in at every crack. Some of the townsfolk were unlikely to recover fully from this ordeal. An international team of counselors was on its way to the area as a result of the harrowing stories of people refusing to sleep, or when they did fall off, waking screaming from the unspeakable nightmares that they experienced. The question of compensation had been raised, and the unanimous opinion of the people of Novgorminsk was that the Americans were to blame, and more specifically the Administration of Bransome Southern University.

Stavros was naturally concerned at the financial implications of the affair, but he set about restoring the pipeline to full working order as quickly as possible. He could not disappoint the people of Sakhalin, whose hopes for a brighter future depended entirely upon the success of his project. More serious was the report that responsibility for the explosion in Novgorminsk was claimed by a previously unknown group, the Siberian National Cultural Fighters. The SNCF made no attempt to justify their action, or to give a reason for it, but they did state that they had demands to make that would be revealed in due course.

In the months that followed life returned to its former delightful pattern. The really notable event during this time was the marriage of Stavros and Irina. The whole of Sakhalin attended the wedding, which was celebrated according to the rites of the Russian Orthodox Church. The day began with great solemnity in the central church of Yuzhno-Sakhalinsk. Priests wearing brilliant robes and high-domed crowns surmounted with crosses wove patterns of enormous complexity around the bride and groom, crowning them in turn, then simultaneously, chanting and scattering incense. Everyone of any significance on the island, the officials of the *oblast* and the city, were sitting in the front pews. A glorious *Te Deum* was sent soaring up into the vaulted roof by a deep-voiced male choir. Irina was dazzlingly beautiful in her white dress; Stavros looked aesthetic. The service lasted three hours and fourteen minutes. Much of this time was taken up with a lengthy address by an Archimandrite, whilst Irina and Stavros knelt together at the altar steps. Stavros could understand virtually nothing of this speech, but later Irina explained to him that it consisted of dire warnings of the consequences of doing most of the things that they had already done.

The reception was held in an aircraft hangar that had earlier been the resting-place of the heavy bombers that had been on the alert to deliver crushing blows to the West Coast of the United States. Now the walls were covered with garlands, the vast floor space was filled with tables laden with local dishes, except for the area in the center, which remained clear for dancing. Prodigious quantities of vodka were on hand for the later stages of the celebration. Stavros and Irina sat at a central table at the edge of the dance floor. Waves of dancers in traditional costume surged back and forth in front of them, the dancing becoming more and more frenetic as the men took turns at punishing the vodka between bouts of violent knee jerking activity. Then to the sweet tones of a balalaika the bridal pair took to the floor alone, to dance an elegant measure. There was much applause, and afterwards the tall, bearded Stavros moved gently from table to table, bowing serenely to his friends, exchanging a word here, making a comment there. The day was a triumph for Stavros, who was genuinely revered by the population of an island that felt that much of modern life had passed them by. Fortunately the newlyweds had left by the time that the party got out of hand. The liberal provision of vodka resulted in a large section of the male population of Sakhalin ending up on the floor of the aircraft hangar, oblivious to the world, and incapable of movement. Stavros and Irina returned to their mansion, happy beyond expectation, and although they had lain in each other's arms many times before, on that night there was a special quality to their lovemaking, which they were never to attain again.

Shortly after the wedding the SNCF struck again. This time the *modus operandi* was different. Out in the tundra, far from any settlement, tracked vehicles were used to rip out a long section of pipe. There was no immediate crisis as there had been at Novgorminsk, no-one was hurt nor any property damaged - no doubt the reason why the SNCF adopted this method - but there was considerable environmental damage. The first indication that something was amiss was the sudden cessation of the flow of sewage at the Sakhalin pumping station. Hurried telephone calls to Irkutsk established that the precious material was being pumped from there in the usual quantities. Once again Stavros contacted the duty officer at Bransome and was assured that everything possible would be done to find out what had happened. It took only a few hours before Bransome reported that a helicopter had located a lengthy break in the pipe, and that it was again clearly a case of sabotage.

Unlike the previous occasion when the pipeline had been broken, this time Stavros was directly affected by the situation. It was now the depth of winter, the break in the line was more inaccessible, and the extent of the damage much greater. It took four days to complete the repairs. The impact upon the people of Sakhalin was immediate and serious. Since Stavros had begun his work the style of life had changed considerably. The supply of electricity had been expanded, and new equipment had been installed in homes, equipment which was useless when power black-outs resulted from the loss of heat at the generators. More serious was the fact that many new homes had been built, including Stavros's own, which did not incorporate the old methods of heating by wood stoves, but drew their warmth from the new heat exchangers that Stavros had installed. The failure of the heat exchangers because of the suspension of the flow of sewage caused real hardship. The beloved new homes froze up and became uninhabitable. The only solution was to move in with relatives or friends who still lived in the old-style peasant houses, and to suffer all the indignities that this entailed.

Of those who had to move out, Irina and Stavros suffered the greatest indignity. They had to ask Irina's parents to take them in, and so soon after their marriage the great man and his wife became refugees. Stavros met the situation with fortitude, but Irina's father made it very difficult to do so. He had accepted Irina's decision to become Stavros's "housekeeper" because of the American's standing in the community, but only with the greatest reluctance. For him it had brought shame on the family. Their marriage had mollified him somewhat, and he had basked in reflected glory on their wedding day, but he did not like or trust Stavros. In particular the younger man's aura of holiness, the savior of Sakhalin, irritated him. And now he had to take him into his house, bear the comments of islanders now critical of the whole scheme, and watch his daughter begin to be disillusioned by it all. He made his unhappiness only too evident, making comments that Stavros did not fully understand, but which he knew to be critical because of Irina's unwillingness to translate them.

Then, a few days later, the SNCF issued its ultimatum. They did not object in principle to American money being used to develop projects like Bransome Southern University's Sakhalin sewage recycling program, indeed they welcomed it. But every person has an inalienable right to his or her own sewage. Nobody can lawfully deprive the individual of the fruits of his labor, or anything appertaining thereto. Consequently piping the stuff away from its source is tantamount to theft, and the SNCF would fight to the death to prevent it. The pipeline would be blown up again and again unless the Americans agreed to develop similar projects in all the communities in Siberia. Stavros was in despair. He and Irina were back in their mansion.

'Don't they understand that this won't work? We can only get enough heat to run an exchanger if we concentrate the sewage from a large area. It just isn't possible to do what they ask.' Stavros made heroic efforts to make contact with the SNCF, without success. Broadcasts were made appealing to them to come forward to discuss their demands, but there was no response. The attacks on the pipeline continued, and the people of Sakhalin gradually came to accept that they must return to the old way of life. The grand design had foundered.

* * *

Galia looked at Ghita with concern. 'You mean that the whole thing is about to blow up?'

'I think so. We had better be careful that we are not dragged down as well.'

Ghita was the Deputy Director of the Ploiesti program. He was a man in his early thirties, tall, dark-haired, handsome. Galia had recruited him soon after the program had been established and J.T. had returned to Bransome. His main attraction, apart from his physical attributes, was the fact that he had good connections with the local political establishment. This had been of great value in providing the infrastructure on the basis of which the program had flourished. BSU now had a wide network of relationships with schools at all levels in Walachia, the region surrounding Ploiesti and Bucharest. Teachers from all over the area came to the Institute to take courses in educational theory and practice, to bring themselves up to date with what had been happening in the West for the past forty years. The enthusiasm of the teachers for the knowledge that was imparted to them was immense, far out of proportion to its intrinsic worth. They were grateful for every idea, every new theory, however outmoded it might be in the schools of Boston, New York or Los Angeles. It was the sheer novelty of having ideas set before them not as religious principles to be learned by rote, but as theories to be discussed, assessed, and if necessary discarded in the light of the evidence; it was so novel that it literally brought tears to their eyes. Their adulation of Galia was embarrassing to her. She was very well aware that some of the concepts that she was responsible for introducing to the students were second-hand, out-of-date, and of dubious worth, but her students refused to accept her protestations about the value of her work. She was the most exciting intellectual figure that they had ever encountered, and they wanted her to know it.

The program had prospered, but Galia had achieved only an ambiguous position in local society. The evident regard in which she was held by the schools and the teachers assured her a special place in the governmental and social circles of Ploiesti and Bucharest, but the "subversive" nature of the content of the courses at the Institute was never far from the minds of the elite who dominated the Romanian political system. But now a completely new situation faced Galia and her lieutenant. In recent months, partly under pressure from outside Romania, a new force had arisen in the political firmament, a reformist group intent on breaking the grip of the Old Guard who had survived the upheaval that had destroyed Ceausescu. The initial help that Galia had received from Gheorge Ilescu, the Director of Public Affairs of Ploiesti, admittedly at a cost of $10,000, had been invaluable in the initial stages of the program, and it was natural she should turn to him again when the local bureaucracy became oppressive, or when she needed the approval of a government department in Bucharest for one reason or another. Naturally, at each stage Gheorge required money in order "to oil the wheels of the government machine", and Galia did not inquire about the destination of the cash that she handed over to him. Initially the Treasurer's Office at BSU had reacted violently to the entries in the accounts from Ploiesti that simply read "Petty Cash - $12,500". Bella Wright, the Assistant Deputy Treasurer, was indignant. 'Where are the receipts? What was the money used for? Sums like this should not be shown as Petty Cash.' However, Oscar Wolf knew how to handle this kind of difficulty. He handed Bella a piece of paper on which was written: 'Normal accounting procedures are suspended for those International Programs that are designated as "sensitive" by Vice President Oscar Wolf. Signed: Fred Zuwicki, President.' There was no further discussion.

The amount of money that had changed hands in this way was considerable. Galia had no qualms on this score. 'If that is what we have to do to operate the program, then that is what we will do.' But now the Reform Group had chosen Ploiesti as the center of its first attack upon the establishment, and targeted Gheorge Ilescu as the political 'boss' of the city. The corruption which everybody had long known about, but which was never mentioned, was now being talked about openly, and in some quarters demands had been made for an investigation of Ilescu's finances.

'What do you think we ought to do?' Galia asked. Ghita was not in a hurry to reply. Eventually he said:

'If Gheorge is actually toppled from power, and if it is shown that we have been paying him off, the Reform Group will make a real meal of it. It will reflect badly on the University, and on the US, and at the worst we could find ourselves arrested on charges of bribery. In addition, we are living in his sister's apartment, at a very low rent, and you can imagine what they would do with that. So we have to do everything we can to prevent it happening.'

'Should we go to the Reform Group, admit what has happened, and say that we had no choice. It was the only way we could operate in this town. They know that as well as we do.' Ghita weighed her proposal.

'Risky! It might work. It might not. There are some very strong anti-American feelings in the Reform Group.'

'What else can we do?'

'We could try a pre-emptive strike.'

'What does that mean?'

'You are very popular. We get Bucharest to appoint you as Mayor of Ploiesti. We make a great drama of dismissing Gheorge, and then we cover up our tracks.' Galia looked at him in total disbelief.

'You must be mad. I'm almost a foreigner; I work for an American university. There's no way they would do that.'

'Don't you be too sure. First, you *are* Romanian. Second, you are popular and attractive.' Galia cast her eyes modestly downwards. 'Third, and most important, I have enough dirt on the people in the Ministry of the Interior in Bucharest to blow them all sky-high if I choose to do so.'

'No! I just can't believe in it. It's not possible.'

'Well, think about it.' Ghita stood up to leave. 'We'll talk about it again tomorrow.'

But in the morning, first thing, Ghita came to her with a crudely printed poster, and placed it before her on the breakfast table. 'Read this. They are getting close. Unless we act quickly, we are lost.'

* * *

The conference room in the Ministry of the Interior in Bucharest was filled with cigarette smoke. The meeting had been in session for two and a half hours, and it was getting nowhere. The Minister of the

Interior, Nicolae Vaslui, was sitting at the center of the table, his head sunk in his hands.

'I will not agree to appoint this..., this person, as Mayor of Ploiesti. She is virtually a Westerner. She is not one of us. She is some sort of liberal. She ran away from Romania. Now she expects to return and take up a position of importance here. It's intolerable. Who knows what she would do?' He threw up his hands in despair. 'Why are we even discussing this?' There was much shuffling of feet around the table. The normally deferential junior politicians and civil servants were being uncharacteristically persistent. The Deputy Minister, Corneliu Brosov, cleared his throat nervously.

'Comrade Minister ...' He choked with embarrassment at this unintended reversion to an earlier mode of address. 'I'm sorry, I mean Your Excellency, we really do not have any choice. This Reform Group is after our blood. Something has to be done in Ploiesti, otherwise it could bring the whole place down round our ears. Ghita has come up with this plan, and we think that it is the best on offer. Quite simply it may save our necks.'

'I know that something has to be done. But why do we have to deal with this woman? In the old days we would just have arrested the trouble-makers, and no-one would have heard of them again.'

'Quite true, Your Excellency. But things have changed. We have elections now, genuine elections - well almost genuine. And then there is the financial aid that we get from the West. But most important is the fact that if we don't agree Ghita thinks that the whole story about the Harghita affair will come into the open.' The Minister jerked upright.

'The Harghita affair. How does that come into it?' Corneliu wiped his forehead with a large white handkerchief.

'It seems that, somehow, a full report on the Harghita affair has been lodged in a bank in New York, and if we don't go through with this appointment the report will be published in the newspapers.'

The Minister went white, then pink, then purple. Then he exploded. 'Who did this? Who's behind it?' He looked around the table at each worried face in turn. 'Who has betrayed us?'

Corneliu spoke soothingly. 'We don't know. But we will find out, and then we will deal with the swine. The main thing is that we have to stop publication of this report, or we are all in deep shit.' The Minister looked at him. That summed up the situation perfectly. There really was nothing more to be said.

* * *

There were, of course, some formalities to be attended to. The current Mayor of Ploiesti was suddenly translated into the Governorship of a northern province. A press conference was arranged at which

Minister Vaslui announced that the Government had decided to embark on a program of municipal reform and that the new Mayor of Ploiesti would not be drawn from the ranks of the civil servants and aspiring politicians, as had been the custom, but would be a 'new face', someone who would bring a fresh approach to the problems of the city. The Government was in the process of reviewing a wide range of possible candidates, and their decision would be announced soon. In the following weeks a rumor circulated in the restaurants and cafes of Ploiesti that the favored candidate was the son of one of the hard men of the Ceausescu regime. The father was in prison in Bucharest, and although the son was not tainted with any criminal activities, it was known that he shared his father's political attitudes. A pall of gloom settled on the citizens of Ploiesti. It was therefore with a considerable lack of enthusiasm that they learned that an announcement was to be made on television on Saturday evening of the government's decision on the new Mayor. When Nicolae Vaslui's face appeared on the screen at 8 p.m. the drinkers in the cafes and the families in their homes met it with cynicism. They hardly paid any attention to his wordy explanation of the great plans for the future, which were under consideration by the Government. When he said that as a consequence of the dawn of this new era the Government had made an exciting selection for the position of Mayor, a few tired eyes were raised towards the screens.

'The Council of State has approved the appointment as Mayor of Ploiesti of Galia Ionescu, Director of the Institute for the Education of Teachers.' In the cafes the remainder of his speech was lost in a tumult of amazed comment, which was rapidly transformed into cheering and applause.

The first telephone call was from Gheorge Ilescu.

'Galia, allow me to offer you my most sincere congratulations. When your name was first suggested to me by Nicolae Vaslui I was delighted, and of course agreed immediately,' he lied. 'I know that we shall be able to work well together, and I look forward to it.'

'Thank you, Gheorge. I think we ought to meet very soon. There are important matters that we have to discuss.' It was agreed that they would meet early on Monday, and Gheorge hung up. Galia turned to Ghita. 'How are we going to handle this? He isn't going to like it.'

'We have to convince him that there is no alternative. I think we can do that.' They spent the rest of the weekend preparing for the difficult tasks ahead. Galia was nervous; Ghita was supremely confident. On Monday morning, very early, Galia, with Ghita at her side, climbed the wide steps that led up to the entrance of the City Hall. A doorman bowed and opened the door for them. As they entered the tall Victorian Gothic hall, the assembled city employees broke into applause. Galia was greeted in turn by the most senior administrators, including Gheorge Ilescu in his capacity of Director of Public Affairs. After the greeting ceremony was over and the employees went off to their duties, the Chief Secretary led Galia to the grand second floor office, looking out onto the main square of Ploiesti, which was now to be her place of work. He put before her a schedule of appointments that had been arranged for that morning so that she could familiarize herself with all that was under way in the city administration.

'Thank you Ion,' she said. 'However before I begin on this list of appointments, I wish to speak with Gheorge Ilescu. Would you please ask him to come here immediately.' The Chief Secretary smiled to himself. So nothing was really going to change around here. She knew who really gave the orders. He left to find Ilescu.

Gheorge entered briskly and sat down without waiting to be invited.

'So Galia, here we are. I expect that you want to know what needs to be done.' Without replying Galia handed him two sheets of paper. He read them through, and then, white-faced, he read them again. Without a word he left the room, went to his office, and within the hour had left the building for good. A memo to all staff was quickly circulated. The Director of Public Affairs had resigned to take up a very important diplomatic appointment as Romanian Consul in Reykjavik. Years later, when Galia was asked what was on those two sheets of paper, she explained that one sheet was a copy of the announcement by the Ministry of Foreign Affairs of his appointment as Consul in Reykjavik. The announcement had been released to the press at 8 a.m. that day. The other was a photocopy of one page of a statement from the First National Bank of Los Angeles relating to the account of one George Lexham.

Life became very hectic for Galia. Although she was still nominally Director of the BSU Institute, it was Ghita who really ran it. In running the city government she had an eighteen-hour-a-day job of enormous complexity. Nicolae Vaslui had only agreed to her becoming Mayor because he thought that she would last only two months at most. But Galia was made of sterner stuff. It was not long before she had mastered the Byzantine structure of the city administration, worked out who was important, or competent, or neither, and learned how to ensure that she knew who was doing what when. More important, however, than her competence at administration, was the fact that she had ideas about policies. She knew what she wanted to do about housing, transport, social welfare, and she knew how to set about implementing these policies. The people of Ploiesti were delighted; the Government in Bucharest was dismayed. The Minister of the Interior summoned his Deputy to his office.

'Corneliu! What the devil is happening in Ploiesti?' Corneliu smiled reassuringly.

'Everything's fine, Minister. All is going exactly as we planned. Ilescu is in Reykjavik. The Reform Group has quietened down.'

'Everything is not going according to plan,' the Minister shouted. Corneliu took a step backwards. He recognized the signs. Vaslui looked set to have one of his funny turns. Usually a funny turn ended in tears for somebody, and it wasn't Vaslui.

'Why is that woman still there?'

'Minister, you appointed her. She seems to be doing a good job.'

'I didn't appoint her in order to do a good job! I appointed her because somebody had a gun aimed at my head. By now I expected her to have disappeared back where she carne from, wherever that was.'

'But Minister, she is a great success, very popular with the local people.'

'Corneliu, you are a fool. In all these years you've learnt nothing about politics. The last thing we want is popularity. Particularly when it's someone like Galia Ionescou who is popular. Governments that seek popularity always end up in trouble. People are fickle Corneliu, they may love you today, but they will crucify you tomorrow. Better to settle for power rather than popularity.'

'Of course, Minister, I understand what you mean. But we had a nasty situation in Ploiesti, and Galia got us off the hook. We should be grateful for that.'

'My God, Corneliu! You must be losing your mind. First you talk about popularity, and now it's gratitude. Soon you'll be singing "Climb Every Mountain," to me. Why don't we dance around the desk?'

Corneliu perceived that this was not a genuine invitation. Something was upsetting Vaslui, but it was not yet clear what the problem was.

'Are you not happy with what the Mayor is doing for Ploiesti?' Nicolae Vaslui flung his arms theatrically into the air, and then lowered his forehead to the surface of the desk.

'Corneliu, now you are on about happiness,' he groaned. 'I am concerned only with staying in office. That is the first and only duty of government. Happiness has nothing to do with it. Sooner or later Galia Ionescou is going to be a threat to me, to us. If she loses her so-called popularity we will be blamed for appointing her, and if her popularity increases she will think that she can replace us and take over the whole of Romania.'

'What do you wish me to do, Minister?'

'Go to Ploiesti. Find out what is going on. She must have a weakness. Something we can use against her.'

'Well, she *was* paying bribes to Gheorge.'

'I know that you fool. My share of the bribes was 40%, and you were getting 10%. Do you think we can use that? We need something we can use to get rid of her. We need someone there that we can rely on.'

'Someone like Gheorge Ilescu.'

'No! He got greedy. If someone hadn't sent us that bank statement from America we would never have known how greedy. He wasn't just ripping off the city government, he was ripping us off as well. What we need in Ploiesti is an *apparatchik,* someone with no imagination, someone like you, Corneliu.'

'Thank you, Minister. That is kind of you. But I do not want to be Mayor of Ploiesti. My wife...'

'Corneliu! Just go.'

Galia lay in bed, ringed by Ghita's arms, snuggling against his naked chest. They had moved out of the Ilescu apartment, and now lived in a modest, but charming house in the southern part of the city. In the months that had passed since she had become Mayor they had hardly had time to consider their personal lives or the nature of their relationship. Ghita, however, was well aware that there was great danger in their situation. Under the old regime mistresses and lovers of the ruling elite had abounded, but within closely circumscribed rules, which were reminiscent of the Victorian age. With great discretion almost anything was possible, because the media only reported what they were allowed to report, but for two unmarried people to live openly together would not have been tolerated. The morality of Leninism-Stalinism could encompass torture and assassination - these were necessary to maintain the integrity of the State - but open sexual immorality was something else. It could lead to the disintegration of society altogether. Since the revolution these attitudes had softened, but only marginally. For the Mayor of a city to live in sin was really not acceptable, and all the more so if that Mayor was a woman. At first the joy with which the people had greeted Galia's appointment had enabled them to gloss over the situation, but already she sensed that people were pointedly talking behind her back at functions which she and Ghita attended together.

'What shall we do?' she asked.

'We have two choices. Either I move out, or we get married.' Ghalia quickly sat up.

'What? Are you proposing to me?'

'I suppose I must be. What do you say?'

'Ghita! This is so romantic. We are lying in bed together, and you ask me to marry you so that you do not have to move out. How could a girl refuse?' Ghita who was very good at macropolitics was not always so sensitive at the level of the individual.

'I'm sorry! Have I done something wrong?' Galia jumped out of the bed and covered her nakedness with a robe. Her eyes were flaming with rage.

'Wrong? Wrong? Have you done anything wrong? Oh, no! You have never once said that you love me, but now you want me to marry you so that you do not have to wash your own shirts. I'm nothing but a meal ticket to you.'

'I thought we had a good arrangement between us.'

'An arrangement! I want you out of this house in the morning. Out!' She pointed imperiously to the door of the bedroom. Ghita, with what dignity he could muster, partially clothed himself and headed for the door, which was being held open by a contemptuous Galia.

'You are making a big mistake,' he said. 'Without me you don't have a chance.'

* * *

Corneliu Brosov knocked on the door of the Mayor's office, and entered.

'Welcome, Corneliu!' Galia smiled at him. To what do I owe the pleasure of this visit?'

'The Minister, Nicolae Vaslui, he thought it might be helpful if I spent a week or so here to give you any help you might need. He is very concerned about you. If there is anything I can do...'

'How nice of him.' Galia pointed to a chair. 'I'm sure there is a great deal that you can do. I am most grateful to His Excellency.' Corneliu looked around.

'How is Ghita?'

'Oh, I haven't seen him for almost a week,' Galia said. 'He is so busy running the Institute now that I do not have any time to devote to it.'

'I'm sure,' said Corneliu. 'Where does he live now? I really ought to contact him. Does he live with you?'

'Oh, no! Certainly not.' Galia was shocked. 'I gave him a room for a short while until he could find something for himself. He has an apartment somewhere in the town. I don't know the address, but my secretary can give it to you.' Corneliu was disconcerted.

'I see. I thought that you and he were...' Galia made no attempt to help him. 'Oh well, I will be here at 8.30 tomorrow, ready to do anything that you would like, Galia Ionescou.'

'Thank you, Corneliu. Till tomorrow.' When Brosov had left the office, Galia sat quietly for a while, and then a smile spread slowly over her face. It boded no good for certain people.

*   *   *

When J.T. had offered her the post of Director of the Fukuoka program, Kasuko Henderson had jumped at the opportunity. When she had left California to return to Japan with Robert Henderson she had undergone a severe case of reverse culture shock. The contrast between the freedom of her life as a student in America and the restrictions of her role as a housewife in Fukuoka was so stark that, although Robert was a good husband, and she loved him very much, she sometimes found herself wishing that she had married someone who would have kept her in America, instead of bringing her back to her native country. She was as patriotic as the next person, deeply loyal to Japan, and very critical of many aspects of American life, particularly the violence of the big cities, the lack of courtesy of the young people, and the sheer idiocy of much of the Californian life-style, but the freedom of women in America, their independence, and their determination to resist any attempt to reassert male domination, had captured her heart. At times she was deeply depressed, feeling that it would have been better if she had never gone to America; then, perhaps, with a Japanese husband she could have lived at peace with herself. But now she would always be torn between her love of her country and her rejection of the role it assigned to married women.

She and Robert had met at a reception for Japanese students organized by the American-Japanese Friendship Group in Santa Barbara. She had been attracted to him in part because he had worked in Japan for some years, was fascinated by it, and sympathetic to many of those aspects of Japanese society which most Westerners failed to understand. At the same time he was a gentle, considerate person, who never tried to dominate her, or to impose his will upon her. They soon fell in love and were married, and inevitably his work took him back to Japan, to Fukuoka. At first Kasuko was overjoyed. To return to her home country, to see her family again, and to have by her side the man she loved so well, what could be better? But life in Fukuoka was less than perfection.

Although Robert had no desire to follow the pattern of life of the typical husband in Japan, he had little choice. His colleagues worked late at the office, until eight or nine o'clock, and then they would repair to a bar or restaurant, eating and drinking until midnight. Almost every evening they entertained customers, or government officials who were important to the success of their business ventures. Robert was always the first to leave, but he rarely got home before eleven o'clock. In order to maintain the respect of the people he worked with he had to adapt to their *mores*. Life for Kasuko was monotonous. Housework, shopping, cooking, and the contact with a few friends in similar circumstances were the stuff of her life. There were compensations, books and music, but her overwhelming sensation was one of loneliness.

Then suddenly J.T. came along and all was changed. Soon after their first meeting in the restaurant he contacted her, explained what he had in mind, and within a week they had reached agreement. J.T. stayed for a further ten days and then flew back to Bransome, leaving Kasuko in charge. The program that she was to develop was different from the ones that J.T. had set up in other countries, in that it involved teaching American students sent over from BSU, who would study Japanese language and civilization during their year-long stay. Kasuko would find accommodation for them, hire faculty, and generally provide them with an experience of Japanese life. She was ideally suited for this job, with her American degree, and her understanding of both cultures. At least she thought she understood both cultures.

After three months of preparation she was ready to welcome the first wave of students, thirty-five in all. She was at the airport to meet them as they streamed off the plane after the long flight from the West Coast. Kasuko and her assistant were in the Arrivals Lounge holding up placards inscribed with the letters BSU. Heavily-laden students began to congregate around her. Kasuko had rented a small hotel near the railroad station that had fallen on hard times. Eventually she intended to place all the students with Japanese families, so that they could really become immersed in the local community, but they would need at least a month's orientation program before they were ready for that. The hotel had been designed for travelling salesmen and Japanese country people visiting the city. Although perfectly adequate for this purpose it was not lavish either in space or facilities, and for this reason it well-suited the budget which Kasuko had at her disposal. The bus eventually reached the hotel, and the exhausted students climbed out. Kasuko led them into the lobby, where tables had been set out for them to register, and to collect their room keys. For some minutes the confusion was total, and then groups of students began to seek out the rooms that had been allocated to them. In spite of their tiredness, most of the students were excited by their new surroundings and in good spirits, calling to each other, comparing which floor their rooms were on, and making arrangements to meet later to explore the town. However, as they moved away to the elevators a small knot of four female students remained in the center of the lobby. Huge mounds of luggage surrounded them. As Kasuko neared them, one said:

'Hey, miss! Where is the bellhop?'

'There is no bellhop. This is not a hotel.'

'Well, you could have fooled me. It sure looks like a hotel. It even says hotel on the front of the building.'

'Well it was a hotel, but now it's a dorm. The student cast her eyes up to heaven, and indicated the enormous suitcases that surrounded her like a barricade.

'O.K! What am I supposed to do with these?'

'Perhaps one of the male students will give you a hand.'

'Right! Could you fetch one for me?'

'You will have to find someone yourself.'

'Oh great! Is all the help like this in Japan?' Kasuko turned on her heel and walked away. As she did so she was aware of the buzz of comment from the four women, who were highly indignant at her behavior. She retreated to the room she had made into her office.

She left the door open, and after a while one of the students who had been in the group in the lobby appeared.

'Can I talk to you for a moment?'

'Of course. How can I help you?'

'Look, I know that this isn't the States, but the room you have given me has to be the smallest room in the world. You can just about walk around the bed and that's it. There is only one small closet. Where am I going to put all my clothes? And the "bathroom" is a joke. It's just a plastic cubicle in the corner of the bedroom. I measured it. It is exactly three feet by two feet five inches. You actually have to stand up in the bath. I have claustrophobia just thinking about it. You have to move me to another room.'

'All the rooms in the building are the same size.'

'There must be some double rooms. Why can't I have one of them?'

'That is a double room.' The student clearly did not believe her.

'You're going to hear more about this, you'd better believe it. My father is a friend of President Zuwicki.' And sure enough, within two hours, Kasuko received a call from Bransome, asking why Adeline had been housed in a slum dwelling, which her father had vividly described to President Zuwicki as a hovel unfit for human habitation, lacking even the most elementary requirements of civilized life. The squalor that his daughter had described, the filth, the giant bugs that infested the room, and the brutality of the local administration, were beyond imagining. However, the father, who was a reasonable individual, felt that if Adeline could be moved to one of the larger rooms which were available, but which for some reason were being withheld from her, she would be able to survive, and would not have to be withdrawn from the program.

The next day Kasuko decided to visit Adeline's room to be sure that nothing was wrong. She knocked at the door.

'Who is that?'

'Mrs. Henderson, the Director.' There was a noise from within, like someone wading through molasses.

'Coming!' A long pause while various scuffling noises could be heard. The door opened slowly. 'What do you want?'

'I'd like to talk to you, about the room.' The door opened further, but only with difficulty, as it seemed that there were various obstructions that had to be removed first. Adeline Giddens stood there, dressed in a dirty white sweatshirt and jeans. Her hair was matted. Kasuko entered the room and looked about her. Clearly there had been some kind of a major eruption in the room. The floor was totally covered in dirty clothes, including panties and bras left where they had fallen, cotton balls, screwed up wrapping paper, and other detritus of unmentionable origins. The bed was stained and filthy, the bedclothes twisted together in inextricable confusion.

Every piece of furniture was covered in a sticky mass of cosmetics, half-consumed food, and tissues soiled by God-knows-what.

'What has happened here?' Kasuko asked. Adeline pouted.

'Nothing! Why do you ask?'

'This mess! It's disgusting. Is this how you live at home?'

'Yes, it is. What's it to do with you? If I had a decent-sized room, I could keep it tidier.' Kasuko filled with disgust, turned and left the room without further comment.

Kasuko was deeply upset by this experience, and it was only after she had spent some time with other students, most of whom were charmed and fascinated by the city and its inhabitants, and could not speak too highly of what Kasuko had done for them, that she began to get the situation into perspective. The following months were a confusing combination of satisfying achievement and frustration. After one particularly happy excursion with the students to a Buddhist temple, where they had experienced the deep sense of tradition that underpinned Japanese society, she was delighted to find that Robert had returned home early, and after dinner they retired to bed to enjoy a rare opportunity to make love. They were entwined in each others arms, their bodies pressed closely together, deep in a long, gentle kiss, when the phone began to ring. 'Ignore it,' Robert said, 'whoever it is can wait.' They lay together, waiting for the ringing to stop, but it didn't.

'I'll have to answer, it may be an emergency with a student,' Kasuko said. Robert turned away with a sigh. Kasuko picked up the phone. 'Hello! Who is this?'

'Walter Giddens. Adeline's father. To whom am I speaking?'

'Kasuko Henderson, the Program Director. Is this an emergency Mr. Giddens? It is after eleven p.m. here.'

'It certainly is. My daughter called me a short time ago. The situation in her room is now desperate, and I demand that you do something about it straight away.'

'What on earth has happened?'

'The toilet will not flush.'

'What?'

'The toilet in her room will not flush.'

'She has called you from Japan to tell you that her toilet will not flush, and you've called me from America at eleven at night to tell me that?'

'You're too right I have. What are you going to do about it?'

'Mr. Giddens, why could she not have reported it to me in the morning?'

'And go all night without being able to flush the toilet. That is completely unacceptable.'

'Mr. Giddens, there are many toilets she can use in that building, and as for the one in her room, she could pour some water down it for the time being.' Robert was lying on his back, looking at his wife as if she was insane.

'Mrs. Henderson, there are certain standards which have to be maintained, and you seem not to be prepared to do that. If you had provided a suitable room for Adeline in the first place, this situation we are in now would not have come about. I insist that you go to her room and sort this matter out.'

'All the other students here are perfectly satisfied with their rooms, Mr. Giddens, and they are all exactly the same as your daughter's room.'

'That is not what Adeline tells me.' The gentle Kasuko came as near to losing her temper as was possible for her.

'Are you accusing me of lying, Mr. Giddens?' Robert sat up and tried to take the phone from his wife. She fended him off. 'I can assure you that what I say is true. I will get a plumber to deal with this matter in the morning. Good night!' and she put down the phone very firmly. She was shaking with anger, and had to walk about the apartment for some time before she could get herself under control.

It took half an hour for Robert to calm his wife, and gradually to lead her back to the point that they had previously reached. They were in bed again, he was caressing her back, and kissing her gently. He slid his hand down, over her naked bottom, and pulled up her leg so that her knee rose along his thigh. He was about to explore further when the telephone began ringing. He flung himself round and grabbed the telephone.

'Who the hell is that? It's past midnight. What do you want?' The sound of J.T.'s voice came along the wire.

'Is that you Mr. Henderson? I hope I'm not disturbing you.' Robert snarled, and handed the phone to Kasuko.

'It's J.T.,' he said, and flopped back onto the bed, making animal-like sounds of rage.'

'Kasuko, I'm sorry to call you so late. Is there something wrong with this line? It's making some very strange noises. Can you hear them?'

'No, I don't think so.' She punched her husband's shoulder.

'That's better. The line seems to have cleared. Kasuko, I'm calling because we've had a report from Adeline Giddens' father saying that she is in some kind of danger. I couldn't quite make out what the problem was. He was almost incoherent, but it seems that there has been some kind of serious plumbing emergency in her room. Have you heard about this? What's happening? Is the place flooded or what?'

'Her toilet won't flush.'

'Sorry! Would you say that again.'

'Her toilet won't flush.'

'That's what I thought you said. Are you sure that that is all that's wrong? Why is her father panicking?'

'J.T.! This is part of a campaign to make me move her to another room.'

'Why don't you?'

'All the rooms are exactly the same. She thinks that I am deliberately keeping her in a small room, and all this hysteria is intended to force me to move her. But there is nowhere else for her to go. Unless you want me to put her in a hotel for a hundred dollars a night.'

'No. I don't want you to do that. But what about the toilet?'

'If there is anything wrong with the toilet, I will have it fixed in the morning. Good night, J.T.' She turned to her husband. 'Why don't we go out to one of your clubs? There's not much chance of any peace here.'

'We could take the phone off the hook.'

'Robert, you are a genius.'

'I know it. Come here.'

After the first few weeks the students settled down, and life became pleasanter. Kasuko relaxed and began to enjoy herself. Bransome had sent her an Assistant Director, a Japanese man, whose name was Hiroshi Honda. He also had spent several years in the United States, but some time ago. Recently he had been working in Tokyo for an import-export firm. Kasuko thought it a little odd that he should have been appointed to work for a university although he had little or no academic background, but she soon realized that he was an excellent business manager, and that the general running of the operation was much smoother after his arrival. She soon left virtually all the day-to-day administration to Hiroshi and concentrated on the development of the academic program, an arrangement which suited both of them very well. One of Hiroshi's major responsibilities was the installation of the communications center that was the first priority for every BSU program site. Soon he had it up and running in the basement of the hotel. He established an office there, where he could be found at all hours, usually deep in conversation with a stream of visitors from the town.

* * *

Part 4

THE CONVENTION

The first limo arrived from the airport. Stavros and Irina climbed out to be welcomed by Janice Hart.

'Hi, Stavros! How are you? It's been a long time!'

'Janice! Nice to see you. I'd like you to meet my wife, Irina.'

'Pleased to meet you, Irina. Stavros and I are old friends.'

Stavros looked at Janice with gratitude.

'Yes indeed! I hope that you two will become friends as well.' Janice led them into the conference center, and across to the desk to register and collect their keys.

'Cocktails in the Main Lounge at 6.30.' She led them to the elevator. 'Oscar will be greeting everyone.' For the remainder of the day the limos deposited new arrivals from BSU centers all over the world, along with many guests, including a number from Washington D.C. By 6.30 everyone had arrived and gathered in the lounge. J.T. was circulating, greeting all his colleagues. The invitations had been sent out by Janice on Oscar's instructions and J.T. was not aware how widely the net had been spread. His first surprise was to come face-to-face with Akiko Takahashi.

'Akiko! What are you doing here?' he blurted out. Then as he saw the hurt look on her face, he took her hand in both of his, and continued: 'I'm sorry, I didn't mean it like that. It's just that the last time I heard about you I was told that you and your husband had gone to Europe. I did not expect to see you again.' She looked confused, cast her eyes down, and said:

'I am most sorry. I should have told you that day in Nagoya, but it was very difficult for me. But Oscar kept in touch with me, and I was very grateful that he asked me to come here.'

'Oscar? I didn't know that he had ever heard of you.'

'Oh, yes! He has kept in touch. I have already met your new Director in Fukuoka, Kasuko Henderson. She seems a very nice person. You were lucky to get her.' Her tone was almost reproachful.

'Yes, indeed. She is married you know. Did you meet her husband? By the way, is your husband with you?'

'No. He is... I will explain to you later.' J.T. had no time to pursue the matter because he was suddenly enveloped in the arms of a small, beautiful, dark-haired woman.

'J.T. I have been longing to see you.'

'Galia!' He tried to disengage himself, but she was pressing her mouth against his cheek, and her arms were firmly round his neck. 'Can I introduce you to Akiko. Akiko Takahashi; Galia Ionescou. Our Director in Romania.' He wrenched her arms away. Galia turned to Akiko, who bowed gently.

'Are you one of his women?' Galia inquired loudly.

'Please Galia, behave.' J.T. looked around the room to see if this exchange had been overheard, as indeed it had. A tall, blonde figure turned and then moved across to them.

'Why, J.T., I have been thinking of you so much since I got Oscar's invitation. I thought we might take up where we left off.'

'Rebecca!' J.T.'s voice took on a hysterical edge. She moved forward majestically and kissed him full on the mouth as Akiko and Galia watched. At that moment, out of the corner of his eye, J.T. saw Aleisha entering the lounge, followed by her maid, to be surrounded immediately by the office staff. She was looking round the room, searching for him. 'Excuse me,' J.T. blurted, 'I must...I've got to go.'

He hurried out of the lounge by a side door, seeking the calm of his office. On the way he met Janice Hart on her way to the reception. She smiled at him.

'J.T., this is going to be fun. I'll see you in the lounge.' J.T. continued on his way without replying. Fun it certainly was not, but the respite could not be long. At 7.30 the welcome dinner was to begin, and he had no choice but to attend. As he entered the dining-hall of the conference center, in quick succession he met Jim and Julia Holcombe from New Orleans, Stavros and Irina Williams lately of Sakhalin, and Robert and Kasuko Henderson from Fukuoka. They all greeted him enthusiastically. He avoided close contact with the cohort of women that had trapped him earlier, but as he had been seated near them at one of the long tables that flanked the hall, he was soon in conversation with them as they waited for dinner to be served. It was not as embarrassing as he had feared, and the evening developed pleasantly, and would have been very enjoyable, if they had not had to eat the food, which was down to the usual BSU standard.

Before the dessert was served, Oscar Wolf rose, banged on the table to gain their attention, and made his speech of welcome. For Oscar it was a lengthy affair.

'Great to see all you guys here. Have a good time!' He sat down. The assembled company was about to return to its drinks and small talk, when the figure of Stavros Williams rose to its full height, and adopted the usual pose of one about to make a carefully prepared impromptu speech, except that Stavros seemed to be rather more nervous than one might have expected, his hands twitching as he stood waiting for silence.

'Vice President Wolf!' he began. 'I cannot let this opportunity pass without saying publicly what has been on my mind now for some time. As some of you here know, before I left for Sakhalin, I was, to put it mildly, a stupid geek.' Some members of the audience laughed, thinking this to be some kind of joke. Those who had known Stavros before, looked down at their plates without a smile. 'I had that combination of arrogance and incompetence that brings quick promotion in certain kinds of organization. But a traumatic experience that happened to me here in Bransome,' he looked down and paused, 'an experience I richly deserved, followed by my time in Sakhalin, working with genuine people, made me realize that there are very real aims and values which we can pursue if we have the guts to do so.' Gathering confidence as he went, he looked around at his audience who had begun to understand that this was not the usual banal vote of thanks to their leader that they were expecting. Stavros plunged on.

'I feel, therefore, that this evening I must share with all of you, dear colleagues, what I have found out about...' His head was thrust forward, an almost fanatical light in his eyes, his right hand raised in a declamatory gesture. Then he froze. The light in his eyes dimmed, and he crumpled forwards across the table in front of him, his face firmly embedded in a dish of BSU cheesecake, which had not set nearly as well as the cook had intended.

There was pandemonium at the table. Irina hurried to Stavros and tried to lift his inert form from the table. She screamed at him in Russian to get up. Others rushed to help her. They lifted him up, and laid him on the floor. A man pushed through the crowd around Stavros.

'I'm a doctor. Let me through!' He felt for the pulse in Stavros's neck. He opened the closed eyelids and inspected the pupils. He tipped back the head of the inert man, put his mouth against Stavros's and forced air into his body. After what seemed an eternity he stopped and checked again for a pulse. Then he began to push against the chest of the stricken man, bearing down with all his weight and then releasing the pressure, again and again. He was still performing this procedure when two paramedics arrived with an oxygen cylinder, and with the doctor's approval, injected streptokinase. They were followed quickly by others with a portable defibrillator, and before the horrified gaze of the dinner guests, administered three massive shocks to the gangling corpse. For it was now a corpse, no longer a man.

The shocked dinner guests were herded out of the room, into the lounge where they sat disconsolately discussing the disaster that had suddenly overtaken them. In a side room Janice and Kasuko Henderson were trying to calm an hysterical Irina. J.T. was consulting with the doctor and the paramedics.

'He was dead when I first got to him,' the doctor was saying. 'There was nothing that could be done.' The paramedics nodded agreement.

'We were here within six minutes of the call,' one said. 'There was no sign of life.'

'What in God's name was it?' J.T. asked, 'A heart attack?' The paramedics looked away, deferring to the qualified doctor. He did not reply immediately.

'We will have to wait for the post-mortem,' he said. 'To be truthful it did not look like a typical myocardial infarction to me. We will have to wait and see.' He turned to J.T. 'I'm sorry, but we will have to call the police. This is not a straightforward case. I don't think that we ought to move him till the police arrive.' J.T. was shocked.

'What are you suggesting? We all saw him collapse. It must be a heart attack.' The paramedics had covered the body with a sheet and were packing up their equipment.

'I'm sorry, but in a case of sudden death like this the police have to be brought in. There is nothing that we can do about it.' When the police arrived, however, they treated Stavros's death as routine. The body was quickly removed. J.T. was asked to provide a list of the names and addresses of those present at the dinner, and after 30 minutes the police had gone.

Oscar Wolf decided that the meetings should continue the next day as scheduled. With considerable difficulty the program was got underway soon after 10 o'clock. The speech for the opening session, to be delivered by Oscar Wolf, was entitled "The Future of Bransome Southern University's International Activities," and had been written, as usual, by J.T. Even the fact that the words being uttered were his own, could not prevent J.T.'s mind from wandering to the events of the previous evening. Stavros had seemed so vital, so determined as he began to speak and then to be cut down in that way! It still seemed impossible to believe that he was dead. And what had he intended to say that had made him so agitated, so fiery? As J.T. looked around the room, it seemed obvious to him that no one else was listening to Oscar's labored reading of the speech. Like him, all their minds were on Stavros and his dramatic exit. As his gaze swept the room, he saw, standing in the doorway, the figure of the doctor who had attended to Stavros the evening before. The man raised his hand as he saw J.T. looking at him beckoned once and then a second time more urgently. J.T., glad to be doing something, slid from his seat, and walked quietly to the door, aware that every single person in the room, including the still-declaiming Oscar, was watching him. The doctor took his arm and guided him through the door, shutting it after him.

. 'Can we go somewhere to talk? I don't know this building.' The doctor was a bespectacled, earnest-looking man in his late thirties. J.T. took him quickly to a small anteroom, he continued. 'My name is Chalmers, Richard Chalmers. I was present last night by chance. Julia, who works in your office, is a friend, and she invited me as her guest. I'm a partner in a practice in the town, on State Street. I'm not a cardiologist, but I know enough about heart conditions to have an opinion about your colleague's likely cause of death.'

'Which is?' J.T. asked.

'That it was not a straightforward heart attack. It was not the kind of collapse that I would expect. He did not crumple up, so to speak, but fell rigidly onto the table, but most important, he showed no evidence of suffering chest pain.'

'What then could it have been?'

'What I saw was more consistent with the onset of a sudden and severe case of total paralysis.'

'I don't understand,' J.T.'s puzzlement was only too apparent. 'What could bring on paralysis so quickly? A stroke?'

'With even the most severe stroke there is a kind of progression, through various stages, usually with facial distortions, and again a kind of gradual collapse.' The doctor lowered his eyes, seeming unwilling to continue without J.T.'s prompting.

'So?'

'Well, to me it looked like the effect of some extremely quick-acting poison. Something that kills almost instantly.' J.T. looked at Chalmers in amazement. He could not forbear to make a sick joke.

'Oh, come on! Even BSU food is not as bad as that! We were all watching him. How could he have been poisoned?' Chalmers shrugged.

'I don't know. Of course, I am only speculating. But I felt it my duty to tell you.'

'Have you told this to the police?'

'Yes. I saw Lieutenant Lubowsky this morning. He listened, then told me that it had been determined that Stavros Williams died of natural causes, and that the file was closed. There will be no post mortem.'

'Isn't that unusual? Surely it is routine to do a post mortem in the case of a sudden death like this?'

'It is not absolutely required. If a doctor is prepared to sign a death certificate, that is usually the end of the matter, and apparently some doctor has done so.'

J.T. returned to the lecture theatre, puzzled and disturbed. Oscar was still ploughing on, whilst most of the audience were becoming desperate. Mercifully, Oscar turned over three pages by mistake, seeming not to notice, and the lecture came to an abrupt end. There was perfunctory applause, and a call for discussion, but as nobody volunteered any comment, the chair hastily terminated the session, and everyone made their way to the coffee room. Janice Hart came over to speak to J.T.

'What are we going to do about Irina? She is alone now. We have to help her.'

'I expect she will want to return to Sakhalin immediately after the funeral.'

'We have already asked her about that. She doesn't want to go back to Russia. She wants to stay in Bransome. As Stavros's widow surely she has a right to do that.'

'Perhaps! But where will she live? And on what?'

'Surely Stavros had some kind of benefits from the University. As for where she is to stay. Well, Aleisha has already offered to let her live with you. It seems that Arab hospitality demands it.'

'What! We only have two bedrooms. How can we take her in?' Janice raised her nose several inches.

'Aleisha seems to think that your sleeping arrangements would make it possible for Irina to share a bedroom with the maid. Irina seems quite eager. And it seems quite consistent with your usual mode of life.' And with that parting shot, Janice turned on her heel, and left. J.T.'s gaze followed her departure mournfully. How did he manage to get himself into these situations? He did not deliberately set out to indulge in unconventional or irregular behavior. It just seemed to happen. He attracted complex life-styles without any intention of doing so. Now he had three women in the apartment. And, worst of all, only one bathroom!

That afternoon J.T. went to seek out Lieutenant Lubowsky at Bransome Central Police Station. The Lieutenant was seated at his desk, wearing a blue, double-breasted suit and a sober tie, his hair smartly brushed. J.T. was taken aback. He had anticipated that the police officer would be wearing a fedora, in his shirtsleeves, his gun holster strapped to his chest, puffing a cigar.

'Good afternoon! What can I do for you?' Lubowsky asked politely.

'I would like to discuss the Stavros Williams case. I'd like to know what happened.'

'What happened was that he had a heart attack.'

'Dr. Chalmers doesn't think so.'

'I know. But the police pathologist does. End of story.'

'Can we request a post mortem?'

'Who is "we"?'

'The University I suppose.'

'No!'

'Who could?'

'His widow. His parents.'

Thirty minutes later J.T. was back in his apartment, talking to Irina.

'Irina. I would like you to request that a post mortem is done on Stavros.'

'I do not understand.'

'I think you should ask them to examine Stavros's body.'

'Examine?'

'To find out exactly why he died.'

'What does it matter?' J .T .sat down and cupped his head in his hands.

'Irina.' He tried to speak as slowly and as clearly as possible. 'It is important to know exactly what happened. Stavros was a young man. Men of his age do not just drop dead. Please, come with me to the police and sign a form requesting a post mortem, an examination.' Irina shrugged.

'I will do anything you wish, Jaytey. I am part of your family now.' J.T., although pleased at her decision, was not so happy with the 'family' bit. However, he quickly took Irina downtown to Lubowsky's office.

'Mrs. Williams wants a post mortem performed on her husband. She is here to sign the requisition.' It seemed to J.T. that Lubowsky was very happy to comply with this request. At any rate he did not make any difficulties. The forms were soon completed. Irina signed.

'Who do you wish to conduct the post mortem, Mrs. Williams?' Lubowsky asked.

'What does he mean, Jaytey?' Irina turned to J.T. with a worried expression. J.T. looked enquiringly at Lubowsky.

'You can either have the police pathologist, who signed the death certificate,' Lubowsky observed,' or you can nominate your own pathologist. At your expense, of course.'

'We will nominate our own doctor,' J.T. said very firmly.

'O.K. Let me know who it's to be.'

'Can I use your phone?' Lubowsky handed him the instrument. Eventually J.T. got through to Dr. Richard Chalmers. 'Can you suggest someone to carry out a post mortem on Stavros Williams?' he asked.

'I'll have a pathologist at the morgue at 2.30.' J.T. thanked him, collected Irina, who hardly knew what was going on, and departed.

In spite of the tragic events of the previous night the spirits of the participants at the College of International Affairs reunion began to return to normal. The pre-lunch cocktail session insured that animated conversation, and even laughter, were to be heard again in the Conference Center. For J.T., however, the situation remained difficult on two fronts. In the first place, he had tried to gain the support of Oscar Wolf for his inquiries into Stavros's death. But he was far from successful in this enterprise. Indeed, Oscar told him that he had been a fool to 'poke his nose in where it wasn't needed.' In the second place, the whole body of the conference had taken up the concept of "J.T.'s women", and delighted in watching as each of the ladies in turn, and in differing ways, paid court to him. But the embarrassment of this situation was as nothing to the nightmare of his home life. Aleisha had decided that it was their duty to take Irina in as part of their extended family, and to treat her as J.T.'s second concubine. The second night after Stavros's death, J.T. arrived home late, after the ladies had retired to bed. He undressed quietly in the darkened room, so as not to waken Aleisha, and slipped into bed beside the supine form under the coverlet, thinking not to disturb her, and to get some much-needed sleep. As soon as he lay down, however, she turned to him and enclosed him in her arms. Somewhat halfheartedly J.T. began to caress her back and to kiss her hair, and then, as she moved closer to him, to run his hand down over her bottom and her legs, pulling up her nightdress, and moving his leg between hers. She clung to him and he was about to become seriously engaged, when the female form in his arms collapsed into desperate sobbing, and cried 'Stavros! Stavros!' J.T. shot out of the bed, switched on the light, and stared in wild disbelief at the figure of Irina, her face contorted in misery. 'I'm sorry, Jaytey, I just couldn't do it. Forgive me!' And her sobbing began again. 'It is too soon, after... Maybe tomorrow night.'

'Irina! What are you doing here? I did not mean you to...I did not know it was you, I swear. This is just unbelievable.' He flung open the door to the other bedroom. ' Aleisha, what do you mean by this?' The women in the other room cowered under the sheets. 'We cannot live here like this. This is impossible. I will have to get out.' He threw on his discarded garments, grabbed up a few belongings, and stormed from the apartment. His only possible refuge was a motel. An hour later, he sank gratefully into bed in a room totally devoid of women, and was soon asleep.

The next day, the last day of the conference, the telephone was ringing as he entered his office at 8.30. It was Richard Chalmers.

'I've been trying to reach you at home,' the doctor complained, 'but all I get is the message that you are not available.'

'Yeah! I'm beginning to think that being unavailable is the most important skill that man can acquire.'

'What? Look, I've had the report from the pathologist. I think we'd better talk.'

'O.K. Where and when?'

'I'll come to your office straight away, if that's convenient.'

'Sure. It gives me an excuse for not going to the first session of this damn conference.' J.T. hung up, and went out to the coffee machine in the outer office. Janice Hart was pouring herself a cup of coffee. Silently she poured another cup and offered it to J.T. He was aware that she disapproved of his "domestic arrangements", and he was embarrassed to face her about it, and at the same time angry that he should have to explain himself to her. He wanted to tell her that he had moved out of the apartment, but could not find a suitable formula for raising the subject. What was it to do with her? He took the cup, nodded his thanks, and returned to his office. Why did Janice treat him as if he was her erring nephew? It was intolerable to have an assistant who made him feel guilty. If she kept this up he would have to find some way of transferring her to another department. He was still feeling aggrieved when there was a knock at the door and Richard Chalmers entered.

'Thanks for seeing me so quickly. I'm in a difficult position. Technically the pathologist's report is confidential to the widow, Mrs. Irina Williams. But as I presume that the University is paying his fee...' J.T. waved a vague hand. He had not really thought about this minor detail. Dr. Chalmers continued, 'I think that you are entitled to hear what Dr. Chang, he's the pathologist, had to say.'

'I think Irina is quite content for me to represent her in this matter.' J.T. said.

'Quite! Well, the fact is that there was no sign of heart disease, nothing organically wrong with Mr. Williams which could have caused his death.'

'So?' What did kill him?'

'That's not easy to say. They will do various tests, but they will take some time. There was one point in the report, however, that Chang wanted me to draw to your, that is to say to Mrs. Williams's attention.'

'Yes, yes! What is that then?' J.T. was becoming impatient with Chalmers's professional rectitude.

'There was a very small puncture at the back of Williams's neck, just above the hair line.' Chalmers looked at J.T. as if the whole matter was now clear, to any intelligent person at least. J.T. waited for further enlightenment.

'Don't you see? No organic disease. A puncture in his neck. That's how the poison was introduced into his body.' J.T. was incredulous.

'You still think he was poisoned?'

'More than ever. There is no alternative hypothesis.'

'When will we know?'

'We may never know for certain. There are poisons like *curare* that are almost undetectable in the laboratory.' J.T. buried his head in his hands. This was becoming almost a routine position for him.

'How could the poison have been administered? You say it must have been a very quick acting poison. We were all there watching him. You were there. Did you see someone come up and stick a hypodermic in his neck?' Chalmers chose not to notice the sarcasm.

'No. But there are other ways.' He paused, knowing that his next sentence would really produce a negative response. 'Such as a blow dart.' J.T. actually lept into the air.

'A blow dart? My God! This is unbelievable. You must be pulling my leg. Did the pathologist find one stuck in him?' Chalmers rose from his chair and made for the door.

'No. But that could be explained as well. Look! I know this is hard to take. If you want to talk about it at any time, call me.' And he left the office.

J.T. made his way to the Conference Center where a discussion was under way about the best way to make financial returns from overseas locations so as to satisfy the University's reporting requirements. When J.T. entered the room a member of the Treasurer's department was in full flood on this subject, but what he had to say was so paralysingly boring that J.T.'s mind began to wander immediately. What with the visit to El Baku and the presence of Aleisha and her companion in the apartment, in recent months life had been so hectic that the tapes that so often ran involuntarily in his head had been dormant. However, the close presence of so many of the women who had played an important part in his life over the past few years had inspired whoever or whatever it was that produced these tapes to new heights of fantasy, and there was little that J.T. could do to control them. There was, however, a new and worrying dimension to the virtual reality show that was being performed in his skull. What had previously been a somewhat lurid, but basically romantic activity, had now turned into a pornographic display of group sex, involving J.T. and five or six females, all of whom were seated in the same room as he at that very moment. Instead of being able to relax and enjoy, J.T. looked guiltily around as the tape remorselessly pursued its course, fearful that in some way the participants in this X-rated video would become aware of what they were acting out. He had just pushed away Galia, who was trying to rouse him in a rather unusual way, had indicated to Akiko that the time was not yet ripe, and was taking Rebecca into his arms, when she said quietly in his ear, 'J.T., I want to talk to you.' He tried to soothe her, gently pushing her head backwards so that her blonde hair was cascading down behind her, only to find that it was becoming entangled with Aleisha's feet as she attempted an athletic maneuver. 'J.T., please.' Rebecca's voice in his ear again. Confused J.T. looked around to see her leaning over the back of his seat from the row behind. 'Can you come outside? It's urgent.' He forced his mind back to reality, and followed her to the door. They went into the coffee lounge.

Rebecca was wearing a low-cut, flowery dress that ended a considerable way above her knees. J.T. sat on a low couch, and she came and sat near him, bending over to touch his knee. He groaned loudly.

'Is there something wrong, J.T.?'

'No! It's just that I am trying very hard to abstain from entanglements at the present time. I need a rest. In a monastery, perhaps.'

'J.T.! Why are you avoiding me? I go back to New York tomorrow, and we've hardly had a chance to talk. Remember those long, interesting talks that we used to have?' She stroked his thigh. 'I learned so much about education from you.'

'Yes,' he said bitterly, 'and then in your report you trashed me.'

'Oh, J.T.! There was nothing personal in that. I was just doing my job. If I'm not critical it looks as if it was a waste of money hiring me in the first place. That's how management consultants work.'

'But don't you have to say something that is actually true?'

'Of course it is nice if we can do that as well. But it's very difficult to understand how an organization really works if you are only looking at it for a couple of weeks.'

'What's the point of it all then?'

'I've often wondered.' She ruminated for a moment. 'I guess it makes everybody feel better. If I say something that the client thinks is useful, then they think the money was well spent, and if I say things that show that I don't really understand what's going on in the organization, then that merely confirms that they were doing it the right way all along. It's a kind of corporate psychotherapy. And I get a nice fee. What's wrong with that?'

'Nothing really, I suppose. It keeps people like you from the fear of unemployment. But it does seem a little like charlatanism.' Rebecca looked vague.

'Perhaps! It's always so stimulating talking to you, J.T.' She was massaging his thigh enthusiastically now. 'But the reason that I wanted to talk to you was that there was something I didn't put into the report because I thought it might upset somebody.'

'That was very considerate of you, Rebecca.' J .T .was worried that he was becoming increasingly sarcastic these days, although no one seemed to notice.

'I know. I do try to be.'

'Well, what is it that you have been keeping to yourself?'

'It's nothing really. I just thought you might consider renaming the College.' There was no understanding response from J.T. 'I mean, the initials, you know. A joke's a joke. But is it wise?'

The afternoon was a rerun of the morning session. An administrator, who had never left the United States except for a weekend in Tijuana, gave a lengthy address on the problems of intercultural relationships. Looking around the room at the assembled company J.T. felt that he could have given a rather more personal and detailed account of the pitfalls of international exchanges than the speaker. His mind was about to follow well-trodden paths when a voice said in his ear: 'J.T. Could we have a word outside?' Rebecca again! And again, conscious of the disapproving looks of the speaker, he followed her to the exit. Once outside he turned to her.

'What's the problem?'

'J.T. I'm in the same suite in the hotel. Remember? Let's go back there to relax and have a drink.'

Half an hour later they were seated at opposite ends of the vast bath, each with a large vodka and tonic. J.T. was admiring the beauty of her chest. 'Rebecca! What did you mean yesterday when you referred to the initials of the College?'

'Well don't you think it's a bit cheeky?'

'I don't know what you mean.'

'Come on, J.T. If you're going to run an undercover operation that's one thing, but you can't then advertise it.'

'Rebecca! I just don't know what you are talking about.'

'O.K! I understand.' She set down her glass, and rose up from her sitting posture. J.T. watched, fascinated, as the water drained from her body, dripping from her pubic hair, running down between her legs. She moved down the bath towards him. She bent over him.

'J.T., you are the most exciting man I have ever met.' She twined her fingers in his hair, pulling back his head, and putting her lips on his, she thrust her tongue in his mouth. J.T. inquired no further about the reasons why she was so excited by him, but gladly accepted the fruits of his inexplicable success.

At the end of a long day the participants in this intellectual orgy were gathering for the final dinner of the convention. Cocktails were served in the anteroom. J.T. was reflecting on the huge cost of bringing all these people here from all over the world. Was it worth it? The knowledge they had gained as a result of it all was trivial. It could have been sent to them in a two-page letter for a few cents, and in any case was it worth having in the first place? True they had all met each other face-to-face, and personal relationships had been formed and consolidated. Or had they? His relationship with Rebecca had blossomed again, but what about Aleisha, Irina, Galia, Akiko and Janice? Not to mention Julia Holcombe. Not so good! He was dolefully ruminating on these eternal verities when Oscar Wolf interrupted the small talk with a demand for silence. 'We have two guests of honor this evening Give them both a hand,' and through the door came Ken Charles and Mike Llewellyn-Proctor. There was a burst of applause, and everyone clustered around them, kissing, slapping their backs, and hugging them. J.T. went across to them and Mike took him in her arms. She put her head against his chest.

'Thanks, J.T. It was wonderful that you came out there to help us. I shall never forget it.' The evening turned into one long party; first, the dinner at the conference center, on to Bransomes' one night spot, then to the Apollo Hotel, where at one point there were fourteen people in the bath in Rebecca's suite, some fully-clothed, others naked, but most of them in their underwear.

Jason Roberts lay in bed in the Apollo Hotel, staring at the ceiling. He had accompanied Ken Charles to Bransome from El Baku after his release from El Khalid, and en route they had met Mike Llewellyn-Proctor in Atlanta. Roberts was leaving his post in the El Baku Embassy to take up a new position in Washington. He had been appointed Head of the Academic Information Section, which had been established on the basis of a plan that he had submitted to the Agency. The idea had come to him when he had observed Ken Charles in operation at BSU's El Baku center. The whole business of intelligence and counter-intelligence had changed since the collapse of the Soviet Bloc, but its importance had not diminished, it had simply changed its focus. The old obsession with military intelligence, to try to gauge the likelihood and timing of a nuclear attack, and to obtain the details of the weapons that would deliver that attack, had gone. But strangely enough the world had not become a simpler place as a result. Indeed it had become infinitely more complex. The behavior of the governments of relatively minor states throughout the world was no longer dictated by the desires of the United States or the Soviet Union. The straightjacket of the Cold War had been loosened. Each little sovereignty felt free to act on its own initiative without the fear of unleashing a nuclear holocaust.

The 'Great Powers' were now at the mercy of every faction in every government of every small state out to enhance its position or to pay off old scores. The kind of intelligence that was required in this situation would not be supplied by 'moles' or 'sleepers' embedded many years ago in government or party structures until the critical moment when these assets could be cashed in, but by vast quantities of information, often very mundane, which could be fed into computers programmed to detect trouble before it manifested itself. This necessitated large numbers of people around the globe, many of them very ordinary people, feeding in this information, however trivial it might seem, so that the computers could crunch it, and a report could land on the appropriate desk in Washington each morning, drawing the attention of the centers of power to any powder kegs which were likely to explode. The need for this kind of intelligence had been clear to many people in the Agency for a long time, but Jason Roberts's achievement had been to make it operational. The remarkable expansion of Bransome Southern University's programs around the world had been no mere coincidence, and nor was the installation in each center of highly sophisticated and extremely expensive communications equipment.

In general the program had been a success, although there had been one or two unfortunate episodes. The business with Ken Charles and Mike Llewellyn-Proctor, although it looked bad at one point, had actually turned out very well. The potential destabilization of the Middle East by feminist revolutionaries had been averted, and the US had come out smelling sweetly on all sides. Seen in retrospect, perhaps the encouragement of Stavros Williams's sewage scheme had been unwise, although there were still a large number of Jason's people located in Eastern Russia who would not otherwise have been there, and, he thought ruefully, they will be there for quite a time clearing up the mess. The Agency finance people had made quite a fuss about his requisition for two million gallons of detergent, but the information they had gathered about dissident groups in Siberia had been worth it. The only real black spot on the record was Stavros Williams's "heart attack". Jason turned over and concentrated on the wall. Damn fool! Why did he have to behave in such a moralistic way? He didn't seem to understand that it wasn't cool to be judgmental these days. And now the widow was causing difficulties. The local police had been cooperative, in a kind of uncooperative way. But Lieutenant Lubowsky clearly was not going to go to the stake on this one. Why should he? At least the Romanian angle was going well. Galia Ionescou was a real gem. She has got those two - what were their names - Corneliu Brosov and Ghita Something-or-other, embroiled in a homosexual plot. Being suspected of homosexuality was still not politically correct in Romania. She was moving from strength to strength. The situation in Japan was developing nicely. Robert Henderson was making contacts at all levels of Japanese society, and his delightful wife, without being aware of it, was the entree to a part of Japan rarely visited by the people in the Tokyo Embassy. Jason moved off the bed and gazed out of the window at the dawn rising over Bransome. It was the first time that he had visited the small town that had become the center of a worldwide intelligence network. The trouble with this idea of his, good though it was, was that to be effective it needed a really large number of informants across the whole world. Could the whole thing be run from Bransome, or would he have to set up other networks run from other universities? The trouble with that was that he could not conceive of finding other universities with such a stunning combination of naivete and incompetence as he had found here. It was too good to be true.

*   *   *

Part 5

THE CANONIZATION

When the convention delegates had dispersed, J.T. turned to the task of sorting out his private affairs. With Oscar's help Irina was moved into an apartment in Bransome, and was provided with a generous pension. Aleisha and her maid remained in J.T.'s old apartment, also with the financial help of the university, and J.T. moved into a brand new condo on the outskirts of the city. Akiko Takahashi had asked to be allowed to remain in Bransome, and, after a remarkably rapid decision by the Immigration and Naturalization Service, she was given a job in J.T.'s office, acting as liaison person with the program in Fukuoka. Ken Charles was also given a job in the International Affairs Office as a Special Assistant to Oscar Wolf. Every morning he could be seen happily raising the flag in Oscar's outer office and supervising the cleaners as they carefully polished the University shield and the trophies that lined the bookshelves in the office of the Vice President for International Affairs. Ken Charles took a special delight in ensuring that every detail of the furnishings and equipment in the building was in working order. Nothing escaped his attention, nothing was too trivial to warrant his passionate care. Light bulbs, toilet rolls, drapes, spots on the carpets, all were grist to his mill. The janitorial staff swore under their breath as he pointed out the merest flaw in their work, and insisted that it be rectified. Ken Charles's days passed happily in these pursuits. He was not required to contribute to the intellectual burden of the University's tasks, and his offers to give the office staff the benefit of his managerial knowledge and expertise, in the form of a series of twenty-four evening lectures, was gently, but firmly, rejected.

The major problem, however, was the body of Stavros Williams, deceased. As a post mortem had been requested, and performed, it was now up to the widow to arrange for the burial, but Irina seemed to have lost all interest in the remains of her dead husband. She now had an independent position, a pension, and a visa allowing her to remain in the United States indefinitely. A new life had begun for her. Any attempt by J.T. to discuss the matter with her was met by a blank refusal to talk about it. 'That is all in the past,' was all he could get out of her. The mortician, however, had a more positive attitude. The storage costs were mounting. Who was going to pay? J.T. went to talk to Dr. Chalmers.

'Should I give the instructions for him to be buried?'

'In the first place, the coroner won't accept your instructions. It has to be the widow. Second, we are still waiting the results of some tests. Third, once he's been buried they will be able to bury the case as well. Our biggest weapon is his body lying there in the morgue. It's the biggest threat we have to hold over them.'

'Them? Who are "They"?'

'The CIA. Surely you realize that. I was reluctant to discuss this case with you at first, because I thought that you must be one of them, working for the College as you do, but then it seemed, unbelievably, that you were genuinely unaware of what had happened to Stavros Williams, so I decided to trust you.' J.T. looked at Chalmers in amazement. The young doctor was becoming almost emotional.

'What do you mean? The CIA? You think the CIA killed Stavros?'

J.T.'s expression of incredulity could have been feigned only if he had been an actor of world class stature. Chalmers was moved to put his hand on the other man's shoulder.

'I'm sorry that it is such a shock to you. How can you not know the kind of people you are working with?'

'I thought I did. But how could *you* be so sure, so quickly?'

'It's not the first time that I have been involved in a case like this,' Chalmers was conspiratorial. 'I was called in when Vittorio Suarez was killed.'

'I'm sorry,' J.T. said. 'I'm afraid that I don't know that case. Anyway, I don't see what it has got to do with the present situation'

'You will. But the most important thing is not to have Stavros buried yet. Wait a while.'

J.T. had other things to worry about, so he took Chalmers's advice. J.T.'s main problem was that, since the convention had ended, Oscar Wolf's behavior had rapidly become more and more eccentric. He no longer seemed to have even the tenuous grasp of reality that he had previously exhibited. He would call J.T. into his office and issue a string of incomprehensible orders.

'J.T! I want you to fly immediately to Tibet. We have the opportunity of cornering the market in yak's milk, but we have to move fast. Those bastards over at Berkeley will beat us to it if we don't act immediately. Oh, and don't forget, the President wants us to handle this situation in Indonesia with kid gloves. Don't foul up!' J.T. was completely ignorant of any situation in Indonesia, and as for yak's milk! He murmured a soothing phrase and departed.

The revelations by Dr. Chalmers about the CIA involvement in the University's international activities had hit J.T. very hard. He was as patriotic as the next man, or woman, and he had no illusions about the necessity of an intelligence system in order to keep abreast of what was going on in foreign countries. He completely understood that if something happened abroad that affected America's interests the Government should know about it, and if an incident occurred which demonstrated that the Government didn't know what was going on there would be hell to pay. He wasn't opposed to intelligence work *as such,* but he did not relish the thought of being so directly involved, and, what was worse, without being aware of it. After Dr. Chalmers's revelations he had stormed into Oscar Wolf's office, and, most uncharacteristically for him, he had banged the desk of the Vice President for International Affairs and shouted out a demand for an explanation.

'Oscar! What's going on? People are telling me that the CIA runs our operation. I've even been told that the CIA killed Stavros. What is going on?'

Oscar looked at him with unusual directness and clarity.

'If you are saying that you don't know what is going on in your own organization,' Oscar said, 'you must either be a rogue or a fool.' J.T. was so stunned by this unanswerable observation that he rushed from the room, and had not raised the matter again. But this was the only trenchant statement that was to emanate from Oscar for a long time. J.T. was left to stew. He either had to resign, or to get on with the job. He chose the latter course, not purely for venal reasons, although he was aware that the prospects for alternative employment were pretty bleak, but because he felt responsible for the many people he had recruited all over the world. He was caught in a web of relationships from which it would have been possible to extricate himself only with a sense of having betrayed those closest to him. With no wife or family of his own he could not envisage a life away from the people whom he had come to like, and in a number of cases in more senses than one, to love.

On a November morning Oscar called J.T. to his office. 'J.T., tomorrow we leave for Sakhalin.'

'What? Why?'

'We have to sort out this business about Stavros. I'm under a lot of pressure to get it sewn up.'

'How will going to Sakhalin help to do that? Stavros is in the morgue in Bransome.'

'I know that.' Oscar's look was vicious. 'We need to contact the people there to explain what happened. That way we can deal with the situation and get Stavros buried.'

'But Irina, his wife, is here in Bransome,' J.T. protested. 'Eventually she will give her permission to bury Stavros. Why do we need to go to Sakhalin?' Oscar was furious.

'Eventually! She won't talk to me. I've tried. She says that it is "of no importance". I have been trying to get her to authorize Stavros's cremation, but she just refuses to sign the papers.' J.T. was unaware that Oscar had been pressurizing Irina in this way.

'Why have you been talking to Irina? I have been dealing with this problem.' J.T. was irritated and suspicious. Oscar waved his objection aside.

'Zuwicki is on my back the whole time. He wants that stiff out of there, *and burned.* You don't seem to be making much progress in that direction.'

'How will going to Sakhalin solve that?'

'We are going to take Stavros with us.' J.T.'s feet left the floor.

'What! I don't believe this. Has everyone gone mad?' Oscar's eyes were indeed those of a man who was not entirely sane. He leaned across his desk and took the lapels of J.T.'s houndstooth Jaeger sports jacket in his hands. His face a few inches from J.T.'s, he hissed:

'Don't give me any more of your crap. I've had it up to here. There's Fred Zuwicki and that bastard Roberts shouting at me all the time to get that creep out of the icebox, and all you do is to take a high moral tone. I've looked into this. We can't bury or cremate Stavros without his wife's agreement,' he shook J.T. rhythmically to give emphasis to his words, 'but we *can* get a license to export him to his wife's homeland.'

'Export him!' J.T. was incensed. "Why is it so important to get rid of Stavros? Could it be that small puncture at the back of his neck?' Oscar erupted.

'O.K! You can be a moralistic, preaching little creep too, if you want. Sure there are things you are entitled to bitch about, but we ran this thing together. You are in it up to your neck. If we don't get Stavros out of here we could both be in very, very deep shit. Do you think that anyone will believe that you are the naive little innocent that you really are? I'm the only person in this world who could give you a genuine character reference,' his grip on J.T.'s jacket tightened, 'but I ain't going to. You stick with me or you are dead!'

The next day saw Oscar Wolf and J.T. boarding a United States Air Force Hercules transport plane at Jackson Field. Stavros was carried aboard, his coffin shrouded in the Stars and Stripes, with a small honor guard provided by US Marines. The plane was bound for England, the only flight with refrigeration facilities that could be found at short notice. As Stavros had now been dead for over a month this was more than a mere formality. If in life Stavros Williams had been a pain, in death he was to prove a positive agony.

During the long flight Oscar and J.T. hardly exchanged a word. Oscar seemed to be interested only in the magazines that he had brought with him, magazines with titles such as *For Men in Need,* or *Ambidextrous and Proud of It.* For his part J.T. sat trying to reconcile himself to being an accessory to a murder. He had never liked Stavros. In his first incarnation Stavros had been arrogant, domineering, hypocritical, ignorant, incompetent, insensitive, ruthless, self-congratulatory, sexist, verbose. Naturally, he had done very well at Bransome Southern. He fitted in. When he had been transformed by some unexplained and inexplicable experience into a caring, humanitarian, priest-like figure, he was only marginally more tolerable. His essential arrogance still shone through. Nevertheless, murder was a crime. People ought not to be killed, even if they were socially unacceptable.

The Hercules landed at the Royal Air Force base at Brize Norton near Oxford. The Base Commander, heavily mustached, having been informed by the Flight-Lieutenant in charge of unloading the cargo that it included an occupied coffin, came out to the aircraft in person. He ordered the RAF Police to inspect Stavros, and to stow him away in the meat store.

'We were not warned that you had a corpse on board,' he said in his clipped British military accent. 'Damned inconvenient. We would have had the Customs' wallahs here and transferred him to the morgue in Oxford. They might think that you are trying to smuggle him in. This is all highly irregular. Against the food and hygiene regulations.' Oscar was unusually placatory.

'I'm sorry, Wing Commander.' Oscar had been well briefed during the flight. 'It is a tragic situation. This young man was struck down in his prime. We have to get him back to his wife's family.' Oscar's voice trembled. 'He was on a special mission. Top secret! You understand.' The moustache under the blue cap with the gold braid did not even quiver.

'Right! Well, we do all we can to help our American cousins, but I want him out of the meat store first thing in the morning. I shudder to think what would happen if some over-zealous cook were to think that the meat was being packaged in a new way, and served him up for lunch. What transport arrangements have you got for tomorrow?' The truth was that Oscar had no arrangements. The United States Air Force faced with an urgent request to remove a cadaver from the territory of the United States had performed its task, and the Hercules was loading for its homeward journey, as they spoke.

'I was hoping that the RAF might have a flight going in the right direction,' Oscar's voice was loaded with admiration for the far-flung tentacles of the British Commonwealth of Nations, 'Kuala Lumpur perhaps, or Singapore. What about Bombay, or Karachi? Anything towards the east would do.'

'This is not a bloody freight company.' The moustache was working overtime now. For several minutes Oscar and J.T. were subjected to the kind of invective normally reserved for an Aircraftsman who had allowed his hair to grow too long. Additionally, the Wing Commander's deep reserves of vocabulary enabled him to cast doubt on the parentage, legitimacy, and intellectual capacity of ex-colonials, parading as university officials, hawking a dead body around the world. Oscar's diplomatic skills, already sorely tried, rapidly ebbed away.

'O.K. Limey!' he screamed. 'This is all the thanks we get for coming over and winning the war for you, is it?' The Wing Commander, once a member of the Oxford University boxing team, was about to declare war on the United States by pasting one of its distinguished university Vice Presidents all over the wall of an aircraft hangar, when his adjutant, who had been standing silently by his side throughout, stepped forward and whispered in the ear of his superior officer. The purple tinge on the face of the Wing Commander gradually faded. He groped for words.

'Harris tells me that we do have one suitable flight leaving tomorrow.' He removed his cap and wiped his brow. 'The Foreign Office is sending some kind of special rations to our Embassy in Bucharest. Seems the poor buggers are starving to death. Your friend will go out on that flight, and you will too. That's it. That's all I can do for you. Harris will see that you get dinner and a room for the night.' He slapped his cap back on his head and stamped off.

Later, in their quarters, J.T. quizzed Oscar. 'Look! If we are working for the CIA, how comes that they have not made all the arrangements to get Stavros straight to Sakhalin? Why did they dump us here? Now we are stuck with this corpse, we have this RAF character shouting at us like we were idiots, and the worst thing about it is that he is damn well right!'

'The CIA had nothing to do with this,' Oscar bellowed back. 'I contacted Jackson Field myself and asked for transport as a favor to the University. I heard that the DA's office were having Stavros examined again tomorrow - today - whatever damn day this is. So I had to get him out. Roberts doesn't know about it - or he didn't when we left.'

'You mean you panicked.' Oscar gave J.T. a look of death.

'J.T. I swear that some day, when we get out of this pile of shit, I will fire you. Don't ever talk to me like that. I don't take that kind of crap from you or anyone.'

'Right! You panicked. Do you think I want your stinking job? You have got me into the most ridiculous situation anyone could imagine, and you expect me to be grateful? Anyway the whole idea of smuggling the body out was stupid.' Oscar fought with himself for several seconds, but in the end he had to ask:

'Why, for God's sake?'

'Because all the important bits of Stavros are in bottles back in Bransome. His brain, heart, liver, etcetera, etcetera. Just ponder on that.' There was no further conversation that night.

* * *

Thirty thousand feet above the English Channel, the RAF pilot was giving a cheery commentary over the public address system: 'Hi folks!' This was obviously his attempt to be welcoming to his two transatlantic passengers. He had spent three weeks on a goodwill visit to Roberts Air Force Base in Idaho, and as a result had become the local expert on all things American. 'We will be routed over northern France, turning south-east near Nancy, crossing into Germany over Freiburg, overflying Munich, leaving Austria to the south of Vienna, taking a direct course over Hungary to make our descent into Bucharest, arriving at approximately 3.45 p.m. local time. I hope you have a comfortable flight. There are 40 cases of champagne in the hold, but they are for the diplomats who have such a hard time in our Embassy. I'm afraid the RAF does not serve in-flight drinks, except tea, of course, which is available at any time.' There was an embarrassed pause. 'The crew would like to express their sympathy about your friend. If there is anything we can do...' There was a click as the PA was turned off. For the first time that day, J.T. spoke to Oscar Wolf. His tone was hostile.

'What do you intend to do when we get to Bucharest?'

'We've got a program there, haven't we? Run by your woman, Galia, isn't it?

'She is not my woman.' J.T. replied icily. 'I did not realize that you were so well informed about our programs.' Oscar waved a vague arm.

'I keep in touch with her. She will do something to help us out.' But it wasn't going to be as straightforward as that. When they were an hour away from Bucharest, the co-pilot came back to talk to the two Americans.

'I'd like to fill you chaps in on what is going to happen when we land. Bit complicated, you see. This is not your regular scheduled air service. We fly here about once a week on a strictly military basis. Our mission is to deliver stuff to our Embassy - documents, food, drink, clothing, guards, weapons - whatever they need. So we never declare anything to the Romanian authorities; we never go through customs or immigration. We have diplomatic immunity, you see. When we get to the airport all our cargo will be transferred to a large van, which will then be sealed and driven to the embassy. You and the..., your friend, will go in the van with all the other stuff. That way the Romanians won't know about you or the coffin. Avoids a great deal of red tape. Dead bodies are the worst for paperwork. You wouldn't believe the fuss that bureaucrats make about moving corpses about. Sorry, got carried away there. Realize how painful this must be for you. The van is refrigerated - keeps the food fresh you see - but the trip only takes about twenty minutes. You'll be OK. Just wrap up well. Best of luck!'

* * *

The Ambassador welcomed his visitors at the door of the Embassy. Before the Second World War Britain had maintained a large diplomatic mission in Bucharest, housed in a vast Victorian mansion, but in post-Ceausescu Romania the mission had been reduced to the bare essentials: the Ambassador and his wife, a First Secretary, three junior diplomats and a few locals employed as secretaries and clerks. They still had the great house, but most of the splendid rooms were empty, except for the dust. The Ambassador's wife had been delighted when she had heard they were to have some Americans to stay in the house. Normally she cooked for her husband and herself in the vast kitchen, which had once provided banquets for the elite, staffed by chefs, underchefs, and an army of servants. The visitors provided an opportunity to get in a cook and a maid for the evening, and enjoy some kind of social life.

'Why are they coming here, darling?' Her name was Claudia. A tall, stately blonde, she had been an eager debutante when she had met the rising young diplomat she was to marry. She had dreamt of hosting magnificent balls in Paris, Washington, Rome. The reality had been a succession of dreary postings in small African states, followed by Eastern Europe, first under communist regimes, and then under even more dreary post-communist governments. Bucharest was likely to be the peak of Frederick's career, to be followed by retirement to some dreary London suburb. 'Why aren't they staying at the American Embassy? They would get much better accommodation there.'

'I think it is some kind of undercover operation. The message I got from Brize Norton implied that one of these people is travelling incognito. Presumably the Americans want to keep this visit under wraps. We always help each other out in this way.' However, even Sir Frederick Jamieson-Brown's *sang-froid* was somewhat dented when the seal was broken on the van, and two men fell out in the last stages of hypothermia. There had been an accident on the road from the airport, and as a consequence of the resulting traffic chaos the journey had taken twice as long as expected. But it was the sight of the coffin, and the explanations stuttered out by Oscar and J.T., that caused the aristocratic eyebrows to rise just a fraction.

'I was told to expect three Americans. No one mentioned that one of them had been dead for a month. Typical, isn't it? The RAF needs to get rid of a corpse, so they bring it here, and gaily fly off back to England. No problem! Just a good story to tell at the pub tonight. You'd better come in and thaw out. Claudia, these men need a hot toddy.'

The whisky had its desired effect and soon Oscar and J.T. were seated in comfortable armchairs in the Ambassador's sitting room. Oscar was trying to explain exactly why they were there, if possible without saying anything that would actually enlighten the Englishman.

'Stavros, our colleague, was the Director of our University program in Sakhalin. We work for Bransome Southern University. I guess you will have heard of it.' The Ambassador made a kind of grunting noise that could have been interpreted as "of course!" Oscar continued. 'In fact we have a program here in Romania, in Ploiesti. Galia Ionescu is the Director.'

'I've certainly heard of her,' Sir Frederick sat up. 'She's the Mayor of Ploiesti. She's not American is she?'

'No, but she works for BSU. Anyway, Stavros started up this program in Sakhalin, which was designed to develop the local economy and to bring the place into the twentieth century.'

'Just in time,' the Ambassador mused, 'considering the twentieth century is over. We won't be able to use that cliché any longer.'

'Right! Well, it seems that Stavros upset some of the local vested interests there. Groups that were opposed to change. So they eliminated him.' That caught the diplomat's attention.

'You mean they killed him?'

'You're damn right I do. A filthy assassination. And right in Bransome.'

'In Bransome? You mean they killed him in America? Not in Sakhalin? Surely if they were going to kill him they would have done it in Russia.'

'No! The local population loved Stavros, worshipped him. They would have lynched anyone who harmed a hair on his head. These thugs had to use a hired killer in the States to do their dirty work.' Oscar was getting carried away He almost believed it himself.

'A hitman,' Sir Fred breathed. He spent much of his time watching videos of American gangster movies. Lady Jamieson-Brown was later to blame her husband's gullibility on this otherwise harmless hobby.

'Right! So we have to get his remains back to Sakhalin, so that the people there can bury him with the honor that he deserves.' Oscar leaned back in his chair, exhausted by this unusually lengthy conversation.

'Fascinating!' said their host. 'But why are you here in Bucharest?' Oscar's inventive ability had already been sorely tested. He had no further reserves of imagination. He looked despairingly to J.T. who had hardly said a word since their arrival.

'Unfortunately,' J.T. hesitated, and then continued, 'the person who made the travel arrangements was incompetent, and we ended up going to England instead of Russia.' Oscar twisted his fingers together as if he was throttling some invisible adversary.

'So the RAF, faced with the unexpected arrival of your friend's body decided to off-load you here. It's a good job that we have a small morgue in the embassy. In the old days they had to be prepared for the possibility that a member of the legation would die and could not be shipped out for some time. Your friend will be well cared for. But what do you plan to do now?'

'May I use your phone to make a call to Ploiesti?' J.T. asked. 'Perhaps Galia can get us out of this difficulty.'

'Of course. But be careful. There have been some complicated political developments here lately.' The British genius for understatement had rarely been deployed with such devastating effect.

* * *

Galia was overjoyed to see J.T. again. She entered the Ambassador's sitting room at a run, arms outstretched, enfolding J.T. and planting an enthusiastic kiss on his lips.

'I couldn't believe it when I got your call. How did you know that I needed you so much? In more ways than one, I may say!' J.T. extricated himself from Galia's embrace, and looked apologetically towards Lady Claudia who had observed this encounter with amusement.

'I didn't know that you needed help, Galia. *We* need *your* help.'

'My help? You must be joking. Did you not read my last report?'

'Report? I haven't seen any report. Who did you send it to?'

'To Vice President Wolf, of course, as I always do. Did he not give you a copy?' J.T. turned to Oscar, who was carefully studying the titles of the books on the Ambassador's shelves.

'Been very busy lately,' Wolf mumbled. 'Didn't get time to read it. What d'it say?'

'I told you that things here were on the edge of an explosion. Those rats Corneliu Brosov and Ghita have turned on me. They have accused me of being an agent of American economic neo-imperialism. Me! A British subject.' She threw a look of agonized entreaty at Sir Frederick. 'I asked the American Embassy for help, but they said that I was nothing to do with them.' She flung her arms around J.T.'s neck again.

'Galia!' J.T. was lost for words. The situation was deteriorating by the minute. 'Look! We came to Bucharest by mistake. We were on our way to Russia. We've got Stavros Williams with us. You remember, he was our Director in Sakhalin.' Galia drew back.

'Stavros? He's dead. I was there when he died. At dinner. In Bransome.'

'Killed by a Russian hitman,' Oscar put in from the general area of the bookshelves.

'We have his body here. In a coffin,' J.T. added.

'But he has been dead for a month.' Galia looked around the room, expecting to see Stavros propped up in the corner.

'In a refrigerated container,' the Ambassador explained.

'We've got to get him out of the country,' J.T. continued. Oscar thinks that we could bury him in Sakhalin.'

'Why not bury him here?'

'The Romanian government doesn't know about him. We smuggled him in from England. That's why we are in the British Embassy.' Galia sat down heavily in one of Her Britannic Majesty's armchairs.

'Oh my God! This could be bad. Really very bad!' Till now, conscious of where she was, Galia's accent had been very British. Now it was deeply Romanian. 'We are really screwed up now.' She turned to Sir Frederick. 'I want to get back to Britain as soon as possible. Please may I stay here, tonight?'

Sir Frederick Jamieson-Brown, Her Majesty's Ambassador to the Government of Romania, had had a very boring career. In all his years in the diplomatic service he had never had to deal with a revolution, a famine, or a war. He was always posted away just before they began, or sent there some time after they were ended.

It was like some good luck jinx. You never got promoted if you were just boringly efficient. No one noticed you. Some of the most successful men that he knew in the service had made the most appalling blunders, but had emerged smelling of roses because of the way they had "handled the situation". He knew that he really should get rid of all these people. They smelled of trouble. But he liked J.T., and he liked Galia very much - *very* nice! And after all she is a British national. So she says. Better get Smithers to check that with London. Really it was the RAF that had got these Americans into this situation. It wasn't their fault. Anyway, I shall be retiring in a couple of years.

'Yes, of course, Miss Ionescu. Delighted to have you. Claudia, we can find a bed for Miss Ionescu, I imagine.' Before Claudia could reply, Galia jumped in.

'I don't want to give you any trouble. I would be happy to share with J.T. We are close friends.' J.T. choked with embarrassment. Claudia laughed.

'No problem! We are broad-minded. With our Royal Family we have to be.'

* * *

'For God's sake, don't make so much noise.' Galia was kneeling over him, her legs wide, pressing her body further and further down, and enjoying it very audibly.

'Darling, you are wonderful.' She continued to thrust at him until she collapsed over him with a long sigh of contentment. 'Thank you, my darling, thank you.' J.T. lay there, his hand caressing her back, thinking not about the body in his arms, but about the body in the basement.

The next morning, Sir Frederick called his guests, those who were alive at any rate, into his office. 'There are a number of matters to which I should call your attention. First, there is a ring of police and troops around the Embassy. Second, the Government of Romania has demanded that we hand Galia over to them. They describe her as a fugitive from justice. She is accused of criminal libel, entrapment of a Minister of State, conspiracy to undermine the Government of Romania, and about five other hanging crimes. Third, the Government of the United States of America has asked if we are harboring two American citizens who have stolen a body, and requests that we deliver up these fugitives, together with the aforesaid body, immediately. And finally, the Government of Romania wishes to know if we are harboring two American criminals, and a stolen body, and if so how did they get into the British Embassy, as there is no record of their having entered the country legally. Not bad for one night's work, is it? I won't bore you with the messages that the Foreign Office in London has been sending to me. I haven't yet worked out what my reply is going to be.' Oscar tried to absorb all this information.

'So when can we leave?'

'You and J.T. can leave at any time. If I surrender you to the American authorities, along with the body of your friend.'

'How do you mean, "surrender us"?'

The Ambassador adopted a patient expression.

'The Americans apparently consider you to be criminals who have stolen a body and removed it from the United States, presumably because you wanted to avoid the detection of your crime.'

'What the hell is going on!' Oscar screamed 'The government knows why I got rid of Stavros's body. Jason Roberts was on at me the whole time to do something about it. Now they are trying to pin the whole thing on me. I'm a fall guy. Me! Oscar Wolf. Well, they won't get away with it. Mr. Ambassador, I claim political asylum.' Sir Frederick could hardly believe his ears. An American seeking asylum from the Government of the United States in his Embassy. It was too good to be true. This was going to be big! He turned to J.T.

'And what about you? Do you claim political asylum?' Before J.T. could formulate an answer, Galia had taken his arm and pleaded,

'Please do. We must all stay here together. Sir Frederick, I claim political asylum against the government of Romania.' Sir Fred was not so sure about this.

'Wait a moment! You say that you are a British citizen. I'm not sure that British subjects can claim asylum in a British Embassy. Never mind, you are entitled to all the protection that we can give you.' Then turning to J.T. again, 'What is your decision?'

J.T. was angry. Oscar has deceived him about the whole nature of the operation back at Bransome, led him into an impossible situation, and now it seemed he was likely to be charged with murder by the agents of a government, *his government,* that had used him in unforgivable way. He had sent people all over the world, believing that he was furthering the cause of international education, only to find that he had in fact been a spy-master. Sir Fred was waiting for his answer.

'I would like to stay.' Galia cheered, and the Ambassador was delighted.

'Good! I will inform London, and then we will talk about our strategy. But first I will get Smithers to break out some of that champagne that came with you. Let's have a celebration.'

The following days were full of incident. Sir Frederick was in his element; London was not very happy. Taking on the Romanians was one thing. Giving political asylum to two Americans, and a body, was something else. True the "Special Relationship" had been wearing thin for a long time, but it was still assumed that the two oldest democracies in the world had a particular respect for each other. Now the British Government was faced with telling the US that they could not deliver up two of their nationals, who claimed they were being persecuted because they had been the unwitting instruments of the CIA. However, political asylum is *political asylum*, no matter where the claimants originated. The British Government therefore issued a statement saying that the claims of the two Americans were being investigated, and that until the investigation had been concluded the men would stay in the Embassy in Bucharest. This process was likely to take weeks rather than days. Galia was delighted. She could look forward to several nights in J.T.'s arms. Sir Frederick was also pleased. His legation would be the center of attraction for the world's media for at least two or three days and his superiors in London would be giving him their full attention for once. Smithers, the First Secretary, was less enthusiastic. He was worried that being associated with a crackpot Ambassador who had allowed a ridiculous crisis to develop between Britain and the US would blight his career.

'This could end in a state of war between Britain and America,' he moaned to his Ambassador.

'Well, that is not unprecedented,' Sir Frederick replied, equably. Lady Claudia, if she had reservations, expressed only one of them.

'It is going to be very wearing listening to Galia and J.T. hard at it every night,' she said. 'In these old houses every sound travels right through the house, but I've never heard anything quite like this before.'

Sir Fred put his arm round his wife.

'Perhaps we ought to drown them out by making a lot of noise ourselves,' he murmured in her ear.

* * *

The British Embassy was situated at 43 Constanta Boulevard. Along the street dark shadows flitted through the night. Men dressed in black from head to foot, each carrying an assault rifle, stun grenades, and a handgun, took up their positions round the house. The Romanian police and soldiers were nowhere to be seen. Earlier, at their base, the Green Berets commander had addressed them. 'Remember, there are three armed British Marines in the Embassy. They are tough guys, but we do not want a shoot-out. There are also women and civilians in there. However, we have orders to get these criminals, and the body that is in there, and we intend to do that, whatever the cost. We have with us Jason Roberts as our political advisor. He will take over as soon as we have secured the building. One further point. We must not carry anything identifying us as Americans, and in the unlikely event that anyone is captured we do not admit our identity. Any questions?' There were none.

The Captain gave the signal. His men smashed down four entrances to the building, rushed inside, weapons at the ready, and took up firing positions. Quickly, Jason Roberts followed them, moved to the center of the imposing entrance hall, and using a bullhorn, shouted,

'Give up! There is no possibility of resistance.' There was a moment of silence, and then the big double doors to the main reception room were flung open. The soldiers braced themselves, ready to fire. A man stood there, in evening dress.

'Come in, gentlemen! You are welcome. We have everything here that you could want.' With a theatrical gesture he waved towards the brightly-lit interior, urging them to enter.

'Careful! It may be a trap,' Roberts warned. Supported by two soldiers, weapons at the ready, he advanced cautiously into the room. It was a large room hung with heavily embroidered drapes; the furniture looked as if it was from the period of the last Czar of All the Russias, tapestried chairs, and no fewer than three chaises-longues. The pile of the luxurious carpet was very long. A glittering chandelier hung in the center of the ceiling. Along one wall was a bar, loaded with every kind of drink imaginable. More striking than the furnishings, however, were the occupants. Everywhere, on chairs, chaises-longues, and even lying on the floor, were young women, dressed in a bewildering variety of styles; some were dressed lavishly in ball gowns which swept to their ankles, others wore miniskirts, and yet others were in their underwear. As Jason Roberts entered they all turned expectantly towards him. They seemed neither alarmed nor surprised by the fact that the two men with him were armed to the teeth. As Jason hesitated, confused, more of his men burst into the room from every door, and from the women rose a gentle babble of delighted welcome. As they surveyed the scene the soldiers gradually lowered their rifles, and then began to move towards the women. 'These Limey's,' one said to his buddy. 'If this is how they fit out their Embassies, I might ask for asylum myself.' Jason barked out:

'Hey! Keep alert there. This could be an elaborate ambush.' He turned to the sole male occupant of the room, the one who had welcomed them. 'Where is the Ambassador? Take me to him immediately' The man, who spoke with a Romanian accent, said:

'I am sorry. We do not have any ambassadors here at the moment. It is a little early in the evening. In fact there is no one in the house. We may have an ambassador, or even two, later on.'

'Are you trying to make a fool of me?' Roberts was becoming angry. 'What the hell do you mean by *two* ambassadors? I demand to see the British Ambassador.' The man threw up his hands in horror.

'Oh, no! That is impossible. He never comes here. The Japanese Ambassador, perhaps. Or the one from Saudi Arabia. But not Sir Frederick.' It began to dawn on Jason Roberts that things were not exactly going according to plan. The man continued: 'Why not have a drink. On the house. Your companions as well.'

'What kind of place is this? Where are we?'

'This is Vasile's,' he said proudly. 'I am Vasile.'

'I think I will have that drink. Scotch on the rocks.' Vasile gestured towards the buxom barmaid. As if they had been given a signal the soldiers moved in on the women, who greeted them affectionately, and before long they were all in animated conversation, clutching drinks served by girls wearing extremely short skirts, which, as far as one could see, and one did try very hard to see, had nothing further beneath them.

Jason Roberts, clutching his glass, demanded of Vasile.

'Is this the British Embassy, or not?'

'The British Embassy? Ha! Ha! An American joke. I see American jokes on the television. Very good!'

'I am not joking. Is this number 43 Constanta Boulevard?'

'No! This is number 34.' Roberts lowered his head into his hands. He would kill that Captain. Three hours later, a happy group of Green Berets made their way through the streets of Bucharest, singing, and occasionally dancing a little. 'That sure was the best undercover operation I've ever been in,' was the verdict of one Top Sergeant. It was an opinion that was generally shared.

*   *   *

At breakfast Sir Frederick addressed the assembled company of "guests".

'It seems that yesterday evening an attack was launched on a brothel just along the road from here. A very well run and attractive brothel frequented by all the top people in government, and by rich foreigners. Not, I hasten to add,' he cast a nervous glance at Lady Claudia, 'that I have ever been there. Anyway, it appears that the attackers, who were heavily armed, thought that they were breaking into this Embassy. They were speaking English, and it is pretty certain that they were Americans, although the White House has issued a statement denying any involvement. It might have been a covert CIA operation to get Mr. Williams's body, and to capture Oscar and J.T. The British Government is not amused, and the Romanians are very, very angry, as they were not informed of the raid, and had certainly not given their approval.' He looked around his audience to gauge their reactions to his news. He obviously considered that there could hardly have been a more auspicious development in this affair. His government was now in a position of moral superiority, its Embassy attacked (in principle at least) by one foreign power, on the territory of another which had the duty to protect it, and all because he, the man on the spot, had offered sanctuary to people on the run.

'In order, therefore, to avoid any further incidents,' Sir Fred continued, 'I have proposed the following course of action, and it has already been approved by the Governments of the United States, Romania and the United Kingdom.'

'You have been so busy, Frederick,' Galia patted his arm. 'You could not have had any sleep last night. We are so grateful.' Sir Fred simpered.

'Just doing my job, you know. The plan is that Romania will give a full pardon to Galia, provided she leaves the country.' Galia threw her arms around his neck and kissed him. 'The United States will guarantee that Oscar and J.T. will not be charged with any Federal crime, and will try to convince the relevant authorities not to proceed with any prosecutions for possible offences against state law.' Oscar and J.T. looked relieved. 'However, the State Department does not want Mr. Williams's body returned to America. For its part the British Government will no longer extend political asylum to you two, and will provide you, and the body, with transport to any destination you wish, except the United States.' Oscar grappled with this all this new information.

'You mean we can't have political asylum?'

'Well, no! There is no suggestion now that you will be subject to persecution, even when you return to the United States.'

'But we can't just get on a plane to America?'

'No! There is the matter of the body. The Americans won't have it back, and the Romanians insist that it leave. They view Mr. Williams as a kind of posthumous illegal immigrant.'

'Could we just leave it here?' Sir Fred decided to pretend that Oscar had not asked that question.

'So you will continue to be our very welcome guests for two or three days while the necessary arrangements are made. But you must tell me by noon today where you want to go. This time we must make sure that you enter legally, body and all, whichever country you go to.' Oscar,

J.T. and Galia had gathered in the living room to discuss their next move.

'What shall we do?' asked Galia. Oscar was wandering about the room, apparently aimlessly, inspecting the furniture without really seeing it. Then J.T. heard, unmistakably, the sound of humming coming from across the room. Filled with trepidation, he turned to Oscar.

'What are you up to?'

'Up to? Nothing! I was just thinking; if you took charge of Stavros, I could go straight back to the States. There are things I should be doing back in Bransome.' J.T. crossed the room.

'Look, I am not a violent person, but I am getting close to the point where it may be necessary for our English friends to supply another coffin - for you!' This was said with such venom that Oscar fell back a pace or two.

'Remember,' he said, 'that I am a Vice President. I can fire you on the spot.'

'Great! That's fine with me. I consider myself fired. Now Stavros is entirely your problem. I will ask Fred for permission to return home straight away, as I no longer have any connection with BSU.' Oscar winced.

'O.K! Let's not argue. Why don't we ask to go direct to Sakhalin?'

'I already asked Fred about that immediately after breakfast. He'd forgotten to tell us that the Russians won't let us into the country.'

'Why not, for God's sake, after all we've done for that place?'

'It seems that the situation in Sakhalin is desperate. Not only is the heat exchanger system not working, but a row developed between Sakhalin and Irkutsk, the town where the pumping station is situated. Irkutsk could not cope with all the sewage that was being directed to it from all over Siberia, so they started pumping it again. This would have made it possible to restore the electricity supply in Sakhalin and provide the heat that they had before.'

'So what's the problem?' Oscar was his old sneering self.

'The problem is that during the winter the heat exchangers, and a lot of the piping, had frozen and been fractured. None of it works. But the sewage began to flow again and poured out everywhere, flooding the countryside. The people in Sakhalin tried to stop it. They blew up the pipe where it came up out of the sea, but that was even worse. Now a sea of sewage surrounds the whole island. Sakhalin is floating on sewage. If we went there now, quite apart from the fact that we would not like the smell, they would shoot us.'

'O.K. smart-ass! What do you suggest?'

'Well, we need somewhere that we can keep Stavros cool until we can bury him. The one place that we have a cold room filled with ice is El Baku. We could stash him there indefinitely.'

'But the electricity supply was always failing there,' Oscar objected, 'and in that heat...'

'Jason Roberts had a generator installed, and they have two years supply of oil on the site.'

'You mean we could park him there, and then go home?'

'We could store the coffin there and give ourselves time to think what to do with it.' Oscar thought for a moment.

'O.K. Let's do it.'

'Please, J.T., can I come with you?' Galia pressed herself against him pleadingly.

'El Baku? Sounds like a good idea. I'll get on to them straight away.' Sir Frederick made off towards the communications room.

An hour later he returned. 'Good! That's settled then. They are quite happy for you to go there. And they will accept the body, provided that it is understood that it is in transit. The one thing they were a bit difficult about was Galia. Sorry, my dear, it seems they had some kind of unfortunate experience with a woman who was associated with BSU. But I convinced them that you were O.K., and they agreed. The RAF plane will be here tomorrow morning.

The ceremony was deeply moving. A Romanian guard of honor was drawn up on the tarmac. Sir Frederick had decided that the occasion demanded that he wear his full dress ambassadorial uniform, complete with plumed hat and sword. The party was driven to the airport in a stretch limousine, with Stavros on the back seat. The television cameras whirred as they stepped down from the car and walked to the aircraft steps. Sir Fred saluted, the Romanian guard presented arms, and the body was removed from the limo. A military band was playing a tune that sounded vaguely like the *Marseillaise*. The effect was rather spoilt when the pallbearers, four baggage handlers, dropped the coffin onto the concrete, where it landed with a loud crack. Everyone held their breath, waiting to see if it would break open, and Stavros would jump out. Thankfully, it held fast, and was quickly gathered up and carried into the plane.

Sir Frederick bade farewell to his three visitors, with a particularly enthusiastic kiss on the hand for Galia. He was driven away, the aircraft door was closed, and the plane began to taxi towards the runway.

The arrival in El Baku was very different. The RAF plane was directed to a special area set aside for military aircraft. No one was there to meet them. Two RAF men helped them unload the coffin and set it down on the tarmac, some distance from the plane. 'We must take off again immediately,' a crewmember explained. 'We have to get to Cyprus tonight.' Minutes later the plane began to taxi again and three disconsolate figures stood in the burning heat beside the coffin. Oscar took charge.

'J.T! You take one end, and I'll take the other. Galia, you bring the bags.'

'Oscar...'

'Just do as I say.'

J.T. stationed himself at one end, and Oscar bent down and grasped the other end of the coffin with both hands. 'Lift!' Oscar called. They tried to stand up, but they could not raise Stavros higher than knee-level. They staggered for three or four feet, weaving dangerously, and then, simultaneously they collapsed, the coffin bumping down hard on the ground. Oscar straightened, wiped his brow, and glowered at J.T. 'For God's sake go and get help.' And with that he sat down heavily on the coffin. 'Quick!'

As he entered the terminal building J.T. saw Ken Charles lining up to go through immigration. 'Ken, what are you doing here?'

'Hi, J.T! I've just this minute flown in from Bransome. I had a message saying that you needed my help. So I came straight away. You know me, your faithful servant.'

'Will they let you in?'

'Sure! We checked. They think that I was quite innocent in that last little affair. They put the whole blame on Mike.'

'I'm sure that's right. Look, it's great to see you, but I can't talk now. I need five or six skycaps, urgently.'

'You must have a hell of a lot of baggage.'

'No! Hardly any; but we do have Stavros. And its hot out there.'

'O.K. I'll deal with this.' Ken Charles, faced with a challenge, began to get things organized, and gratefully J.T. left him to it.

For the next few days the BSU compound provided a pleasant haven for the harassed travelers from Bransome Southern University. Servants ministered to their needs. Ken Charles managed, heroically, to provide some alcohol. Galia was ecstatic, each night reaching ever-greater heights of sexual athleticism. They even forgot for a time the presence of Stavros Williams in the cold room. Eventually, however, Oscar Wolf became restless.

'We can't stay here forever,' he said to J.T. one morning.' Apart from anything else I can't take the noise at night any longer. I'm amazed that broad can still walk. It sounds like you are using her to pound nails into the floor. Christ, I haven't had a woman for weeks.' J.T. was offended.

'I can't see that you have anything to complain about. We wouldn't be here if you hadn't been party to a criminal conspiracy and then lost your nerve.' Oscar found it impossible to endure the change in J.T. The younger man, who had previously been so quiescent, so polite and so obedient, now made no attempt to hide the contempt he had for Oscar. J.T. took every possible opportunity to hammer home Oscar's responsibility for their present predicament, and no threats of future retribution could deter him. Finally Oscar cracked.

'O.K! That's it! I'm going down to that damned Embassy and demand that they do something. I've had enough of all of you and of this place. I'm getting out.'

Ambassador Anstey, remembering his previous encounter with Oscar Wolf, was not surprised when his visitor entered looking as if he intended to kick ass.

'I demand to be allowed to go back to the States,' were Oscar's first words, as he marched across the carpet towards the Ambassador's desk. The Ambassador neither rose from his chair, nor extended his hand in welcome.

'You are free to return to the U.S. at any time. There are no Federal or state charges filed against you. Present yourself at any port of entry and there will be no difficulty.'

'What about the body?'

'That's your problem. The Government of the U.S. accepts no responsibility for it. You must dispose of it.'

'But what about his wife? She may not like us dumping him just anywhere.'

'The last I heard she didn't seem to care what happened to him.'

'Can't you ship him back to the States?'

'No!'

'It's that bastard Jason Roberts that got us into this. He was supposed to be on your staff, but in fact he is CIA. Get him to deal with the body.'

'Jason Roberts was a Counselor in this mission. He has been reassigned. There is nothing further to say.'

'I am a Vice President of Bransome Southern University. I won't be treated like this.'

'You are a stupid little man with an inflated view of your own importance. You don't rate here. You are nothing. I can just about bear it when people are competent, but arrogant with it. You are arrogant *and* incompetent. Oscar was incoherent with rage. He launched himself across the desk towards Anstey intending to shake him until he realized how important a Vice President of BSU really was. The Ambassador pressed a buzzer. Two Marines, resplendent in blue dress uniforms, white caps and white gloves, entered the room.

'See that this "gentleman" leaves the Embassy. Immediately!' They each took one of Oscar's arms, lifted him bodily from the floor, and with his legs waving wildly, carried him from the room. Without visible effort, they carried him to the Embassy gates, which were opened by the sentry, and threw him into the dust of the street. The gates clanged shut behind him.

Bruised and humiliated, Oscar Wolf lay there for some moments, gradually becoming aware that the figure of a man was standing over him. Oscar looked up. The man, dressed in a white *jalabia* trimmed with gold, bowed.

'Effendi, may I help you to your feet.' He extended his hand and pulled Oscar upright. Oscar saw that he was a distinguished-looking Arab, bearded, with piercing black eyes. 'Allow me to introduce myself, sir. My name is Sharif. I can see that you are in need of help. I suggest we move away from this place. I would be honored if you would accompany me to my humble home. It is not far from here.' The humble home proved to be an extensive mansion, with courtyards perfumed by flowers, and cooled by fountains. Oscar cleaned himself in a bathroom fitted out as luxuriously as any in Manhattan, and then joined his host, who seated him on a couch, and inquired what he wished to drink.

'Please do not feel inhibited. In this house the desires of our guests are paramount. We have gin, vodka, whisky, brandy...'

'A gin and tonic. Please!' Without Sharif appearing to have to do anything a servant appeared and offered a long glass to Oscar who took it eagerly and drank deeply.

'You are in trouble, my friend. How can I help you?'

'Why should you help me?'

'It is our duty to help those in need. The Koran is very clear on this point.'

'It's a long story.'

'Time is no object. You are a guest in my house. The evening meal is being prepared. We have many bedrooms.' From somewhere deep within the house came the sound of music, and of female laughter. Oscar stretched himself out on the couch, took a deep swig of his gin and tonic, and began to talk.

'It's nearly ten. Where the hell can he be?' In spite of himself, J.T. was worried about what could have happened to Oscar. 'I'm going to call the Embassy.' The information that Vice President Wolf had departed soon after five, and that they had no knowledge of his later movements, did nothing to soothe J.T.'s nerves. 'You don't think that he has ratted on us and flown back to the States?' he gloomily asked Ken Charles.

'Who knows? Anyway, he's not much help in a crisis. Let him go!'

'Sure, but it makes me mad to think that he can get away with murder, literally, and then leave us holding the body.'

But Oscar Wolf had not returned to the States. Three days later he was back in the compound, filled with a new enthusiasm.

'We're all going to El Khalid. Get ready as quickly as possible.'

As they drove through the great gates of El Khalid, they were welcomed by Jason Roberts. He led them inside, and soon they were seated in a cool, comfortable room, being served with long drinks and sweetmeats. A man wearing western clothes joined them, but whom J.T. recognized as the person he had known as His Serene Highness the Governor of El Khalid. Ken Charles spoke up.

'Hey! What's going on? Why have we come here? This place gives me the creeps.' Roberts smiled.

'I'm sorry, Ken. This place is really a CIA safe house. Sharif here runs it for us. The Government of El Baku turns a blind eye. We had to keep you in the dark last time. I won't go into the details now, but I can assure you, you were never in any danger here.'

'You could have fooled me.'

'The point was to fool other people. Anyway, I have brought you all here to explain a plan that I have evolved. This is, I'm sure you will all be aware, a top-secret matter. It has support at the highest level of our Government. Our network, operated through BSU, has been of great value, but it was too diffuse, too thin on the ground. We were concerned about possible threats from many quarters; now we have identified the real problem, the real threat. Muslim fundamentalism; that is going to be the enemy for the next fifty years. We have to combat it, to infiltrate it, to subvert it. That is why we are here. We will start a new religious movement, a kind of global religion that will combine the major elements of Islam, Christianity, Bhuddism, Hinduism, Shintoism. You name it, we'll have it. We shall start it here in El Baku. No other Arab country would allow us to get a foot in the door at present, but eventually their own citizens will set up clandestine churches, and when that happens they will be in real trouble.'

'But none of us are religious. We are not Arabs or Iranians. No one will believe us,' J.T. protested.

'That is the beauty of the plan. It is obvious that this cannot be a CIA plot to undermine Islam, *because* we are not using Arabs, Iraqis or Iranians. That is what the CIA would do. You are just a group of obvious nuts, who would not be used by anybody in their right mind. So you have to be genuine.'

'But we do not know enough about religion.' How can we develop a new religion if we know nothing about the subject?'

'That's where Sharif comes in. He won't be here at El Khalid. He will have to distance himself from this operation, but he will feed us ideas that we can use.'

'Why should we do this? We want to go home. Why should we spend months or years in the desert working on this crazy idea?'

'You won't. You'll be travelling a lot. This will be the headquarters of the sect, but you will be setting up branches all over the world, including the U.S. We shall be targeting Muslims in Russia and China, North Africa and Turkey.

'I want nothing to do with it. I have never signed up for the CIA. I want out.'

'No one leaves the Firm. We have plenty of ways of keeping you in line. Anyway, we've got enough photos of you with several women in very interesting poses, to destroy you, if you don't cooperate.'

'What women? How did you get them?' Jason took a sheaf of photographs from the desk in front of him.

'Well there's Galia here, of course; Akiko, Rebecca, the one's with Rebecca are *very* special. Then we have Aleisha, and Julia, those would cause a real stir in the South. Then there's one of you in bed with Irina...'

'OK! OK! I get your point. You had someone filming me all that time?'

'Oh! That's routine. You're connected with BSU, so we needed to know *everything* about you.'

'What about me?' The Vice President entered the discussion for the first time.

'Oscar, we've got more on you than we have on J.T., and the photos show that your interests are more...varied, than J.T.'s. And we have plenty on Zuwicki and that whole crew.'

'What about Stavros? He's the reason we are here. What are we going to do with him?'

'He is vital to the plan. When Sharif heard about Stavros he knew that we were on to something. He is going to be the central figure in this situation, more important than any of you. We have already removed him from the cold room at the compound. You will see later why he is so significant. But that's enough for now. Over the next few weeks there will be a lot to do. We will develop the plan in detail, but we also want you to have a good time. There will be plenty of good food, a great deal to drink, and lots to do. So, enjoy!'

Indeed, the following weeks were enjoyable for J.T. He and Galia shared a luxurious apartment, servants attended to their every need, they rode together through the desert in the cool of the evenings, afterwards they ate sumptuous meals, and then retired to their apartment to make love, lingeringly and thoroughly, until late into the night. They assumed that their couplings were being recorded for posterity, but far from being inhibited by this knowledge, it fired them to achieve greater heights of noisy satisfaction, and they occasionally directed friendly comments to the unseen cameraman.

J.T., although resentful at being forced to participate in this plot, even took pleasure in the daytime activities, involving as they did the study of the history of world religions. Experts were flown in from Germany and Britain to instruct the conspirators, and frequent briefings were given by Sharif on the approach that they were to adopt. It was an elaborate game, being played out in an Arabian Nights setting.

* * *

Fred Zuwicki, President of Bransome State University, was in a bad mood. The staff of the Office of the President knew he was in a bad mood because he had fired three people that morning. His average was one a week, and it has to be said that this did have the effect of keeping his underlings on their toes, but three in a morning was an indication that the situation was seriously threatening. At this rate they would all be gone by the end of the week. The cause of the President's ill temper was that Vice President Oscar Wolf was due to arrive from El Baku that afternoon, and Zuwicki was undecided about how to deal with him. On the one hand, the fact that Wolf and his lieutenant J.T., had disappeared without warning, taking with them the body of Stavros Williams, and that they had been away from their desks for several weeks, had involved Zuwicki in a considerable amount of work, something from which he expected his subordinates to shield him. On the other hand, the fact that Oscar had not been around had been a considerable relief, and Zuwicki had certainly been happy that Stavros was no longer in the country. The President was inclined to fire Oscar, partly because it was some time since he had fired a Vice President, and he did not want to get out of practice in that department, and partly because he had become bored by Oscar. He and Oscar were very similar in character and it was that which had initially led Zuwicki to appoint a man who had no real qualifications for the job to an important position in the University, but now Oscar's crude incompetence grated on Zuwicki - it was too much like looking in the mirror. He still had not completely made up his mind what to do, when Miss Adams showed Oscar Wolf into the room.

'Where the hell have you been,' was his greeting to Oscar, although Zuwicki knew exactly where Oscar had been and what he had been doing.

'Hi, Fred! Good to see you.' Oscar slumped down on a couch. Zuwicki decided definitely to fire him. 'I am here to tell you,' Oscar continued, 'that we are really on to a good thing this time.'

'Which is?'

'Religion. We can become the center of *the* biggest movement in the history of the world.'

'Why should we do that?'

'Because there is money in it. Lot's of money.' Zuwicki began to revise his opinion of Oscar. 'We can build an enormous Ziggurat on campus.'

'A Zig...what?'

'A Ziggurat. It was a kind of temple in ancient Mesopotamia. It was like a pyramid, but instead of sloping sides it had steps all the way up. So the High Priest could perform at the top. It will attract millions.'

'People or dollars?'

'Both. We set up an Institute of Pantheism. We have a television station to broadcast the services. We collect money to finance it, and we run the whole thing from BSU.'

'Where do we get the money to build it?'

'The CIA will give it to us.'

'Why?'

'Because they think that this new religion will destroy the Muslim fundamentalists.'

'Will it?'

'Hell, Fred, I don't know. What does it matter? We get the bucks.'

'What about the Faculty? They might object.'

'You've never worried about that before.'

'True, but we've never done anything quite like this before.'

'We can give them all big travel grants. That always shuts them up.'

Zuwicki pondered all this new information. Maybe he ought to wait a little before firing Oscar. Then a thought struck him.

'Why do we need this Zig thing? Why not just a big church?'

'That's the whole point. This religion is meant to appeal to everybody. So we start with a temple from the earliest religion of all.

Then we add on bits of all the other religions. It will go down big.' Zuwicki was beginning to warm to the idea.

'O.K. But you mentioned a High Priest. Who will that be, then?'

'Didn't I tell you? Ken Charles, that's who it will be.'

* * *

As the sun rose and flooded the desert surrounding El Khalid with brilliance, Galia stirred and shook J.T. awake. He absent-mindedly patted her bare bottom, and turned over to resume his sleep.

'Get up, you slob! Jason has asked me to design costumes for us. I want you to give me some ideas.'

'Know nothing about it.'

'Pull yourself together. I need your help.' J.T. opened his eyes, and then shut them again as the strong light struck his retinas.

'I feel awful. What did we do last night?'

'We ate until midnight, we drank until 2 a.m., and we made love until 3.30. What's your problem?'

'What time is it now?'

'It's already 7.30, and we've done nothing.'

'I'm dying. Let me depart in peace.'

'J.T.! This is serious. What kind of costumes should we wear? Do you think I would look good dressed as a nun?' This concept was so bizarre that J.T. sat up and scrutinized the beautiful naked body seated by him on the bed. Even in his fragile condition his hands began, almost of their own volition, to stretch out towards her. Galia pushed him away.

'Please, J.T. Help me!'

'O.K. You have to realize that we mustn't seem to be connected with any established religion, certainly not Christianity; but on the other hand we must not *offend* any other religion. So you cannot look like a nun, but you have also to remember that Muslim women must cover their hair.'

'So what do I do?' J.T. gave up all thought of further sleep.

'Let's have breakfast, and then we'll talk about it.'

The problems of devising a religion that would please all and displease none were not limited to the mode of dress to be adopted. It became clear at an early stage that it would be very difficult to adopt any kind of symbol or icon that did not offend in some respect. So the new religion, of necessity, became one of extreme simplicity and, indeed, a kind of purity. It combined humanistic ideals with a benevolent deity; it expressed sympathy for human frailty without condoning excess. A careful analysis was made of the rituals of the major religions of the world. Rather than try to combine them, as Oscar Wolf thought they were doing, the only acceptable solution was to reduce ritual to an absolute minimum, consisting only of actions that could be reconciled with the practices of those religions, without aping them.

The first public service was held at BSU. J.T., Galia and Ken Charles flew in from El Khalid with twenty-five Supporters who had been recruited from around the world, from Asia, Africa, Europe and Latin America. Jason Roberts and Sharif remained discreetly somewhere in the background. There had not been time to build the Ziggurat, which was to be constructed out of blocks of stone. It would eventually be sixty feet high, surrounded by an arena banked with enough seating to accommodate several thousand people. At the summit would be a level surface for the conduct of the ceremonies. Today's ceremony was to be performed in the football stadium on a specially built wooden structure, consisting of a number of staircases leading up to a platform at the top. Although the event had received a great deal of advance publicity, only a few hundred people had assembled by the time that the service was to begin. The atmosphere was jovial, most of those present treating it as a "happening". Laughter and bantering conversation echoed around the almost empty stadium. There was a complete absence of reverence. When the procession of celebrants filed onto the platform, the tone changed, but only marginally. Out of common politeness the laughing and talking were subdued but not eliminated.

They were dressed in long, flowing robes, fashioned after the style of the ancient Celtic druids. Each garment had a hood that could be left casually draped over the head, or drawn tightly across the brow. The robes were of different colors - white, green, yellow, blue, brown, and black. The central figure, that of Ken Charles, was robed in bright scarlet. They positioned themselves in a semi-circle facing a podium on which had been set a tall, rectangular object covered with a white cloth. Ken Charles approached the podium, the worshippers around him sank to their knees, and as he raised his arms in a dramatic gesture, the cloth fell away, revealing a glass case, more than six feet in height, and in it the bearded, robed figure of Stavros Wiliams. Stavros's face projected a sense of calm, of peace, of total serenity. The effect of this apparition on the spectators was profound. They fell silent.

They looked up at the figure in awe. Many sank to their knees and raised their hands prayerfully. Ken Charles was intoning a liturgy. The Supporters filed down from the Ziggurat, and each taking a member of the audience by the hand, led them one by one up the steps to stand before the figure of Stavros. There each person expressed himself or herself in any way that seized them, some standing with bowed head, some kneeling, some prostrating themselves on the floor, and then moving down the other side of the Ziggurat, to stand subdued, and in some cases tearfully staring up at the vision above.

J.T. had not taken part in the ceremony. He felt that he had discharged his responsibility by being the stage manager, and did not actually have to participate in the performance. In fact the whole business was distasteful to him, and it was only Jason Roberts's threats that kept him involved in the charade. He had daily contemplated open defiance, but he was seriously concerned about the consequences if Roberts were to use the photographs. He suspected that no other university would give him a job, because Roberts would not hesitate to send prints to any prospective employer if J.T. defied him.

J.T. followed Ken Charles into the stadium, to the room that he and the male Supporters were using as a robing chamber. Charles pulled his scarlet robe over his head and, standing before the mirror, began to rearrange his hair.

'I think that went well,' he said.

'Astonishingly well.' J.T. was puzzled. 'It seemed as if they were really moved by it all.' Ken replaced his jacket.

'It was quite natural for them to respond to the solemnity of the occasion.'

'Well, yes! But some of them were in tears. How could they take it so seriously?' Ken, ready to leave, turned to address his friend directly.

'Look, J.T.! I don 't think that you should adopt this carping attitude. Religion is of great importance to many of us, and when people have a deeply spiritual experience, perhaps for the first time, it is bound to affect them.' J.T.'s puzzlement turned to open astonishment.

'A deeply spiritual experience? Ken, are you beginning to believe this stuff? We made it up, remember?'

'That doesn't mean that it isn't valid. Who knows what mysterious hand lay behind what we did, who was directing us.'

'Mysterious hand? That was Jason Roberts, and you know what he's up to.' Ken began a stately move towards the doorway.

'I think, J.T. that you should show more respect. Some things cannot be explained by simple logic. Sometimes we just know what we have to do.' He drew himself to his full height, and went out to meet those members of the congregation who were still in the stadium, waiting patiently for the chance to speak to him. J.T. stared after him. The last time he had heard that tone of voice was when Stavros had been explaining his sewage scheme to him on Sakhalin.

In bed that night, J .T .lay on his back, staring at the ceiling. Galia was at his side, her head on his chest, his arm around her shoulders. ‘You know, it was strange today,' he said. 'When you and Ken and the others were on the platform I was watching the people there. At first they were treating the whole thing as a joke, laughing and talking. Then, when Stavros was unveiled, the atmosphere just changed totally. They went quiet, some were crying, others were kind of awestruck. I can't understand it.'

'I can. It affected me in the same way.' J.T. pushed her away and sat up.

'You? It got to you? I can't believe it.'

'I find it difficult to believe it myself, but I was up there, remember. When that cloth came off, it was as if I had been hit between the eyes. I still feel kind of shell-shocked. Ken was *really* impressive.' J.T. shook his head slowly in disbelief. That night, for the first time for several weeks, they went to sleep without making love.

In the weeks and months that followed, the retinue moved from town to town, country to country. They began in South America, where they met with strong resistance from the Catholic hierarchy, but with enormous enthusiasm from the *peons.* A sweep through Eastern Europe was a complete failure, with almost empty halls wherever they appeared. They flirted with the fringes of Islam, in the Lebanon and in Northern India, but in both places they were met only with polite curiosity. After a brief recuperation in El Khalid it was agreed that they should return to Bransome where the Ziggurat had now been built.

The site chosen was a mile away from the campus, set in a secluded park. The Ziggurat had been constructed out of rich basalt. The polished stone gleamed darkly, a mysterious pile, with steps rising up to the top, front and rear. At the summit a kind of altar had been erected, with a high back, set rigidly upright, and the glass case containing Stavros was already in position, covered with a white cloth. Completely circling the Ziggurat was a bank of earth, nearly as high as the Ziggurat itself, covered with turf, and with stone seats fashioned from the same black stone, arranged in tiers around it. Access was through tunnels that pierced the circle at its base.

Word of the earlier ceremony had spread and more than a thousand people were present when Ken Charles led the celebrants up the steps to the summit. Since that first occasion little had changed in the ceremony, except that Ken Charles now had a more prominent part to play, addressing the assembly for some minutes before he unveiled the figure at the center of the stage. This had the effect of heightening the anticipation of the audience, so that when he turned and flung his arms on high, and the cloth dropped from the altar, a deep sigh was expelled from hundreds of bodies. The scenes which followed were extraordinary. Some preferred to ascend the stairs on their knees, others climbed with their hands held high above them, but all were deeply moved. Many were reluctant to move away from Stavros once they had reached the space in front of him, staring up at his face as if transfixed The Supporters gently moved them on. It was difficult to bring the ceremony to an end, as many worshippers, for that is what they were, tried to ascend the steps twice or more. Eventually, the attendants were able to clear the people from the arena, and the glass case containing the body of Stavros was carefully carried down.

Jason Roberts looked angrily around the room. 'I don't understand it. We are getting nowhere in the rest of the world, but here in the States we seem to have started some kind of forest fire. They are going crazy out there. So far there are plans to build thirteen Ziggurats in Los Angeles alone!'

'And what is wrong with that exactly?' Ken Charles was frosty. 'It simply reflects the fact that people need the kind of spiritual comfort that we are giving them.'

'And it's bringing in a lot of cash. Fred Zuwicki is happy,' Oscar said. Ken Charles rose from his chair, his hand raised in admonition.

'I've had enough of this. The University has no right to use religion as a fund-raising activity. It is scandalous, it's...blasphemous!' Oscar looked at him in amazement, but before he could speak Galia burst out:

'I agree! Any money that is donated ought to be passed on to charity, not used to provide a new twenty-room mansion for the President of the University.' Oscar scowled. As they all knew, the plan was that when Zuwicki moved into his new University house, Oscar would get the present presidential home, which, although it consisted of a mere fifteen rooms, was still a cut above Oscar's ten-roomed hovel.

'This is all beside the point,' Jason Roberts tried to regain the initiative. 'This whole operation was begun as a way of undermining the spread of Muslim fundamentalism. All we have achieved so far is to upgrade Zuwicki's domestic arrangements. That's not going to look too good in my report.' Ken Charles was still on his feet.

'I warn you,' he said. 'I will not tolerate this. Neither you,' he gestured towards Roberts, 'nor you,' he fixed Oscar with a look, 'will use this movement to further your own rotten ends,' and he swept from the room. J.T. had not taken part in the discussion, feeling as he did that his career, perhaps his life, had reached its nadir, and that nothing now could possibly save it, so it was Galia who broke the silence. She crossed to where J.T. was sitting.

'I'm sorry, J.T. I'm moving in with Ken. He needs me. I'm really sorry,' and she followed Ken Charles from the room.

* * *

Jason Roberts was in earnest conference with the Assistant Secretary.

'This man Charles is totally out of control. He seems to think that he really is some kind of prophet. He won't take instructions. And now he wants to break free from Bransome Southern. He says that they are just a pack of greedy crooks.' The Assistant Secretary stood looking through the window at the tourists crowding the Mall.

'Well, he's right there. Probably he wants the money for himself.'

'No, I don't think so.' Roberts looked worried. 'I think it is more serious than that. If he just wanted to make a profit we could deal with him, but he doesn't want money. I think he really believes that he has a mission in the world.'

'To do what?'

'To do good.'

'Oh, that! Then we really are in trouble. What can we do about it?

* * *

Part 6

THE CONCLUSION

J.T. sat in his office in the College of International Affairs. It was like old times. Both he and Oscar Wolf were back in their former roles. Jason Roberts had released them from their obligations to the Institute of Pantheism. The decision had come very suddenly.

'We have decided to let Ken Charles go it alone with this religion thing. You have done everything that we asked. Thank you!'

'What about the photos? Can we have the negatives?'

'They are the property of the Federal Government. I don't have the authority. Sorry!'

J.T. settled back into the quiet routine of a small college town. The immediate sense of relief at no longer being involved in an operation in which he did not believe soon gave way to feelings of loneliness and isolation. Things had changed during the months of his absence. Galia was, of course, travelling around the world with Ken Charles, and others had also found consolation elsewhere.

Akiko Takahashi had left her job at BSU and had opened a Japanese restaurant in the town. She had met Bruce, an antipodean, who had come to the U.S. to set up a course in TAFL -Teaching Australian as a Foreign Language - but whose accent was so harsh that no-one could understand a word he said. He was, however, an extremely good cook, having spent many years in the outback living off the local fauna. Under Akiko's tuition he soon adapted to Japanese cuisine, and together they ran a very successful business. Beneath his rough Australian exterior he was really a very gentle human being, and Akiko came to love him deeply.

Irina Williams had spent many hours listening to Dr. Richard Chalmers trying to convince her of the importance of pursuing the true cause of her husband's death, until one evening she decided that there was only one way to take the good doctor's mind off that subject, and they spent four and a half hours in the study of general comparative anatomy, until Richard could take no more, and fell asleep in her arms. As she pressed his head close to her bosom, she smiled seraphically. She had made inquiries about the style of life and income of American medics, and as a consequence she had decided that it was her duty to give Richard every kind of support. They were married in the Episcopal Church in Bransome. Aleisha, tiring of being trapped in J.T.'s old apartment with her maid, had gone back to belly-dancing, and could be seen performing twice nightly at the Bransome Holiday Inn. When the performances were over she held court in the newly designated Arabian Nights Bar, and the room occupation rate by corporate account client's went so high that the walls of the manager's office were filled with special commendations. J.T., desperate for female company, had tried to tempt Rebecca Vogelsang back to Bransome, but after a number of fruitless attempts to contact her on the telephone he had written to her and received a reply which clearly indicated that her current investigations into managerial behavior were absorbing all her energies.

As is so often the case when someone who is 'indispensable' is away, the office routines in the College of International Affairs had been gradually adjusted to take account of J.T.'s absence, and he now found it difficult to reinsert himself into the administrative process; the members of the team jealously guarding their new responsibilities. As a consequence he spent long periods in his office staring into space, his mind ranging over the events of the recent past, and the relationships that had waxed and waned. He felt that his life, at the age of thirty-three, was already in decline, and that there was little left to look forward to.

The main burden of the extra work that resulted from J.T. taking off on his travels had fallen on Janice Hart. She had in effect replaced him, without formal recognition of her new role by the University, either in salary or in title. On his return, J.T. had suggested to her that she ought to be promoted or recompensed in some way for the work she had done, but she appeared reluctant for him to raise the matter with Oscar. She presented the same cool, competent, detached manner towards him that she had formerly adopted, and for his part J.T. saw in her simply the valued colleague that she had always been.

Oscar Wolf's career scaled new heights. The inflow of cash from the Ziggurat movement continued to increase, in spite of Ken Charles's opposition, as Bransome Southern University had carefully taken out a patent on Stavros as a 'medium of communication', and received royalties from his every public appearance. Zuwicki had moved into his new mansion, and was transported everywhere in a chauffeur-driven, white Rolls-Royce. Oscar had also taken up his new abode, and had been given a lavish entertainment allowance so that almost every evening he was host to a party of one kind or another. Some of these parties became rather wild, attracting the attention of the local press and on one or two memorable occasions of the local police as well. There was talk of nude bathing parties in the big pool at the back of the property, and of the uses to which the bedrooms were put, but these rumors were never substantiated and the deployment of large detachments of campus police discouraged the attentions of busybodies.

The urgent buzzing of his telephone broke J.T.'s reverie. Oscar's voice rasped in his ear.

'Get over here. Something's come up.'

Oscar was in a really bad mood. A year ago J.T. would have been terrified by the signs - the ferocious looks, the angry voice - but no longer. He saw Oscar for what he was, a bully of mediocre intellect.

'What's the problem, Oscar?'

'The problem is that Jason Roberts wants to pull the plug on Ken Charles and his whole operation.'

'That's not surprising. It's not working out the way he planned it.'

'So what! Who cares? Ken has done a good job.'

'You mean he has brought in a lot of money to the University?'

'Too damn right he has. And we want to keep it coming in.'

'Who are "we"?'

'Zuwicki and me.'

'Zuwicki and I.'

'O.K. I'm glad you agree with us.'

'That's not what I meant, Oscar. I meant... Oh, never mind!' J.T. continued. 'Why does Roberts want to stop Ken? Even if he's not destroying Islam, why interfere with his "mission"?'

'It seems that the damn fool is getting involved in politics. He's making pronouncements during his so-called services. Urging people to support liberal causes, even endorsing candidates for election. Some Senators and Congressmen are pretty riled up about it. Religious figures don't normally do that. Support liberal ideas, I mean.'

J.T. realized that the situation was more serious than he had thought.

'Yes, I can see that would irritate some people.'

'Damn right! So what are we going to do?'

'Surely, this is a matter between Jason and Ken.'

'What! Do you realize how much money we stand to lose if Ken's operation folds?'

'Anyway, what can Jason do? He's not financing Ken any longer.'

'Do? What can he do? We're talking CIA here.' Oscar was becoming hysterical again. 'Sometimes, J.T., I get the feeling that you are not really on board. I overlooked your behavior in Europe and El Baku. I guess you were under strain, but if you don't pull yourself together we may have to part company.' With that he indicated that the interview was at an end, and J.T. left the room.

'The fact is that I don't really care if I do leave Bransome. I'm fed up with Oscar, Zuwicki, and that whole crew. They are such hypocrites. They are supposed to be running a place of learning, but all they are concerned about is money and power.' Janice Hart stared open-mouthed at J.T. She had never seen him like this, so filled with anger. On his return from his interview with Oscar she had been in the outer office, and on impulse he had called her in and told her what Oscar had said. 'I've a good mind to go back there, and chuck this job in straight away,' he concluded grimly.

Janice involuntarily placed her hand on his arm 'Oh, J.T.! Don't do that. Look! Why don't we go out to lunch, and talk about it.'

At lunch, over sandwiches and coffee, J.T. poured out his sense of outrage at the manipulative style of the administration of BSU, its false values, and the unpleasant people who headed it up.

'And now they want me to protect Ken Charles against Jason Roberts's schemes, purely because they want to safeguard their business interests in his "mission". They don't give a damn about what he is trying to do, or what he stands for.'

'What will you do?'

'I'm in a Catch 22 situation. I either cooperate with the CIA, or I try to keep Zuwicki in the style of life to which he has become accustomed. What a choice!'

'Surely the main thing is to help Ken. He seems pretty sincere, and that's important.'

'That's true! You know, it's strange how people change. Ken Charles always seemed such a geek, interested only in stupid things, and now he's conducting this crusade, and I have more respect for him than I have for any of the other people in this damn university.' Once again Janice felt the need to comfort him, squeezing his hand in hers. 'The odd thing,' he continued, 'is that Stavros seemed to go through the same kind of transformation. Most of his life Stavros was a real jerk. He didn't give a damn for anybody except himself. Now, look at him, he's become a saint!'

'Yes, but he *is* dead.' She would have liked to add, 'and we are alive, and should make the most of it.' But she did not.

'True, but he changed well before his death. When I visited him in Sakhalin, he was a different man. He had undergone a religious conversion.' Janice leaned towards him across the table. Her expression was earnest.

'J.T.! I have wanted to tell you about Stavros. I feel so guilty. I am responsible for his death, and for so much else that has happened.' J.T. looked at her in amazement.

'Why on earth should you be responsible for Stavros's death?'

'Because I...did something, which unhinged him, and changed his whole life,' and she went on to describe the episode in the grass. 'All that has happened since then is the result of what I did, and now it seems that it might be the reason for you to leave Bransome.' She was close to tears.

'Janice! I had no idea. But it's not your fault. You mustn't blame yourself.' They continued discussing the situation for some time without arriving at a conclusion. J.T. consulted his watch. 'It's time we were getting back to the office.' He looked at her gratefully.

'Thank you! You've been like a sister to me.' She stared bleakly at him, and rose to leave.

* * *

'For God's sake! He's gone too far this time. He's come out in favor of National Health Care.' Jason Roberts banged the desk in front of him. Unfortunately, the desk he was banging belonged to President Fred Zuwicki. Zuwicki fixed him with a ferocious glare.

'Don't you give a damn about the freedom of speech in this country. What about the First Amendment?'

'I care about the First Amendment as much as you do. That is, as long as it suits me. I demand that you stop him.'

'I can't. Even if I wanted to. And I don't want to.'

'You are going to regret this Zuwicki,' and Roberts slammed out of the office.

* * *

'J.T., I don't understand what's happening.' Ken Charles had flown into Bransome, and hurried straight to J.T.'s office. 'Galia and I have been called to Washington. They want us to testify before some congressional committee. They say we are "subversives", using religion to promote liberal causes.'

'Well you are. The trouble is that you are too good at it. You're getting a following.'

'I just say what I think. Is that a crime?'

'That depends on what you think. Look, Ken, why not draw back from political issues. Just go on with the religious stuff and keep away from endorsing candidates for office or telling the Government where they went wrong.'

'The "religious stuff", as you call it, is meaningless unless it has some application to the way you conduct your life. Surely you see that.'

'I see the most amazing situation. We invented this religion because the CIA thought, insanely, that it might be a challenge to the influence of Muslim fundamentalism. Now you are using St.Stavros to push liberal ideas, and Fred Zuwicki and Oscar Wolf, whose political values are drawn from Genghis Khan and Attila the Hun respectively, are trying to protect you from those nasty conservatives in Congress. The whole thing is bizarre.'

'I think you might be a little more sympathetic to Ken and me,' Galia interjected. 'After all, we are your friends.'

'O.K. I'll do what I can, but for the moment I don't see what I can do.'

* * *

'Today, this University stands at a critical point in its history.' President Zuwicki, splendid in cap and gown, was making his Commencement address. 'For hundreds of years in this country we have defended academic freedom and the right of our citizens to express their views without fear. Now we are faced with a challenge to these hallowed rights.' Serried ranks of brightly robed academics observed him with disbelief, hardly able to restrain the shocked gasps that rose in their throats. This was the man who systematically harried any instructor who expressed views with which he disagreed, and who had ensured that tenure was denied to teachers who expressed the slightest criticism of his administration. 'Voices are raised today in our land decrying the sincerity of a member of this University who is preaching a gospel in which he believes. He is a man of unimpeachable integrity, yet he is labeled as a subversive influence, and even the administration of this great and renowned University is subjected to intolerable pressure to try to silence him. I pledge that we will support him and his work, as an earnest of our commitment to the most sacred values of our society.' There was a bemused murmur of agreement, and a splattering of applause.

* * *

'J.T., we've got to get rid of Ken Charles. He's a dope.' Oscar Wolf was pacing his office carpet like a caged animal. 'Zuwicki is hopping mad. It's either Ken Charles or us.'

'What has he done now?'

'He's starting a new political party to contest the next mid-term elections. It's to be called "The Keep America Right Party". Zuwicki said he was to clear his desk by 5 p.m. today. Trouble is, he doesn't have a desk.'

'But last week the President said that he would support Ken whatever happened.'

'Look, don't try to understand the higher politics. You're not equipped for it. We've got to find a replacement. We've got to keep the money coming in. What about Galia? A High Priestess might go down big. And she's quite a looker!'

'She would not desert Ken. She is devoted to him.'

'She gave you the elbow when it suited her.'

'That was different. I think you will have to look for someone else. And frankly, I don't want to be involved. It is nothing to do with International Programs.' As J.T. left Wolf gave him a malevolent look.

* * *

'Ken has been arrested.' Galia was distraught. 'He's been accused of embezzling University funds. It's ridiculous. He wouldn't do that.' Janice had found Galia weeping in the outer office and brought her in to J.T.

J.T. tried to comfort her.

'They'll never make that stick. Zuwicki has framed him. They want to shut him up.'

'We've got to do something, J.T. We can't let them get away with this.' Janice entreated. She was almost as upset as Galia.

'The University has already issued a statement,' Galia sobbed. 'Because of the charges against him he no longer has any connection with BSU.'

'I'll go and bail him out'

* * *

There were more people in the arena than for any of the earlier services; the news of the arrest had spread fast. The benches were crowded, rank upon rank, up to the topmost layer. The atmosphere was electric; anticipation was high, but for what no one knew. The glass cabinet, shrouded in its white cloth, was in place. The procession of acolytes entered, and began the climb to the top of the Ziggurat. At the rear walked a figure dressed in scarlet robes, but instead of the tall, impressive form of Ken Charles this High Priest was diminutive, and of shambling gait. Janice, standing next to J.T. near the foot of the steps, gasped:

'It's Oscar!'

There was a murmur of disapproval from the crowd. As Oscar began the ascent of the steps, the normally pious assembly became increasingly agitated and angry. People began to shout abuse, and shrill whistling rang across the arena. The Supporters, troubled by the noise, paused in their climb, and turned around to face Oscar as he continued to mount the steps. Uncertain whether to continue on or to confront Oscar, the robed and hooded figures looked down the steps, and there at the base of the Ziggurat stood Ken Charles, his scarlet hood thrown back, and beside him Galia. As they began to climb the steps, the crowd began to clap. The Supporters waited till Ken and Galia reached the level where Oscar stood, and when after a moment's hesitation he moved to one side and allowed Ken and Galia to pass, the procession continued on its way to the summit to the acclaim of the crowd. From that moment, the service was the most moving that they had experienced, and when the saint was unveiled, nearly every member of the congregation fell to their knees, arms raised high. Ken Charles turned, and was about to begin his address.

Two groups of men, each six in number, emerged from the tunnels under the stands and began to race up the steps at the front and rear of the Ziggurat. They were dressed in dark combat gear with handguns strapped round their waists. They reached the plateau at the summit of the Ziggurat, and six of them ran straight towards the glass case holding St. Stavros and began to lower it, whilst the others tried to secure Ken Charles and Galia. The shocked Supporters, becoming aware of what was happening, ran to the rescue, grappling with the intruders. As the glass case became horizontal, the commandos began to run for the top of the steps at the front of the Ziggurat, carrying the case with surprising ease. There they were met by ten or twelve men and women determined to prevent the body of the saint from being taken away. A tug-of-war ensued, with the wildly tipping glass coffin being pushed first one way then the other. Some of the attackers who had been restraining Ken and Galia, detached themselves and rushed to the aid of their fellows, who were hard pressed to withstand the greater numbers of the enraged Supporters. The sudden force of four or five men hitting the melee at the edge of the platform gave it a momentum which resulted in a total loss of control, and in front of the horrified gaze of the worshippers surrounding the Ziggurat the coffin fell onto the top step, smashing into a thousand pieces as it hit the dark basalt. The body of the saint shot out, and began to tumble crazily down the steps and as it fell it began to disintegrate. First, the face, which proved to be no more than a mask, dropped from the head as it smashed on a step, then an arm, and then a leg were torn from the body. Shortly before the corpse reached the foot of the steps, the torso itself was rent asunder, and before the astonished eyes of the assembled worshippers a great quantity of dollar bills, of varying denominations, burst out and began to drift about in the light breeze of a Bransome Sunday afternoon.

*   *   *

‘I just can't understand why they did that!' Janice was near to tears. 'Ken and Galia weren't doing any harm.' J.T. and Janice had finally left the arena after the crowds had dispersed. After Stavros had disintegrated, the attackers had swiftly fled from the scene, but they had carried Ken and Galia off with them, bundling them into cars that had driven away with screeching tires.

'They have become too much of a threat, that's the problem. The CIA manipulates the whole program, and now I am not sure that the reasons that Jason Roberts gave us for embarking on the business of this new religion were really what was behind it. When you think about it we were crazy to imagine that we could undermine Islam in that way. What we do seem to have done is to cause some kind of crisis here in the U.S. Ken and Galia have been called to give evidence to a congressional committee, and if they do that the balloon really will go up. So they had to be removed.'

'You don't think that they are dead?' Janice's face was beginning to crumple. 'If Stavros was killed...'

'No, I don't think that,' J.T. replied hurriedly, without conviction, 'but I've got to find out.'

J.T. had been in the office of President Zuwicki only twice before. Then its grandeur and gravitas had overawed him. On those earlier occasions, however, he had not stormed in uninvited, banged the presidential desk, and demanded an immediate explanation.

'What the hell is this all about?' Zuwicki scowled. 'I don't have to give you explanations. If there is any explaining to be done, you'll do it.'

J.T. leaned across the desk. 'If you do not tell me what is going on, I swear I will take you by your miserable little neck and STRANGLE YOU.' Zuwicki recoiled. His right foot crept towards the buzzer which would alert the campus police to the fact that their boss was in mortal danger, but before he could reach it, J.T. had moved swiftly around the desk, and swung Zuwicki's chair round so that the younger man towered over the cringing administrator. 'Where are Ken Charles and Galia Ionescou?'

'How should I know? Who are these people?'

'They are your employees. Your colleagues. They were kidnapped yesterday on this campus by armed men, on the campus of the university of which you are president. Didn't you hear?'

'Oh them! Yes, I heard something about it. It's being investigated.'

'Look, Zuwicki! Either Ken and Galia are set free within twenty-four hours, or I will go to the newspapers, and I will tell them everything I know about International Programs, about Oscar Wolf, about Jason Roberts, and about you.'

'About me? What do you know about me?'

'I know that Oscar Wolf was just carrying out your orders,' J.T. lied. 'That you have been working with the CIA from the beginning, and that you have been taking regular payoffs for services rendered.'

'Zuwicki tells me that you are making him miserable,' Jason Roberts said. 'That's not very nice of you. Even if he is about the nastiest piece of work I have had the misfortune to be associated with.' Roberts had arrived unannounced in J.T.'s office only hours after the latter's conversation with his superior. 'He says that you want to denounce him to the newspapers. Why would you want to do that?'

'Look, Jason! If anything happens to Ken and Galia, I swear I will see that you, Zuwicki, and Oscar go to jail. If it's the last thing I do.'

'O.K., calm down. Nothing is going to happen to them. They are just being kept out of circulation for a while. I promise you that they will be all right. Galia will be sent back to England, and Ken will be given a good job back in El Baku.'

'Just like Stavros I suppose.' Jason Roberts looked weary.

'J.T., I assure you that I had nothing to do with that. It was a mistake. It's true that we wanted to keep Stavros quiet. He found out too much about our operations in Siberia. It was embarrassing. We had been running the SNCF, the Siberian National Cultural Fighters that is, for several years. They did a lot of jobs for us in the early eighties. Then they went wild and started to do unauthorized operations on their own. So we stopped paying them. That made them mad, and when they heard about Stavros's pipeline they decided to blow it up to get their own back. Eventually Stavros contacted them, and they gave him the low-down on all our business in Siberia, including what our "engineers" were up to. That's what he was going to reveal at the dinner that night.'

'So you had him killed.'

'No, it wasn't like that.' Roberts's expression was pained. 'We had a staff meeting to discuss the situation, and Oscar was there. He had just been forced to attend a University Drama Society performance of T.S. Eliot's "Murder in the Cathedral", and he kept muttering, "Who will rid

me of this turbulent priest?" Well, this young fellow was present at the meeting. He had been working for some time on different ways of eliminating people like Castro and Saddam Hussein, but the Agency wouldn't let him test them out, so he took Oscar at his word. I swear that nobody gave him authority to kill Stavros, and I was pretty annoyed with him afterwards. I expect my people to consult me about that kind of thing. Anyway, there was an internal inquiry and he was switched to another section. There will always be a black mark on his record, and it could affect his chances of promotion adversely. A pity, because he's pretty good at his work.'

'That's clear from the job he did on Stavros. It must have been difficult for you.' The sincerity in J.T.s' voice indicated how deeply he sympathized with Jason's dilemma. The tall man looked doubtfully at J.T.

'So are you satisfied? No more threats to Zuwicki.'

'No, I can't say I'm totally happy about all this. What was the point of this whole religious bit? Did you really think that it would bring Islam to its knees?' Jason roared with laughter.

'Oh, that was really great. One of the best things we have ever done. I was sure that you would just ridicule the whole idea. Particularly with your academic background.' J.T. swallowed hard. 'But Sharif said that you would run with it,' Jason continued, 'and he was right.'

'What was it about then?'

'Well, we're always needing to move money about the world, large sums of cash to pay people off. So what better way than in the body of a saint? It worked really well until Ken began to get above himself, and Oscar got greedy and thought that he could grab a whole consignment for himself. So we had to close the whole thing down. We made a bit of a botch of it as it happens, but it should turn out all right. Anyway, can I assume that we shall not have any more trouble from you?' J.T. took his time before replying.

'On two conditions. First, that I hear from Galia and Ken that they are safely in England or El Baku.' He paused.

'And the second condition?'

'That Oscar Wolf is fired from his job at BSU.'

* * *

'Why should I fire Oscar?' Zuwicki had joined J.T. and Jason Roberts at the latter's request. Roberts shrugged.

'Ask him.' He gestured towards J.T. Zuwicki fixed the younger man with a malevolent glare.

'So! Why?'

'Because a man like that should not work for a university. Look at the things he has done. He is a disgrace to American education.'

Zuwicki turned to look out of the window at the peaceful campus scene. He considered for a moment and then turned back to his two companions.

'O.K. I will guarantee that Oscar will resign as Vice President for International Affairs immediately. Within the month we will hold a farewell dinner for him. And you, J.T., can make the speech bidding him farewell.'

'Why me?'

'I think it would be highly appropriate, as you are the cause of his resignation.

* * *'

In the five year's since J.T.'s appointment to the faculty of Bransome Southern University he had never felt as spaced out as at this moment. Sitting near to the President of BSU, he was soon to rise to give the valedictory address for one of the President's closest henchmen, Vice President Oscar Wolf. The Great Hall of the Alumni Building had been cleared of its usual rows of metal seats to make way for tables set for the dining pleasure of the Trustees, top university administrators, faculty members, local business people and politicos, and their partners. The hall buzzed with their conversation, bursts of laughter rang out, and raucous remarks were shouted from one table to the next as the liberal supply of alcohol took its toll. Waiters and waitresses bustled between the tables, juggling trays loaded with plates and calling orders for drinks and water to their colleagues. Dessert and coffee had been served. Zuwicki nodded to J.T. It was time.

'President Zuwicki has asked me to deliver the address this evening to mark the resignation of Oscar Wolf as Vice President for International Affairs. This is indeed an important day in the history of Bransome Southern University. I have worked with Oscar for several years, traveled the world with him, and closely observed his administrative style. Few people are better qualified than I to give you the real low-down on this man.' Some members of the audience tittered. What a hope! 'Perhaps in order to get things in the proper perspective, I should say something about myself, otherwise you may be puzzled about what I

have to tell you.' J.T. paused and looked around at the faces turned towards him. He could pick out Janice, her eyes cast down, rather embarrassed that he might possibly make a fool of himself. 'I am, essentially and above all else, a coward.' This time the laughter was more robust 'If you did not know that you would never understand how it was that I came to accept what I did accept, or to behave as I did behave.' The audience sat up a little straighter. This was definitely not the tone they had expected. 'I needed a job desperately. And when I got one, working for Oscar Wolf, I was determined to hold on to it at all costs. And that's how I got drawn into this incredible mess. I mean, of course, the administration of Bransome Southern University.' There was a momentary disbelieving silence, and then an outburst of wild applause from the faculty members present. The Trustees, Zuwicki and his minions glowered.

'The other thing that you should know about me is that I am naive. I know that most of you will find this difficult to believe, but it took me a long time, years in fact, to realize that Wolf and Zuwicki were not really interested in education.' Shouts of "You must be kidding!" from some of the more inebriated members of the Faculty.

'No! No! I mean it. I really thought that beneath their ugly exteriors there burned a passion for the advancement of knowledge, for the enlightenment of the masses. But in reality all they were concerned about were their salaries, and their perks, but above all for the exercise of power. They love power. They glory in it.' The chorus replied 'We could have told you that.'

'I know that now. I guess most everybody in this university knew it except me. That's why this evening I ask for your understanding, for your forgiveness. You probably all thought I was one of them, and I can see why you would. But let me dwell for a moment on the central character of this tragedy. Stavros Williams was well known to many of you. He was a typical rising young BSU administrator. He poured scorn on the likes of Zuwicki, but in reality he was a Zuwicki in the making, an arrogant, opinionated, self-serving person, whose basic incompetence led him to treat people with contempt.' The face of the President of the University was now puce. He stood up, banged the table with his fist so hard that two glasses fell over, and he shouted: 'Get out! You're fired.' His wife took his arm and dragged him back down to his seat. Nothing was going to make her miss this. It was the most exciting thing that had happened in many years.

'But Stavros underwent a change of heart, what he himself described as a spiritual conversion,' J.T. continued. 'I won't tell you exactly how that came about, but it turned him into a caring, sensitive

person. True, he was no more intelligent than before, but his incompetence was easier to bear. However, he was destroyed by this University, and by the person whom we are gathered here to honor this evening.' Oscar, consumed with rage, waved a fist at J.T.

'You'd better be careful. Remember, we have some evidence that could end any miserable career possibilities that you still might have.'

'He means some photos showing me in what are usually described as "compromising situations". Well, I've decided that there is probably a good market for this kind of material, so who cares what they do with them.' Whoops of encouragement from the rear of the hall! 'This man,' he pointed to Oscar Wolf, 'used the University as a vehicle for an arrangement with the CIA to conduct espionage around the world. And when Stavros was about to reveal Oscar's involvement in this dirty business, Stavros was eliminated. Stavros was a creep, but he did not deserve that. The worst aspect of the whole affair is that, after his death, Stavros was used as a front for smuggling money abroad, in order to pay off the people who were doing Oscar's dirty work.'

There was uproar in the hall. Oscar was on his feet, shouting threats at J.T., Zuwicki was banging the table to try to restore order, half the audience was raging against Oscar Wolf, and the other half wanted to lynch J.T. It was no longer possible to make himself heard above the din, so J.T. sat down, sipped his wine, and watched as the dinner party dissolved into warring groups, in some cases having to be restrained from coming to blows. Some of the younger faculty rushed over to congratulate him, whilst some senior members of the administration came over to accuse him of being a traitor, biting the hand that fed him.

Eventually Zuwicki's manic table banging restored some semblance of order. He glared around the room. 'I have an important announcement. I want you to know that the Trustees met earlier this evening, and they decided that the vacant position of Provost of the University should be offered to...Oscar Wolf. And I am happy to be able to tell you that he has accepted. I know that he will bring the same dedication and distinction to this post as he did to the position of Vice President for International Affairs.' Bedlam ensued. J.T. quietly found his way to the exit, where Janice was waiting for him.

'J.T.,' she said, 'that was great. I love you.' They left the hall, hall in hand.

* * *

10798301R00109

Made in the USA
Charleston, SC
05 January 2012